Best Friend
for Hire

A Novel by
Mary Carlomagno

D1469132

A POST HILL PRESS BOOK

Best Friend for Hire:
A Novel
© 2017 by Mary Carlomagno
All Rights Reserved

ISBN: 978-1-68261-260-6
ISBN (eBook): 978-1-68261-261-3

Cover Design by Ryan Lause
Interior Design and Composition by Greg Johnson/Textbook Perfect

Post Hill
PRESS
Post Hill Press
posthillpress.com

Published in the United States of America

For Lulu

A phone call at 9:05 on the first day back from holiday break can never bring good news, especially when it comes from the newly appointed, heavily coiffed, senior executive vice president Susan Thornton-Smith, dubbed STS by her corporate minions, who longed to create a sense of intimacy where none had previously existed. This, however, would not be the case for me. I was ready for my promotion; in fact, I had been at my desk for an hour already making sure everything was 100% perfect for today. My new hot pink crocodile iPad case was lined up with its office accessory family. The iPad itself was just one of the many things I was going to buy to celebrate my promotion to Publicity Director.

Being Assistant Director was a big job at my company, despite the fact that there had never been a director for me to report to. It had only taken me T-E-N Y-E-A-R-S to make it from Assistant to Assistant Director. When "STS" came up on my phone screen, my heart leapt in excitement. I got it, I thought. Maybe there was even a little surprise breakfast being planned. I dreamed of that office deliveryman bringing trays of treats to successful executives. Really successful people never sneak a bagel with a schmear at their desk, but are served mini-muffins on faux silver trays and drink their coffee out of real china cups and saucers. Finally, I thought, this would be me.

My fantasy was cut short by STS's voice saying, "Please come to my office when you have a sec."

When you have a second or "a sec," of course, was "boss" code for right now. It's like when you ask for the check or more water at a restaurant and you say, "When you have a chance." Everyone knows you really mean now. I paused for just "a sec" and triple-checked my appearance in the mirror: Banana Republic navy pantsuit with a tasteful silk cream tank underneath—check. Tory Birch medium heel pumps—check. One piece of interesting, but not too interesting, jewelry—check. This outfit was the uniform for publicity girls in all the major publishing houses citywide. Like army lieutenants serving a higher-ranking officer, we needed to look neat and appropriate and blend in with the rest of the army. Like good little soldiers, we knew our place. That was all about to change today. Symbolic hot pink iPad case in hand, I marched toward my superior's office with confidence.

Once in the inner sanctum of STS's world, I looked around at what corporate success looked like, or in this case, corporate excess. Her new corner office had floor-to-ceiling windows framing Manhattan skyscraper views. As I entered, the Park Avenue interior designer was busy arranging and re-arranging seating areas, while Felicia, Susan's assistant, hung pictures of Susan posing with the owner of the company, Susan with her dog, and a third picture, which appeared to be of the owner of the company and Susan's dog. A steady stream of flowers was being delivered to congratulate STS on her new position. Did those same deliverymen have arrangements with my name on it, I wondered. Thinking for sure that they did, I tried to make eye contact, hoping there would be some secret recognition from one of them. You're next, their knowing stare would indicate. Once the flowers had been delivered, I would sail in, only to have the department assistants hoist me on their shoulders and carry me down the executive hallway.

As I was creating my fantasy, my thoughts were broken by a sound like a record being scratched. Susan was disengaging herself from her headset, causing a piercing chirping noise. As she faced me, her smile faded as though she realized that she had some less celebratory business to take care of. I was beginning to sense a publicity tragedy that only I could handle. The job of the soon-to-be Director of Publicity is never over. Bring it on, I thought. I could solve this dilemma in a hot New York minute. We'll have just enough time before we head into the conference room for my petite muffin breakfast.

Most of my publicity dramas revolved around Smith and Drake's star author, Dr. Ursula, the self-proclaimed self-help guru whose career I had managed for the last five years. Her bestselling books kept the company afloat. I was convinced this meeting was to discuss the incident at the Holiday Gala event last week at the 92nd Street Y. Trying to head this sour news off, I offered, "Listen, I know what you're going to say. I left a message for Dr. Ursula and she promised me that this would never happen again." "This" was a heated discussion with Charlie Rose about who donated more this year.

"Already handled," I reassured my new superior.

But STS was not interested in this story; in fact, it appeared that this was the first time she had heard about it. As she let out several long exasperated sighs, a long needle was being poised near my hot pink promotion bubble. She launched into the few words that no employee is ever equipped to hear, much less one who is expecting a promotion.

"I can't believe I have to do this, Jessie."

STS seemed off her game, clearly not a good start for the company's number one public relations executive. With just a

3

few minutes to go in her routine, she could still pull out a couple of additional jumps and stick the dismount, but the entry move would cause some deductions. This was clearly not the way either of us thought this morning would go. She was regaining her composure and realizing her place in her new office among her new furnishings. I was beginning a slow descent into unknown waters. I felt like I was slowly falling off a cruise ship, and we all know that once you fall off one of those ships, you can never get back on. They simply keep sailing without you.

I was hoping for a report of a drama, waning sales, or a threat to leave; any of these would be welcome problems to alleviate the cloud of doom that, thanks to STS, was now hovering over my head. In that fraught environment, I grasped for something to control, adjusting and re-adjusting my leather notebook, fiddling with the clasp on my "statement" piece of jewelry. Holding on to some sort of corporate ritual that would root me back here where things were normal and familiar. But as STS began to stammer and employ phrases like, "It's not you, it's the company," and "The company is belt-tightening," and "You had a good run," the purpose of our meeting was becoming as clear as the meaning of these corporate clichés. Sensing the finish line in sight, STS abruptly hit the speaker button and talked directly into the phone.

"Let me go ahead and call Rita in Human Resources. She can help you sort out the details."

STS offered her trademark smile, one used many times before on unsuspecting recipients. Then, in an attempt at closure, she swept from her side of the desk to mine with her arms wide open. She waited for me to move forward to be enveloped in a farewell hug. She held on a bit too long for comfort, reminding me of a reality show where the competition has just been voted off while the cameras are still rolling. I was so caught off guard by the display of affection that I reciprocated by patting the Armani-clad executive on the back. I could feel the bones of her back as STS began to disengage from me. It was like hugging a xylophone.

My mind raced. Did I just get fired? Grappling for some sense of understanding and, at the same time, feeling badly for STS and her awkward bony embrace, I could not think of anything to say.

"Don't worry, Susan, you'll be all right," was all I could come up with.

As if STS suddenly became aware of herself and her position, she broke off the embrace and quickly stepped back to her side of the glass-and-chrome desk. It was as though I was contagious and she wanted to set up a buffer zone between the two of us before she could be infected too.

Within 15 minutes, I had gone from the A-plus list to the F-minus list, left on the exit ramp with no idea how to get back on the highway. Stunned, confused, and still wondering if I, indeed, had just been fired on my first day back from vacation, I replayed the chain of events that had brought me to this moment. I retraced the precise wording, but the words, *"you are fired, canned, finished, terminated, as in you no longer work here,"* had never been spoken. But I was certain that I would not be attending any of the launch meetings scheduled for later that day, nor would I be lunching with the rest of the marketing department tomorrow. Clearly, I would not have to kick in for Bob in accounting's birthday party later in the week, nor would I take part in the company Super Bowl pool. All these calendar details would be left open-ended, as a result of this overarching news item. It was doubtful that Rita or anyone else could sort out any of these details.

Perhaps it was a misunderstanding, a fledgling hope that dissipated as soon as Rita in Human Resources explained

COBRA, severance, and stock options all tied up neatly in my farewell package from Smith and Drake. My 10-year corporate career was wrapped up in two sheets of letterhead that required one signature. The package, as it were, did not even merit its own presentation folder. I took the two stiff pages and awkwardly placed them in my hot pink crocodile iPad folder. They did not fit in there, either, so I just jammed them in. But the pages still stuck out, making it impossible for me to zip the folder closed. My need for everything to fit in its proper place would have to wait; the more pressing issue was that I was clearly out of a job.

I left the executive wing quickly, hoping not to be seen by anyone. I was going against traffic; a swarm of employees was heading into the conference room. I hugged the wall with a smile plastered on my face, acting as though I had to go back to my office to retrieve something. But my façade was not convincing. Those who did see me looked at me sympathetically. Perhaps they were on that cruise ship, prepared to leave me behind as well. As I made my way back to the publicity pit to gather my things, I heard STS regain her composure completely as my former officemates sang, "For she's a jolly good fellow." I knew then that the boat truly had sailed on without me. The croissant deliveryman arrived, and Smith and Drake carried on. For everyone but me, it was business as usual.

At my desk, I tried to stuff the accumulated detritus of my career into a canvas book bag. None of the items seemed to have anything to do with me: a Walt Frazier basketball, a memento for putting Walt on tour; a call sheet proving the number of times I had called *Good Morning America* to book Dr. Ursula (proof of work that would only be needed in this office); a copy of Strunk and White's *Elements of Style*. As a first-time fired person, I was uncertain what was mine, fearing I would be escorted out by guards on the lookout for purloined office supplies or proprietary files. Would a lobby tug-of-war erupt if I were to take my Jessie De Salvo stationery or a rollerball pen that was clearly property of the company, not this former employee?

To make matters worse, I had no one to confer with. Most of the company employees were down the hall eating a catered breakfast courtesy of STS, my corporate husband Daniel was out on tour at the nation's colleges with three feminist authors and my assistant Emily was out of the office that day looking at wedding venues in New Jersey. Otherwise, both would have been in at 8:30 a.m., as they were every day. Daniel's office was dark, its door closed, and Emily's computer was off, which only increased my feeling of abandonment. I now worried about their future, as well. With the entire pit empty, I peeked up one last time from my desk and swore I heard someone say, "You don't have to go home, but you can't stay here." Only this time, instead of being at The Garage in Hoboken at 3 a.m., I was stone cold sober and had no place to go at all. And so I picked up my canvas tote bag and my basketball and left the office. For the first time since college, I was without a job and without a clue.

I hurried to the staircase to avoid bumping into people near the elevator. On the first two flights going down, my heel caught on my pant leg, causing a tear that nearly made me do a header all the way down to the lobby. As I gathered my shoe in my hand, my basketball freed itself from my grasp and began its noisy descent to freedom, its thump-thump-thump echoing up and down the stairway. I made a feeble attempt to chase it and lost the entire contents of the bag, just barely catching the hot pink, now wholly symbolic, iPad case. The rest of my desk contents were strewn between the sixth and seventh floors, waiting to be gathered up again, stuffed back into the bag to be set in their usual positions in my new place. In my mania not to be seen by the judgmental eyes of former co-workers, I had grabbed items blindly, this would prove to be a problem.

Standing in line at the New York Waterway Ferry waiting for the one that would take me home, I searched in the sudden downpour for my missing umbrella, which was the only item I needed. To make matters worse, the rip in my pant leg was threatening to turn my pants into a skirt, and my shoes were so waterlogged from the rain that I might have been better off going barefoot. I still had not located my umbrella as another problem unveiled itself. A recent Keratin hair treatment, which was designed to calm my curls, was beginning to back-fire. Between the rain and humidity, the curls had decided to stage a protest, and now my hair was curly on top and poker-straight on the bottom. Crossing the Hudson can sometimes be a wonderful adventure, one that people even pay money for on vacation, but today this journey was about as pleasant as crossing the River Styx.

Soaked, cold, and alone, I began to make my way back to Hoboken. The rain was subsiding a bit as I made my way off the Ferry. The Manhattan skyline was now behind me and, equipped with only my office essentials, I trudged toward my apartment. Washington Street, the main street in Hoboken, was also going through some changes. The majority of business in this step-sister to Manhattan had predominantly been bars and clubs. In the last 10 years, these old-school, former mom-and-pop shops and seedy saloons were now sushi bars, day spas, and baby stores. It used to be that Hoboken was a quick stop where post-college kids who could not afford "the city" did a few years' stopover on their way to greater things, like a better job that could afford them more expensive and cooler apartments in the city, or a marriage that would eventually beckon them to the suburbs of New Jersey or Long Island. These post-college kids were now mommies and daddies and had no plans of leaving anytime soon. Now the entrance to what used to be Kelly's Tavern on upper Washington Street was a hip wine bar boasting a mommy lunch with a complimentary glass of wine. Outside a stroller valet lined up the expensive trolleys with names like Bumble Ride and UppaBaby.

Despite the fact that it was only 11 a.m., a tavern that was near Derek's studio apartment—he was my on-again, off-again boyfriend—seemed a better choice than sitting in my apartment, alone. The last conversation I had had with Derek was two weeks—or was it two months—ago. Grasping for something familiar, I was certain that he would be in town just where I left him, working away on his screenplay. Going to a bar on a Monday morning would normally be unthinkable for a working girl like me, but obviously there were others who did not share this belief. Inside the darkly lit tavern was a group of people who did not work in offices. Many had set up shop here, pounding at their laptops. What were they working on? Novels, job searches, online dating profiles? Among these purposeful, yet casually dressed, day workers was a cozy couple nestled in the corner banquette, deep in discussion and drinking impossibly large café lattes. Their breakfast was a deep contrast to the mini-muffins and small croissants that I had left behind at Smith and Drake just an hour ago. Things already seemed out of joint. In my heart, I was hoping a TV journalist would pop out of the shadows and tell me this had all been a big joke. But life is never really like a reality show, and no one should know that better than a publicist.

I plopped myself down on the first bar stool I could find and summoned the heavily tattooed, mutton chopped bartender, which was no easy task since he was transfixed on an impossibly tall woman who looked as if she just walked off the pages of German *Vogue*.

"What can I get ya, ma'am?"

Ma'am? Was he talking to me? When did I become a "ma'am?"

My reaction may have startled him, because he stopped for a moment and really looked at me as if trying to figure me out. And then, much to our mutual surprise, I ordered a mimosa. As he reengaged in the witty repartee at the more fashionable end of the bar, I struggled not to make comparisons in our appearances. Suddenly self-conscious, I headed off to the bathroom to assess the damage of this morning's events. I wanted to fix myself up a bit before seeing Derek. Even though we had not been as close recently, I knew that he would be willing to meet me for a drink and some sympathy. There would be a great reunion as he would sweep me into his arms and let me know that even though I was a workaholic, he would take care of me, look after my well-being, and generally become an entirely different person. He would get a day job and with that money support me until I got back on my feet. Confidence can often be increased on an empty stomach and a strong morning cocktail.

When Derek's phone began to ring, not only did I hear the ringtone on my phone, but also the actual ring sounded in the bar. A quick scan of the bar offered no further clues or recognition to what had just happened. Everyone was just where he or she was supposed to be. Even the cozy couple did not budge. The bartender, whom I can assume was now taking a pity on me, served me another mimosa.

When you are sitting alone at a bar, you are conspicuous. There is an urgency to explain why exactly you are alone. When two people meet at a bar, the entire scenario changes. You have someone in the world, regardless of any kind of terrible things have happened. The joining at the bar makes things better and seems to absolve everyone of whatever happened before or will happen after. It is quite Zen really. If someone were to meet me, I would get just a bit closer to normalcy, feel less alone, less fired, less humiliated. The phone rang again and this time more loudly. That *is* Derek's ring; I know this because he has a distinct ringtone. It's the theme song from the television show *Cheers*. The ring was coming from inside the bar, close by. It was the phone that was sitting on the table of a couple huddled together cozily in the corner banquette. The couple still engaged in their oversized coffees, so deep in cuddlesomeness that the phone went unanswered. I slunk down from my bar stool to investigate this awaiting injustice and then it happened. My eyes met the male star of this happy couple rendezvous. And it was Derek. Derek was the man snuggled up with a woman who had her back to me. A woman so engaging that he would avoid my SOS calls, twice. Add jealousy, rage, and embarrassment to my long list of now swirling emotions.

Like most terrible events, things started to move in slow motion. I looked at Derek, he looked at me, and we both looked at the phone, confused about what exactly to do next. He finally answered the phone. We stood for a moment and spoke into our receivers, confused by the fact that both of us were indeed in the same bar, just a few feet away from each other. And then, after what seemed like several awkward minutes, his companion turned to face me. It was Allison, as in Allison my next-door neighbor and friend. We all just stared at one another for a beat and then another beat, our glares ricocheting off one another like billiard balls. I was certain everyone in the bar would turn around and notice this showdown, but the day workers continued to frantically type away. Moving toward the table, I had the sense that tumbleweeds were moving toward us like a scene in one of those old western movies when the two gunfighters draw their revolvers on a dusty street.

Disheveled, phone in hand, I took the first step and moved toward their table. There is something about catching someone red-handed when they have committed a crime, an "A-HA! I've got you moment," which should make the discoverer feel justified. But this discovery did not do that for me. Before I could crystallize the humiliation, the outrage, and the shock of this turn of events, Allison stood up and started coming toward me, clearly with the intention to hug me. What was going on today that everyone delivering bad news felt the need to hug me?

"Jessie! What a surprise, it's great to see you...or *is* it great to see you?"

Derek, equally confused by my two phone calls (more than I had placed to him in the last six months) and my presence, coupled with my unexpected appearance, also began to show concern.

Not only were the two collaborators not surprised to see me, they seemed to be happy to see me. As if to say, we have done nothing wrong. Everyone knows we've been seeing each other, everyone but *you*. I was beginning to sense a theme to this day. Everyone seemed to know something that I had obviously missed. Still not convinced that these two were, in fact, together, I asked the obvious.

"What are you two *doing*?"

"Having coffee."

"Together? You're having coffee together?"

It was clear that this was not the first time these two had had coffee together. Allison, sensing my unsteady footing, reached over and placed her hand on top of Derek's, her Tibetan beaded bracelet making a little clinking noise against the mosaic tiled table.

"Babe, let's give Jessie a little time to regroup in this space," Allison suggested to my—I mean, her—boyfriend.

Regroup in this new space? Who talks like that? I had regrouped just enough for now, thank you very much. I had been "regrouped" all morning in fact. Again, the unease of newness set in, along with queasiness. Derek nodded to his partner and moved a chair closer to me as if I would fall face first onto their lovely table if I were not guided into the actual chair. He shot a conspiratorial look to his Allison, which indicated that this was not a chance meeting, but that this super couple had been familiar for some time. Derek was somehow expecting this conversation and was at ease. As if it was predetermined when I stood him up (again) five months ago. Derek had been waiting for me to show up for a post-work drink when he received a familiar text, "Rain check, work drama." That text had excused me from any prior commitment. This was part of a long string of stand ups and last-minute cancelations that had comprised our dating relationship. As I had been texting that fateful night, Derek was beginning a new relationship in real time right on my doorstep.

"We just started talking," Derek began.

"And haven't stopped," Allison finished.

Allison, who had just moved in a year ago, had not been aware that Derek and I ever had a romantic relationship. She further explained that a guy like Derek was very hard to come by, and that once he had said that he was free, she did not hesitate to "scoop him up." *Who could blame her?* I recall her saying something about the heart does what it will, but the second mimosa was beginning to have its effect, otherwise I would have corrected her and said "the heart does what it wants, not "will." That doesn't even make sense, but her voice seemed to trail off as I stared hypnotically at the small rose tattoo peeking out of her gauze tunic top.

To add insult to awkwardness, my so-called boyfriend and my so-called friend immediately wanted to know exactly what had happened to me, and from the beginning.

"Let's discuss this as a family," Allison coaxed. The usually complimentary Derek was inspecting me closely, as if he could not quite figure out what had happened, my odd appearance coming into better focus as I got closer.

"You don't look so good," he said. The understatement of the century, I thought to myself.

The bartender had taken notice, more interested now in my demise than his doppelgänger. I felt even more conspicuous in his presence. He delivered a third mimosa to our table. A good bartender, like a good publicist, is usually one step ahead of bad news. Placing a loose curl behind my ear, I instantly tried to reinvent myself as a carefree girl just taking some time to join her friends for a casual morning cocktail. To make sure he knew that I was not a complete basket case, I muttered, "You can put that on my tab."

"We can settle up, later," he said and gave me a sly little salute.

Feeling like it was time for me to go for the second time that morning, I grabbed my bulging tote bag. Just then, out of the bag rolled my long sought umbrella, which proceeded to pop open to its full size right in my face. When I opened my mouth in surprise, all that came out was a high-pitched squeal. Oh, yes, this was shaping up to be a real bestseller of a day.

I left the warm cocoon of the bar and began the sobering walk back to my nearby apartment. Shifting my glance downward toward the slick sidewalk, I proceeded slowly, methodically, still afraid to arouse interest from passersby. My stealth return was nearly complete until my inquisitive dry cleaner and neighbor spotted me.

"No work today?" she probed.

"No, no work today," I said out loud, and then to myself, no work tomorrow either or the next day or the day after that.

"Okay, I like your pants, enjoy your vacation. Bye-bye."

I was relieved to be inside my first-floor apartment without any more spectators to respond to. The apartment was dark, blinds closed, and there was little evidence that anyone lived here. A half-read manuscript was strewn on the couch where I had left it last night. The neglected galley kitchen was tidy, too, no evidence of meal making, wine drinking, or use at all. Not even a coffee cup from this morning to suggest the warmth of a home.

It was as if someone else, not me, were making this house tour. Pausing in the first room of the railroad apartment, my things looked oddly unfamiliar. The apartment had a straight-forward layout, one room leading to another and another in succession. A true Hoboken railroad apartment that had never quite felt like home, its very layout almost designed as a metaphor for my life. During the weekend my parents helped me move in here, my very first apartment where I would live alone, they had also noted its long, tunnel-like design.

"You're not renting an apartment, you're renting a hallway," my father commented with a combination of dissatisfaction and utter amazement. And he was right; looking around this apartment, it did not seem welcoming, or even familiar, for that matter. It was like a picture that has hung in your bathroom for years and suddenly you look at it, really look at it. And you say something like, *how did* that *get there?* Here I was in the hallway starting to itch uncomfortably from my dysfunctional outfit.

I started shedding the painful reminders of the day, depositing the entire suit into the garbage can, and the shoes, now beyond repair, quickly joined it. The troublesome tote bag was in the middle of the living room floor, now demanding even more attention than it had already seen today. I scowled at it and turned away from its hideous presence, determined to take the world's hottest shower. Once inside the shower, I turned the water faucet to "Hot" and kept on turning, making it hotter and hotter, until finally the water in its post-war plumbing started to run cold. Another signal that time was up. I slipped into a fuzzy warm-up suit, even though I had no attention of working out. Looking like a retiree returning to Boca after a long summer in the Northeast, I was preparing myself with athletic wear. The most active I planned to be was to sit on my couch and watch daytime television, a luxury in which my workaholic life had seldom given me the opportunity to indulge.

In some sort of technicolor nightmare, a super close-up of Dr. Ursula was on the screen. Once again, she had inserted herself into my world, without my even recognizing her entrance. It was a repeat of the *Dr. Phil* show we taped last fall.

And no sooner did I lock in on her chartreuse Chanel brocade jacket, which very few women can pull off, the phone rang. My mother, another well-intended inquisitor, was calling.

How did she do it? I had been home for five minutes, and she called me. Sooner or later I was going to have to talk with her, sooner or later I was going to have to start telling people my sad news. But I somehow thought that sooner would have been a little more than the five hours I'd had to acclimate to my out-of-work status.

"Jessica, what are you doing home?"

"I left work early."

"What's the matter?" she probed, her psychic powers at full alert.

The thing about my mom is that she knows things before they happen. More than maternal instinct with her, this is all about her Sicilian upbringing and all its crazy superstitions. As a child, I had thought that everyone believed these myths. One day, I said to my friend Jan, *hey, you've got a string on your pants, that means you're going to get a letter,* and she looked at me like I had three legs. She was not the first, nor the last. In my family, every time your ears would ring, you asked people for a number. This number corresponded with a letter in the alphabet, and that letter began the first name of the person who was talking about you. Sounds simple, really.

Most of these superstitions foretell bad news or things to look out for. Sicilians are a suspicious group, always thinking that someone is out to get to them. Today, they may have a point. So with all this stored psychic knowledge, Ma calling me at home in the middle of the workday should have come as no surprise. But with all the unexpected happenings of the earlier part of the day, it was safe to say that my Sicilian sense was off, at least slightly.

"I knew there was something wrong and just as I was about to call you, I saw Dr. Ursula on the television and I thought, this must be it."

Here's the other thing about my mom—she lives for television. Conversations with her include full updates on the *Real Housewives of Wherever*, the *Big Brothers*, the Food Network stars, and all those other instantly famous people who develop a huge overnight following. All of her useful information comes from television, mainly *The View* and *The Young and the Restless*. Most of them she does not even enjoy, but she has to keep up with them, if only to point out their mistakes and make sure that her kids don't ever follow in their footsteps. And the worst part of all this media fascination is that she is a big fan of Dr. Ursula.

With quick brushstrokes, I relayed the whirlwind events of the morning. In truth, I had no intention of telling my mother or my family about any of this, but without time to prepare a suitable cover story I began to spill like one of the reality stars she watched so intently. Like a good audience member, she listened to my intriguing tale. This was the second time I had recounted the story, and the fact was that I really had no idea how I wanted to feel. This was one journey for which there was no road map. I had never been fired from anything, ever, before.

With this lack of experience, instead of being angry, I was more embarrassed.

A persistent thought at the back of my brain was there was something I could have done differently—but what? That pesky feeling that you cannot lay your finger on something, a nagging feeling that keeps bringing you back repeatedly to the same series of events, wondering if you had tweaked the story just slightly, how you could have changed the outcome. All I could think of was a sort-of *Glamour* magazine "before" shot of me.

The "after" shot was a blank, black box. But my mother did not see it that way.

"Have you heard from Dr. Ursula?"

I was stunned by this question and the fact that the entire conversation was quickly slipping out of my control.

"Um, no, um," I ad libbed, "why would I?"

"It's just good manners, dear, after all the work you did for her. I thought she would call; she is such a compassionate person."

The compassionate person line really hit home. My mother had tons of compassion, but it was usually misplaced, and misplaced in heaps. Celeste De Salvo, the youngest of three sisters, certainly had a keen eye for observation, a habit she was now liberally sprinkling all over my work events. At times, her advice and commentary were direct, even cutting, but compassion was always her underlying theme.

"If I can't tell you the truth, then who can?" was her *modus operandi*.

Her abounding compassion was best observed in the big media stories, like Tonya Harding, *poor thing*, and Teresa Giudice, oh the orange suit. I would then have to remind her that Tonya "poor thing" Harding had arranged to have her teammate clubbed in the knee, and that the Teresa Guidice was sent to jail because she did not pay her taxes. She fell for the media spin and used her Catholic forgiveness to let these situations allow her to take the high road. In make-believe land, she, like Oprah, was living her best life adopting an all-knowing, saint-like quality. In real life, though, the opposite was usually true; when it came to one of her children, she was usually short on compassion and understanding. We needed a firmer hand, apparently, than an ice skater or a superiorly coiffed tax-evader.

"I just cannot believe she did not call."

"It's just bad etiquette," she continued to hammer home the point.

Frankly, I didn't know how much the good doctor knew about what had happened. Did she have something to do with my firing was another thought I couldn't keep out of my head. Again, I tried to trace the Rube Goldberg-like chain of events that had led up to my dismissal, but still I came up with no coherent answer.

"Ma, does it really matter?"

"It always matters; doing the right thing is important."

This right and wrong theme figured greatly throughout my upbringing. As the daughter of two Sicilian parents, it was not easy. Sicilians are known for their arrogance in much the same way as the country is known for its scenic vistas. Sicilians set themselves apart from other Italians; being on an island that so many other cultures tried to conquer only contributed to their bellicose nature. All those civilizations could not be wrong.

"Besides, Ma, she is still on the boat."

"What does that mean, still on the boat? Like your father, not off the boat?"

"No, literally. She is on a boat."

My mother's reference was to the slang phrase for Italians who were so old-fashioned that they never got off the boat that had originally delivered them to America from their unsophisticated Italian villages. But in this case, the good doctor was actually on a boat, a big one, the Norwegian Line's "New Year/ New You" cruise that would not be docking in New York Harbor until tomorrow. Even though my mom was more media savvy than most 70-year-old women, there were some things in the modern world that needed a more detailed explanation, and this was one of them.

"Cruise travel is lovely. I can see why the doctor would want to do that. I went on a cruise, you know, before I had you kids."

"Ma, I know...you told me...um, can we get back to the other conversation we were having?"

"Well, Jessica, it's really time to move on, let's stop dwelling, things end when they are supposed to, dear. Not longer, not shorter, all according to God's plan."

And just as the referenced religious comment, hurled from on high like a lightning bolt, I saw that there was another caller on my line. And the conversation with Ma, for now, would have to wait. I rushed her off the phone to see who was on call waiting, a concept that, after all these years, she still had trouble grasping. Why would you make another call wait to pick up another caller who is waiting, she riddled. And as usual, I had no retort for my mother's lock-tight logic.

"Maybe it's Dr. Ursula," she said as I hung up to take the other call.

It was Emily, my assistant—oops, make that former assistant—who was in full-blown panic mode. I tried to reassure her, as much for my benefit as her own, that everything was just fine.

"Em, things end when they should, not before and not after," paraphrasing the words that I had just been chagrined to hear my mother use.

Young, naïve, first-time job assistant Emily did not know what to make of this sage advice. She was a well-manicured, giddy girl with a high-pitched voice who always seemed like she was about to break into applause at the slightest piece of good news. Not surprisingly, the slightest bit of bad news could always be expected to turn her into a basket case. An incessant up-talker, she had the unusual habit of constantly asking questions, and before anyone had a chance to answer her, she would answer those questions herself. That emotional exterior made her immediately likable, and her sensitivity to everyone else's needs made her the perfect publicity assistant.

"I am just so sorry that I was not there when you left...a bride's work is never done, as they say."

In an instant I was transported to the mania that Emily's wedding had created. It was as if she turned a switch to become an entirely different person when talking about Jordan Almonds and peonies. At least something had remained the same in my topsy- turvy life; not even my getting fired was going to stand in the way of Emily's wedding preparations. And for that, I felt thankful.

The sun shining through the blinds woke me from a fitful night's sleep. It was Tuesday and I had nothing to do. But more than an absence of task, I was struck by an absence of purpose. Yesterday's late afternoon phone calls had given way to an ominously quiet atmosphere this morning. In my world, busy was currency: the busier you are, the more powerful you are; the less busy you are—well, you get the idea. Save for a late night text exchange with my office husband, Daniel, the lines had gone ominously dead.

From my bedroom, which was situated at the front of my railroad apartment, I passed through the living room, which still carried the physical and emotional remnants of last night: empty water bottles, a Hot Pocket wrapper, the half-read manuscript, its pages now strewn across the floor, and, of course, the tote bag still waiting for its contents to be given a new home. I was starting to relate to the tote bag's displaced status. Feeling edgy amidst all this accumulated stuff, I rummaged through the pile and located my iPad, which looked defiant in its hot pink case. As I reached for the power button, an errant piece of pesky clutter got in my way and I idly brushed it aside.

It turned out to be the severance package from my now former employer. Even though Rita in Human Resources had urged me to sign on the dotted line yesterday, I had the presence of mind to wait and review later. Like a good procrastinator, I decided to save reading these documents for another time and instead began to sift through the detritus of the living room, beginning with the coffee table.

Procrastination, by definition, is the opting out of one task to choose a more pleasurable one. I knew this because instead of reading the documents or cleaning up the living room, I chose to surf the web to find the true meaning of procrastination. Further reading suggested that procrastinators are really just putting off the inevitable. In other words, that nasty task you just put off will still be waiting for you when you return, and may even be less desirable. With that bit of internet wisdom, I started purging the top layers of the coffee table.

Within an hour, I had cleared the coffee table of 20 old magazines, most I had never read, the half-read manuscript (written, by the way, by the niece of someone at work), two unmatched flip flops, three tubes of lip gloss, and one of those cushy balls designed to relieve stress. Finally, I freed a yoga mat that had somehow trapped itself under the bottom rung of my coffee table. By this time, I had managed to fill two garbage bags and two recycling bags. One thing I saved was an inscribed copy of *Smart Blonde*, Dr. Ursula's first book. If times got really rough, I might have to sell it on eBay. On my way to the recycling bins outside, I started rehearsing my responses to anyone wondering why I was home on a workday. As if there were a giant "F" for "Fired" on the front of my hoodie, I felt like a community outcast, like an unemployed Esther Prynne. I planned to take control of the dry cleaner first. I walked down the block to confront her by surprise before she could see me.

"Beautiful day for a vacation," I blurted out to her.

"Beautiful, yes, beautiful, nice weather, don't work too hard," she replied, little realizing the irony of her innocent comment.

"You, too," I responded.

There is a rule in media training that no matter what the interviewer asks, you stick to your copy points. Most authors rarely prompt an interviewer to intentionally throw them off or embarrass them in some way. Especially my self-help authors, most of whom were diet gurus, advice columnists, or fitness specialists dispensing top-10 tips on how to lose weight and live a healthier lifestyle. I would tell them to stick to the key messages of the book and to enjoy themselves. Once, I even told household guru Peggy Post to lighten up. After all, she didn't start the Iraq war; she just liked seeing napkins folded nicely.

It was now time to take my own advice. And that, my dry cleaner friend, was how these conversations were going to work in the future. I knew it wasn't such a big thing to clean up your living room and walk outside in the sunshine, but I was starting to feel a little better, a little closer to normal and less like a vampire, forced to shun the light of day.

This sense of self-empowerment I was experiencing was pure Dr. Ursula. Thinking about her immediately launched me back into a frenzied state that Emily and I referred to as Ursula time where we were acutely aware of all of her comings and goings, her media appearances, her lunches, even her downtime. At any moment, we knew where she was, whom she was with and where she was going next. It was our job to think for her, be two steps ahead of her, to take care of her, and, most important of all, keep her happiness utmost in our minds.

I wished now that I could divorce myself from our professional relationship and ask her for her advice. What would Ursula tell me to do? In truth, I missed her. She was difficult, but she was my difficult. I knew how to handle her in crisis; shouldn't it work the same way now that our roles had been reversed? But they weren't. As I tried to take my own advice, I was reminded of how difficult taking care of her could be.

During last year's sales conference, for instance, the good doctor had been waging her own defensive. The Smith & Drake sales conference was a long-standing publishing company tradition, which involved transporting the entire staff, complete with all the attendant office politics, to an off-site location, preferably some place warm, such as a resort in the Bahamas. Ironically, most of the conference was spent indoors, in freezing cold conference rooms, rendering the pools, tennis courts, day spas, and other resort amenities completely useless.

At this particular conference Dr. Ursula's credibility was being used to defend her latest controversial book. Wonder boy editor-in-chief Alex Sheffield was on the podium, providing a convincing argument about her track record and media appeal. Almost immediately, he met some resistance from the chain store sales manager who, although not officially, was really in charge of the company. Were it not for good sales numbers from a big stores, such as those in her accounts, Dr. Ursula and others like her would be forced into the murky world of self-publishing. It was the great equalizer in a way. Once thought to be the slayers of small independent stores, these big box retailers held sway to such a degree that they were now the saviors for some fortunate authors, enabling them to be published on their say-so alone.

Online giants were another factor, but could not deliver the visceral impact of Dr. Ursula's life-sized cardboard figure outside a storefront in the Mall of America. Lilly Crowley, of the superstore giant Winters Books, was the first to break ranks, as she was one of the first female sales managers in publishing and had enough experience and power to speak her mind without consequence.

"Why is she doing a male-bashing book?"

"I don't want to see men as useless. I like men. I even like you, Alex," charmed the good doctor.

Alex shifted and re-shifted his papers, organizing his rebuttal. He interjected some salient points about reaching a new audience and new market. There was plenty of room in the market, he said persuasively. But Lilly would not budge. She lingered on each word in her reply, making her southern accent even more distinct.

"Winters won't touch that book."

Winters Books was based out of Nashville, Tennessee, deep in the Bible Belt, where "women's lib," as Lilly explained it, was a real threat to hard-working families. I loved Lilly, although her usual commentary was a public relations minefield. Thank goodness I never had to media train her for *The Today Show*. She may have taken credit for the Iraq War, in fact. Her liberal use of the words "women's lib" always made me chuckle but they would likely have offended most modern women.

"They just won't take it, Alex. And I am not sure that I even want them to."

This statement transformed the stylish top editor into a struggling senator grappling for balance between the blue and red states. Regardless of his media training and obvious charm, the group of sales managers in the middle of the room were already choosing sides. Dr. Ursula's readers were women, conservative for the most part, who had strong family values; they would read about empowerment, but this new departure would have them wondering, right along with the red states. As Alex floundered in his own verbal quicksand, the room was becoming unruly.

"She isn't saying that marriage is a bad institution; it's just that she thinks all people should be able to get married, but probably some shouldn't."

This compelling urban argument did not increase confidence as Lilly persisted.

"Winters won't touch that book."

She repeated in much the same manner as the condemnation speech by Pontius Pilate to the onlooking crowd that crucified Christ. Alex was truly on a cross of his own making. The title of the book alone, *Marriage Sentences*, was enough for most conservatives to condemn it. And to run a publishing business, you need people to buy books, plain and simple, even if you don't agree with a book's message. But this was taking free market capitalism a bit too far. Not to publish a book because one account doesn't support an author's views seemed shortsighted, to say the least, but that is where the business was heading, whether any of us liked it or not.

Dr. Ursula was going to have to score big on her welcome to dinner speech this evening, taking place in the Aloha Ballroom. But before that, we all had damage control to attend to. Dr. Ursula, Alex, and I planned an impromptu emergency summit in the Ocean Vista suite. While Alex and I discussed strategy, the good doctor searched in her Hermès bag for the perfect lip color.

One might have questioned the look and style of such an accomplished therapist, which was more Vegas showgirl than degreed researcher. A leggy blond who empowers people who are less good-looking and not as smart had endless media appeal. Her Chanel suit was cunningly tailored to reveal half of her thigh, the look reminiscent of naughty young Hollywood starlets who, once empowered, were more than happy to show a little leg.

"Men are not capable of long-term, monogamous relationships." Her comment revealed more about her current situation than the subject of the book launch.

"Look, no one needs to know that Timothy has left," I redirected.

"We can spin it in the press to seem that you got too successful and he couldn't handle it. You were going in different directions.

"This is really what you want to say, isn't it?"

Timothy, her husband of 25 years, had recently left her for a younger woman, a holistic health counselor who was more open to his needs, dietary or otherwise. While concentrating on the relationships of others, hers had fallen apart. How ironic. That evening, she approached the podium with a steady confidence, but we knew that she was disguising wounds that would take time to heal. No one wants to follow a wounded soldier into battle, even if she is clad in $1,000 shoes.

Like so many times past, while waiting in the wing, Dr. Ursula asked me for a final cross-check, which meant cleavage, lipstick, and hemline. I gave her the customary thumbs up as she made her way into the room, her insecurity fading as she grabbed her notes and mock-up book jacket, and charged into the breach. This time, it was me giving her advice, which, ironically, was her own.

"Keep moving forward."

Fed up with my own inertia and the helplessness associated with having to explain unemployment to everyone who did call, I conquered procrastination and finally read the exit letter in its entirety. I was moving forward, as well. In signing the agreement letter in my corporate unwelcome package, I was entitled to outside help from an outplacement firm. Outplacement is a program for downsized corporate executives to find out how to get back to the wonderful world of corporate America, a goal that seemed ill-conceived, if not insane, at the current time. At first, the idea was out of the question; why would I want to spend time with all those unemployed people? My mother summed it up with one simple statement.

"You are unemployed, too, dear."

Firmly placed in humbling reality, I finally bestirred myself and left the relative security of my apartment to attend my first meeting at Morris, Field and Benjamin Counseling Services located right above Grand Central Station in midtown Manhattan. The location was perfect for any Metro North commuters who had recently been fired. I joined the realm of off-peak commuters. It reminded me of traveling in Los Angeles, where there is no rhyme or reason to the traffic. It was just constant; it made me wonder if anyone was actually getting to his or her destination, or if they were trapped in a constant traffic circle.

It was clear that working in a high rise from 7 a.m. until 7 p.m. was not the only way to make a living. People were setting up their virtual businesses in coffee shops where they could enjoy supersized coffee drinks and free Wi-Fi. Landscapers and cleaning ladies were tending to the million-dollar brownstones. Realtors double-parked along Washington Street in an endless exercise of borrowing keys from other realtors to show million-dollar townhouses. Nannies strolled with the children of those who lived in those million-dollar brownstones. In my town, at least, none of the people looked like they needed a big office to appear successful.

But more than busy activities, these people had purpose. They had the larger question of, "What do you do?" nailed.

There was simplicity in this reply. "I am a gardener, a realtor, a nanny, a roofer." Each had a marketable skill. In MFB's welcome brochure, the determination of marketable skills was highlighted as a company cornerstone.

The thought of returning to a corporate environment where a prison like cubicle awaited did not seem commensurate with the deep understanding of the cracked psyche that outplacement promised to heal. After all, the ejector seat that was my office chair was still hot from launching me out into the path of finding myself just days ago. Confident that some sort of activity was better than none, I now forged ahead through the whirlwind of Grand Central Station. Once through the recently opened global food markets and a 35-floor elevator ride, with a 365-degree view of the atrium shops below, a visible and conspicuous ride ultimately delivered me to the dark-paneled offices of MFB.

The first stop was an interview with the placement director, who assessed where I should be in the corporate workplace by asking a series of seemingly unrelated questions. Based on my answers, and what I could only speculate as my lack of math skills and business acumen, my job recommendation was to work in public relations at a media company. Well, we all know how well that had turned out.

Before making my way down to door number two, I stopped at the impossibly cheerful receptionist to secure the oversized ladies room key. Somehow, even ladies rooms these days had velvet rope-like entrances. Pleasantries were exchanged about the changing weather and how hard it was to find just the right cardigan for the weather. Mine, as Diane shared, was just right and very "smart."

"Thanks so much, Diane, now you have a great day," I replied.

Maybe life at outplacement could be cheery after all. As I was heading for the ladies room, I passed a large glass-windowed conference room where an enthusiastic speaker was introducing today's topic. She scrolled with a large erasable red marker on a wipe board.

"Empower Yourself through Entrepreneurism." Even though the marker would likely be wiped off in the next session, no doubt entitled, "How Did I Get Here Again," the speaker seemed convincing enough. Attendees scribbled notes and adjusted their positions. Poor souls, I thought to myself.

Frustrated by my lack of empowerment, I breezed by dismissively. In fact, I breezed myself all the way out of the building, vowing never to attend again. It was not until I reached for my wallet to pay for some vegetable samosas at a kiosk that I realized I must have taken the bathroom key with me. And like it or not, now I had to return to the scene of the crime tomorrow. My theft of this item would certainly not sit well with Diane the receptionist, especially not after we had shared so much personal information.

The great thing about being laid off and having so much free time on your hands is that you finally have enough time to spend with friends you've been neglecting during all those long workdays and business trips. The unfortunate part of this scenario for me was that I had no friends outside of work. Inherent in friendship was the idea of being there for them, listening to their problems, being accepting of their faults, essentially providing a buffer to the cruel and unfair realities of the world. But intrinsic to these elusive friend relationships was the idea of reciprocity, a concept I had been unfamiliar with over the last 10 years.

If you were not related to my work life, I was unable to perform the necessary maintenance that a good friendship entails. My only friends were from publishing, more specifically, people from my old company. In need of authentic conversation and camaraderie after a grueling first week out of work, I was looking forward to spending time with people I knew.

Lunch had been planned with my semblance of a support system, Emily and Daniel, at a French bistro located not far from Smith & Drake. I settled into a corner booth in the back of the restaurant, where, hopefully, we would not be noticed by any Smith & Drake personnel who just happened to walk in. Emily spotted me and began her signature handclapping as she galloped past the bar to arrive at the booth, literally jumping for joy at the thought of us getting together. I stood to greet this overwhelming welcome, which was the least I could do under the circumstances. She lunged forward with a huge, clingy hug that caused me to grab for the banquette to keep myself from falling. I ended up banging my head on the specials board chalked in French on the wall behind me.

"OMG. You look super skinny, just perf. Did you lose weight?" she asked.

Emily had a habit of using the conversational equivalents of texting initials such as LOL and OMG. She would regularly punctuate her conversations with "perf" for perfect and "ridic" for ridiculous, as though life was too short to fill out all the other syllables in those words.

Funny thing about being on the outside, everyone seemed to think you look different, better, less stressed. Perhaps what Emily was picking up on was the absence of frenetic urgency that had existed during my usual workday. Today, I was calmer than what she had been used to seeing.

Daniel swept in behind her, trying to wrap up a caller who was reluctant to say goodbye. He rolled his eyes and gestured with his hands as if the caller could actually see his visual cues to end the conversation.

"Gloria Steinem..." Emily mouthed to me.

"Yes...yes...the third button, the one with the little bird... yes...yes it's cute. Of course, call me if you need more help. Ok. Ok. Ok. Ok. Bye-Bye."

"Funny thing about these thought leaders, they can duke it out on the Fox channel, but half of them can't figure out how to send a tweet," Dan remarked.

In minutes, I was swept back into the mania of office politics. Because we had so much ground to cover, Daniel had brought an agenda with him so that no topic would go uncovered.

The very first topic was STS and her decision not to replace me. Instead, I learned from Emily, she had doled out my authors to the existing staff, causing even harsher work conditions than usual. Publishing houses were known for this tactic, asking people to do double work without any extra compensation. Management assumed that people were clamoring to work with a prestigious author. In reality, booking hotels and radio show appearances for Dr. Ursula, or Dr. Oz, was the same kind of mundane work.

This was only one of the many misconceptions people had about the publishing industry. Another was the perception that people enjoy it or that publishing people are called to the higher purpose of getting essential information to the public. And last, the culmination of the above, which was that people who enjoy their work and provide a service should get paid less. Publishing, like Zen Buddhism, was a struggle. Of course, this theory began with the large assumption that authors are nice and interesting people. And many of them are—until you work with them. There is a publishing cliché that asks what the best kind of author to work with is. The answer is, simply, a dead author. I did not share that belief every day, but some days I did. We all did.

Publicists were envisioned to sit in media green rooms all day long, eating free catered food and getting showered with accolades. The accolades were rarely, if ever, delivered, and on most days publicists felt like order takers overwhelmed by the pesky details of limo services, flight departures, and restaurant reservations.

And Daniel was smack in the middle of a week's worth of pesky days wrangling his authors' travel plans. He was so busy that he had little time to sit down, much less eat. I was honored that he had managed to get away from his desk to see me.

"Seriously, this has been the first time I've had lunch in the last three weeks, and I don't care how busy I am, I was not going to miss seeing you."

Apparently conditions at Smith & Drake had deteriorated from a place where people work really hard to a slave labor camp. Aside from the usual "take more work and like it" philosophy that most publicity departments were built upon, the climate of the company had shifted since STS became the newly crowned queen of all things.

"She is ridic with the power thing," Emily added. "I used to think she was a really nice lady, but I guess it's because I never had to deal with her directly. You were amazing at that," she added.

My role as buffer, support system, and all-round fairness monitor had not been replaced, and with STS on a power trip not unlike Stalin during the Purges of the late 1930s, the entire structure had turned into a dictatorship. In truth, all this bad news was making me feel quite good for a few reasons. Not only had I been good at my job, but also my work friends really missed me, a lot. In the absence of having any life outside work,

I had done a pretty good job picking these two people to be my support staff. Sure, I hired them, but they actually liked me, and I liked them.

I missed being with people who knew me, knew that I did the right thing, supported me in any event, and this knowledge made me feel like I was not only good at my job, but also a good friend.

"She cut my expense budget for Naomi Wolf's tour in half and gave it to Gloria Steinem..." Daniel said. And then he paused for dramatic emphasis. "Out of nowhere. STS had lunch with Camille at the Gramercy Tavern, got starstruck, and started making promises to her that I'll be forced to keep."

"And now we have to keep them. We have a new name for these people too. FOS. Friend of Susan," Emily chimed in.

Admittedly, I was no expert on acronyms or friendships at that point, but STS having any friends at all seemed unlikely to me based on the way she treated her co-workers. I was confident that my actions were never like hers. I was a much better friend than she was. In her defense, the author lunch can be a confusing event for those who have never attended. Susan, as a super-executive in the firm, rarely had the chance to interact with authors; she was usually in boardroom meetings with financial people and stockholders. Her foray into my world was new, and she greedily scooped up the perks of her new job. So what if she made promises that someone else would have to keep. She was the boss.

All of this information was starting to add up. How could they afford to keep me on staff with the expensive demands of STS? My dismissal had been because of her, not because of my performance. It was because there was not enough money to keep me and satisfy her extravagant habits. While it was comforting to know that my performance was not the reason for my dismissal, it was sad to realize that my job could so easily be reallocated for a greedy executive's frivolity.

"And that's not even the half of it. She and Alex Sheffield are at war. And the entire office is being forced to choose sides because of one new addition to the self-help list," Daniel explained as he crossed off item #2 on his list.

Our Salade Niçoise and unsweetened ice tea arrived unnoticed as we feasted instead on this agenda item. Dan had been forced into the Alex camp after adding the unruly Dr. Ursula to his roster of high maintenance authors. He and Alex Sheffield worked closely to fend off another threat of her jumping publishers. The children's publisher, Newberry Press, had approached her to write a Young Adult novel. To get the doctor to stay at Smith & Drake, Alex and Daniel had pitched the idea of a series of self-help books aimed at adolescent girls. Of course, she loved the idea of shaping all those young minds and making them Dr. Ursula acolytes for life. I was glad I had missed out on that ego boost.

They had little time, though, to relish the victory of keeping Dr. Ursula on the list when another FOS popped up. This time STS had signed up a three-book deal with her new best friend, Goddess Marina. Goddess Marina was a fixture on the Manhattan lecture circuit. Her sold-out workshops, the Corporate Kama Sutra, likened finding the perfect career position to finding the perfect sexual position. Apparently, one was easier to achieve than the other, but her claim was that you could rarely have one without the other. With the big news of a national syndicated television show on the horizon, publishers around Manhattan were clamoring for the book rights to Goddess Marina's maiden offering.

Maybe it was because I was overwhelmed by the power of reading *The Power of Intention* which has the working principle that people are all connected that made me think that I knew the Goddess Marina, even though we had never met.

While the premise was certainly compelling and would no doubt sell many books, I was unsure that the material could be applied to real life. But that did not seem to be necessary to gain success in the television world, where licensing deals and sponsorships gave people brand name credibility overnight.

On some level, while it felt good to know that my leaving had caused such chaos, I took no joy in seeing my colleagues suffer. On the outside, I wondered if there was some way I could help. And just like that, the universe answered. Not only was Emily dealing with a new boss, sans the Jessie buffer, but also she was knee-deep in wedding plans after her wedding planner had abruptly quit the week before.

"What happened to your planner?" I asked.

"She eloped."

It seems that the wedding planner had had it up to her eyeballs with wedding planning and instead of planning her own took off with her fiancée for unchartered Caribbean territory. She simply could not stand to plan one more wedding, even her own. This was all recounted to Emily via text from the tarmac at the Charlotte Amalie airport in the U.S. Virgin Islands.

"Isn't love grand?" remarked Daniel.

Daniel was the only person I knew in a stable relationship. He and his partner, Patrick, had been together for 20 years and were not convinced that a showy wedding was for them or anyone else, for that matter, gay or straight.

"We were gay before gay was gay…you know what I mean?"

I was not really sure what he meant, but I nodded in solidarity because that's what friends do. I had found something to fix. Emily needed me again, this time to help with her wedding. Before Emily went into any more detail, I took a deep breath, took a pause to increase the suspense of the moment, and volunteered to become, of all things, a wedding planner.

"I can do it. I can plan your wedding."

"REALLY?" said Emily.

"Really?" said Daniel.

"Really," I said.

This leap of faith into the high pressure of world of wedding planning seemed logical for many reasons. First, the couple would be married in New Jersey and I was from New Jersey. Second, I wanted to continue to be viewed as "amazing" in her eyes. And last, I needed to find something to do. None of these reasons were good ones, mind you, but I wanted to be back in the mix and this was a good way to do it. Emily was ready to start the following weekend when Brendan, perhaps already fatigued by coupledom, was heading back to Villanova for a boys' weekend.

The couple had graduated two years ago, but they conducted many aspects of their life together as if they were still in college. Many of their friends had moved in together to save on rent in Manhattan, or went solo in the lower-costing boroughs. Emily and Brendan lived the city life during the week, but on the weekend returned to their college routine, bar crawling till 3 a.m., waking up late, and heading to brunch after noon to consume large amounts of fried cheese and bacon. And they'd then repeat the entire process all over again on Saturday evening. This behavior had somehow convinced them that they were ready for marriage.

Daniel and I referred to this rushed Generation Y union as the starter marriage, as opposed to my peer group, the generation Xers, who meandered into their 30s, married solely to career, a choice that usually resulted in a complete forfeiture of all other unions. The few people I knew who married young also divorced young, and were out there again looking for husband or wife number two. In the end, it all equaled out, I figured.

Emily was not the typical princess bride type. Upon first glance, you would think her a tomboy, a little heavyset, probably an athlete of some sort, but always impeccably groomed. She had embraced the new pampering trend where you can get a manicure and pedicure upon a moment's notice for $20 or have your hair blown out for $45 (with a complimentary glass of wine). The competition for walk-in appointments was so fierce and the demand so great that nail salons outnumbered coffee shops and sushi places combined. And what modern girl could ever get her hair straight enough? A salon that could combine mani, pedi, and blow out was sure to be a gold mine. Note to self: Think about opening multi-purpose salon.

Crazy straight-haired brides made most people uncomfortable, with their unreasonable demands and unrealistic expectations. But I did not expect any of these behaviors from Emily, who was an easygoing, make-no-enemy kind of person. As her first boss at her first job, she was enamored by my confident (or jaded) career woman independence. She viewed me, she had once said in a moment of candor, as "like so much more than a boss."

But, come to think of it, I really didn't know much about Emily outside of the office. Emily as a bride had a more direct side. And before you could say role reversal, I had signed up to work for my old assistant.

"This is perf! It's like I am your boss now!" she giggled.

"OMG." Daniel added.

OMFG, I silently amended. What had I gotten myself into?

Before I could ponder my new role as a wedding planner, I had to
return the errant bathroom keys to MFB. My intention was
to slip them back into their slot without Diane noticing. Keys
returned to their vertical metal home, I would then attend to my
new life's purpose, Emily's wedding. But like most of my life as of
late, I couldn't bank on things going as expected. My new MFB
support team had a different plan for the morning. They had an
order to things; accustomed to the emotionally fragile state of
ex- employees, they were used to people wandering off the reservation, which is why they had put stringent controls in place.

The second round of counseling was scheduled for that
morning, designed, no doubt, to mimic the meeting-heavy
schedule of the corporate world. We were being re- trained to
live on the outside once again, like prisoners receiving group
therapy or drug addicts being scared straight. The counselors
were preparing us for our precarious return to the world of
employment and would not be stayed from that mission. Diane
greeted me once again with a smile. And I tried to make it look
like I just arrived back from the ladies room. If she knew that I
was the key thief, she thankfully did not let on.

"Jessica, here's your name tag, and the conference room is
down the hall to the left. Follow your group down the hall past
conference room A to conference room B."

Like a mindless sheep, I followed the person in front of me to conference room B, another glass-enclosed room, barely distinguishable from its next-door neighbor, conference room A. Our next instruction was to pick up one oversized piece of paper.

"Be sure to write your name on both sides, so that everyone at the table can see your name," Christine, the moderator, explained. Then her tone turned cautionary.

"Bring these nametags to every meeting. You will only get one."

Some of us did that little breathless gasp where you start to laugh and then realize that no one else is laughing, so you stifle yourself and make it look like you are coughing or suppressing a sneeze. She wasn't kidding. Christine was one of those quintessential human resources people who uses the "icebreaker" to ease the awkward tension when people who do not want to be in a meeting together are placed in a meeting together. Icebreakers are supposed to make people more at ease, but usually the opposite is true.

Regardless of the awkward nametag transition, we realized quickly that anonymity and a sense of humor, for that matter, were no longer an option. Once reserved for people who have real troubles, like alcoholism or gambling, we could not keep our names to ourselves and soon all would be revealed. Names on the table, we awaited our next instruction, which Christine was parceling out in an effort not to overwhelm us.

"First, I want you to tell us what you did in corporate. And then tell us what you want to do, outside of corporate." The latter part of her two-pronged question caused puzzling looks on some faces, while others were busy jotting down notes. Perhaps coming up with better descriptions or ways to lend more importance to their former positions.

Chad Braddock, a handsome, lean, graying at the temples type, got the ball rolling. His former position as the CEO of Sierra Nevada Salsa, the nation's largest salsa manufacturer, met with approval from the group. Despite the obvious show of support for salsa, Sierra Nevada sales had been slipping lately due to a host of competitors, and were no longer considered the number one salsa. Chad, like the condiment he produced, felt similarly demoted. Caught up in the wave of sympathy from the group, he neglected the critical part two of the question.

"And...what would you *like* to do..." Christine prompted, speaking in a melodic way so as to encourage Chad to finish her sentence.

"It's pretty unlikely that I'll stay in the premier condiment business," Chad admitted. "I still like food, but I'm not sure that I want to work in it...."

"Thank you for sharing, Chad," Christine said, then circled the room with her eyes.

"Who do we have next?"

All eyes shifted to the nametag of Linda Swanson, a bespectacled, matronly looking woman in a navy blue polyester pantsuit. A small New Jersey perfume plant had recently ousted Linda when Estee Lauder purchased the company. Although she preferred not to name the company, she explained where the plant was located and the fact that they made Elizabeth Taylor's White Diamonds, providing clues to a mystery that otherwise only perfume trade insiders could have been able to solve.

"I would like to launch a glamorous perfume under my name," Linda blurted.

"Terrific, Linda...just terrific."

Kate Maddson spoke next. She had revolutionized the umbrella. Sam Frankel had a miracle vitamin that would increase energy and sex drive. One latecomer, who rebelliously did not put out a nametag, was interested in importing house-keeping staff from China. Apparently, lots of people in Asia *will* do windows, he joked.

The members now moved their gaze down the assembly line of confessions to me.

"Hi, I'm Jessie Desalvo and I was a book publicist for Smith & Drake. And, well, the only thing I can tell you is that after this week the only thing I know is that my boss and I have finally have something in common. Neither of us wants me to be a book publicist again."

Chad Braddock started laughing and was soon followed by most members of the group, and while I had not intended my admission to be comical, it was hard not to laugh out loud at the sheer impossibility of it all. I let out a relieved guffaw, the first release of laughter I had had in days. It felt good. Christine directed her attention to the next person, and Chad gave me a wink.

All of the examples showed people trying to find a life beyond corporate, a life with a new direction; whether those paths would lead to anything remained to be seen. These were purpose-filled people asserting themselves.

After our introductions, Christine encouraged "open networking." Networking with the unemployed seemed a little counterintuitive to me, but there we were. All of us now leveled by our dismissal, equal in our rejection, but each with varying degrees of anger, depression, and confusion to deal with. Some of the more experienced MFB members jotted down names of entrepreneurial bloggers, and networking groups like Le Tip that met at Starbucks in Battery Park on alternating Thursdays. We compared notes about where to find even more conversation, and, in turn, even more confidence building.

This world of seminars and lectures was not foreign to me. Most of my career had been spent booking authors, from Warren Buffet to Marianne Williamson, in places like the Learning Annex and the General Assembly. When looking on the websites of these establishments, it seemed that more and more professionals were teaching seminars with catchy names like "Start Your Own Start-up" to "Living Supersized in a Downsized World." Ex-corporates could choose their flavor of empowerment, whether it was the law of attraction or an office with the proper feng shui. What plagued me was not the lack of help out there, but just exactly what kind of help I needed.

I was also struck by lack of anything to talk about, so while comparing notes with Linda Swanson, the soon-to-be perfume mogul, with no real career news, I panicked and mentioned my newly landed position as a wedding planner. It seemed that in my absence of having any specific career goal, keeping busy doing something, anything, would help me with this career transition.

"I really like helping people," I told Linda with all the confidence of someone who has no idea how to help herself, much less someone else.

"If you're in the business of helping people out, I have a project for you," said a woman decked to the hilt in a Chanel brocade jacket and designer denims.

"You should see my closet." Enter today's featured speaker, Caroline Hendricks, a recent alum of the program, who was here to share her story about building a custom art business online.

Eager to keep the conversation going, I added, "I love going through my closets. When I realize I hate everything inside, it gives me license to buy new stuff."

Nearby, Chad Braddock was shaking his head. No doubt his wife was able to fill a closet or two on that Salsa salary he had brought in through the years.

"Mars and Venus. Mars and Venus," he quipped as he exited the conference room.

Following Caroline's compelling story about selling emerging avant-garde art to her formal stable of Wall Streeters, the group began to file out. Linda Swanson was first to hit the lobby and grabbed for the ladies room key. In full cattle mode, I followed her, letting her shoulder the responsibility for taking and returning the key to the ladies room.

Back in conference room B, Jerome Shiffman had settled himself in front of the wipe board, where he now drew in green (erasable) marker a large oval structure on top of a pyramid. His nameplate in place on the podium, he was ready to tell us all about his new company, Forbidden Fruit. He held up a large spiky piece of fruit, which he explained held magical properties that would make you live longer and better and provide you with the energy of a teenager. When pouring samples of the juice for the group, he made sure first that no one was planning on driving or using heavy machinery following this meeting. Another icebreaker, or a legal disclaimer; I'm still not sure.

After the initial nausea and gag reflex had worn off, it was, as Chad put it, "not that bad." Jerome asked the group to become sales representatives—cue the pyramid diagram and an instant job opportunity was born! Network marketing is the new catch-phrase for what Amway did in the 1950s; get other people to sell things for you. As the group grows the people on top take a cut of the profits from the people they recruit. In a perfect world, everyone gets richer and richer. The goal is to avoid being the person on the bottom.

Today, Jerome wanted to fill spots 1 through 12 on his personal food pyramid. Passionate about this juice, Jerome was so personally vested in the company that he had stocked up on several cases that were now being warehoused in his living room. His take-charge attitude was as refreshing as his strange little juice samples. All in all, the group was enjoying his corporate comeback story, which had begun five years ago when he was let go from Lehman Brothers, where he was selling sub-prime mortgages.

His "never going back" moment happened when he sat on his couch and proceeded to build a business there. Most interested in his story was a fellow financial services refugee, Lillian Gorman, who had chosen the route of spiritual empowerment to heal her corporate wounds. Upon being ousted from her cubicle, she chartered the first flight out of JFK to Arizona. While visiting a spiritual retreat in Sedona, she was romanced into sinking her 401(k) into a condo near the red rocks. Lillian had cornered Jerome and was already signing on as a salesperson.

"There are no coincidences. I am salesperson number one," she boldly declared.

She was no doubt buoyed by the cosmic energy and recent real estate purchase in Arizona. This job was perfect for her and she, too, could work from her new Southwestern-patterned couch in Sedona.

As the final war stories were relayed, network meetings jotted down and articles circulated, Christine excused the group, reminding us once again to take our nametags, for next time! Before I could leave, Christine met me at the door and handed me her business card and home address.

"Can you be at my place on Sunday?"

And of course, I could be.

6

The subway ride to Caroline's apartment in Astoria took longer than I thought, but nothing was going to bring me down. I was officially back in the work force. I had gained a client; even the word client made me feel important, needed, necessary.

Caroline wanted to discuss her wardrobe. Unclear about exactly what to expect, I felt confident that I could easily maneuver myself around her closet and tell her what looked good on her and what didn't. Maybe this could be the start of my career as a fashion stylist. Even though I had no formal training at the House of Dior or a degree from FIT, I loved clothes and, well, you have to start somewhere. Note to self: Get a copy of French *Vogue* for the ride home.

I thought it would be important to present a classic look, so I was appropriately attired for the occasion in a tailored pair of navy trousers and a Kelly green sweater set. I purposely chose an outfit that was not too bold, something that would be non-intimidating, like an outfit an author might wear to be interviewed on *CBS Sunday Morning*.

I arrived a few minutes late and was prepared to apologize profusely for my tardiness. I hate being late for anything and being late for my first client meeting bordered on the careless. But some people had a looser grip on time than I did, and Caroline was one of them. Caroline did not answer when I rang the buzzer, so I waited in the lobby for 10 minutes, pondering whether I was in the right place at all, or maybe I had gotten the date and time wrong or worse, *had completely misunderstood what I was supposed to be doing here.* I double-checked my voice mails, my texts, even my GPS to make sure that I was in the right place at the right time. I was. After the third ring, I was buzzed in without a word. Caroline answered the door, clad in a towel, turban, and bathrobe. Caroline immediately commented on how "charming" I looked.

"I just got back from the gym. Pardon my appearance."

Her appearance looked pretty good to me, robe or not. She was about my age, well proportioned; one might describe her as a handsome woman with a girlish figure. She was nearly six feet tall. She offered me a drink and a snack before taking off her towel turban, revealing a thick blond mane of hair, which she immediately tied up in a clip that she had holding her robe together.

My attention was diverted from her suddenly plunging neckline to a tray of fresh strawberries along with a pitcher of water with cucumber slices. The tray was perfectly appointed, the berries were perfectly ripe, and the Kate Spade dessert plates and matching juice glasses looked like they were part of a window display at Bed Bath & Beyond. I was right. They hadn't been used before. When I commented on them, she said, "Just got them. T.J. Maxx, $14.99. I mean, you can't go wrong."

Like a sartorial harbinger, these small pieces of information that she shared told me a lot about her habits. When I gazed around the room, I noticed a bundle of unopened shopping bags whose contents had yet to be worn as well. Like little guideposts to the stores along Seventh Avenue, Loehmanns, T.J. Maxx, and Barneys were lined up next to one another in what appeared to be address order. It looked like on her way back from the David

Barton Gym in Chelsea, she had done a little retail exercising as well. Perhaps that's what had delayed her.

"I thought we would start in the walk-in closet," she said. And instead of excusing herself to change into clothes, she simply led me into the next room. The "walk-in closet" was more like a walk-in room, complete with a center island, and featured two Henry VIII-looking chairs in case, while you are getting dressed, you needed to take a break. Perhaps the overwhelming number of shoe choices might make you lightheaded and in need of a place to rest.

"I just don't know where to start," she explained as she looked around the room, which was actually larger than some Manhattan studio apartments I had been in.

Frankly, I didn't know where to start, either; there were more clothes here than the stock room at Bloomingdales. I took a deep breath and surveyed the custom-built closets that lined the walls; were there four or five?

"Why don't you tell me what you need the most help with?" I adopted a prescriptive, doctorly tone like when you go for an exam and the doctor asks, "Where does it hurt?"

"I guess before we start, I should tell you my little secret."

I expected her to tell me about her recent trip to Shopaholics Anonymous, an admission that I would expect based upon the fact that she had a garment rack full of newly purchased items with the price tags still on them. The rolling rack was like the ones you see being pushed through the streets of the garment district to transport the latest season from designer showroom to Macy's for a quick trunk sale. I had never seen one in someone's home. Mainly because no one had the room for this and secondly, because no one has this much turnover on merchandise requiring that new arrivals wait outside the closet until more space could be cleared. Another clue was the dressing room floor, which was covered with shopping bags from Bloomingdales, Bergdorf's, and Bendel's—the three Bs of high-end retail.

"Maybe I should just show you?" she said. And before I could say buyer's remorse, Caroline had taken off her robe.

"I had lap band surgery," she confessed.

I had never seen lap band scars or surgery scars of any kind before, nor was I comfortable with a near six-foot-tall naked woman casually conducting a conversation with me about her body. I was in new territory on both counts. The scars were about three inches in length and made a zigzag square pattern down the length of her belly. I tried my best not to react and make her feel uncomfortable, but she was not in the least bit fazed. I was the one who was uncomfortable, and I had a difficult time figuring out where to set my vision.

"Pretty invasive, huh? They really don't tell you what it will look like. But apparently, they fade over time."

She explained that once you have this surgery, you have to eat less and less and in the last few weeks, after losing 65 pounds, she had actually gained back five pounds. She was ashamed, horrified, and panic-stricken over the weight gain. That was why she had asked my help.

"And now, I just have nothing to wear," she said with what had to be the most ironic comment I had ever heard.

Her dilemma was further exacerbated by the fact that she was not wearing a stitch of clothing. But I secretly suspected that the opposite was true. Could she really be without anything to wear with all the clothing options around her? I was overwhelmed as well; I collapsed in one of the Henry VIII chairs to regroup for a moment, as though weighed down by the conundrum she had just saddled me with. I already recognized the first stage of recovery: denial. She was in complete denial about what her problem truly was; it was not that she did not have anything to wear, but way, way too much when it came to wardrobe options.

"Let's take it slowly, one closet at a time," I said.

I suggested a tour through the closets where she could pick out some things to try on for me. This was a great solution, because not only would it give me a sense of what fit her, but it would also get the naked woman who stood in front of me into some clothes.

Closet number one was filled with fur vests and animal prints; frankly, it looked more like an exhibit at the Museum of Natural History than a workable wardrobe. I dismissed going through this one first; it was too big of a bear to handle. Closet number two was "fancy," she told me. This was haute couture, high designer, and featured fewer pieces, but some big space suckers, like a full-length Yves Saint Laurent ball gown that had never been worn and spread out to take up seemingly half the closet. Okay, I'm exaggerating. It was really just a quarter.

"It's insane, I know, but I got a great deal on it."

"And where exactly did you plan to go in that one?"

"Nowhere really, but I thought it would be a good thing to have," she fumbled.

When I pulled out a Joan Vass two-piece black ensemble with cutaways, Caroline explained that she thought it might be fun to dress like one of the Real Housewives of New York. Of course, the tags were still on this outfit. Because things worn on reality television are never actually really worn in reality.

"Fun?" I asked. "Are these outfits having any fun in your closet? You know what's fun, taking that $6,000 and heading to the Caribbean. That's fun."

I said it jokingly, but good humor often has a darker side and I was getting a little annoyed with this blatant waste of money. But Caroline responded in kind.

"That would be fun, and I have the perfect thing to wear."
She pulled out a sequin-accented sari skirt that, yes, would be
perfect for the islands.

"Now you're talking," I said, "except I think maybe the
sequins might be a little much..."

"Ya think?"

"Yeah, I think."

I didn't want to make the woman feel bad by letting her
know that $6,000 for two outfits, even if they were a good deal,
was not money well spent when you don't wear the items and
you keep them locked up in your closet for three years. I was
ready to move from anger to acceptance, but she needed a little
more encouragement.

"How about we sell them on eBay to recoup some of your
losses? I'm sure someone needs a ball gown to attend a fundraiser or a Real Housewives Halloween costume party."

She loved that idea, mainly because it might open up some
more discretionary shopping dollars and also provide more
space in her crowded closets. Whatever the reason, we had to
move these pieces out of her working wardrobe and release
them back to where they belonged, which was any place but
here. I immediately conjured up a picture of the husband and
wife setting loose into the wild their beloved lions at the end of
Born Free.

Getting back to basics, I realized, was the key to success. And
a little tough love wouldn't hurt, either, I reckoned. I instructed
Caroline to pick out an everyday outfit she felt the best in. Two
pieces she loved, that she wore, over and over again, because
they made her feel good. She immediately picked out a black pair
of tailored Michael Kors trousers and a perfect white button-
down blouse from the French shirt maker Anne Fontaine.

"This is my uniform," she shared with me.

Trying it on put us both at ease. We had our basic template for what this woman actually wore. But the truth lurking inside closet number three was her true secret: 25 outfits, identical to the one she was wearing. The problem was they were all different sizes, each representing one step on her journey to weight loss.

"Those used to fit, those never fit, these might fit," she itemized them for me. Like Goldilocks, she was starting to make some hard decisions.

In an effort to establish some middle ground, I took out all the pieces that represented the extremes; she had sizes 2 to 14. The pants she had on were a 10 and fit perfectly, five pounds or not. We quickly eliminated the size 2s, the 4s, the 6s, and the 8s. As we did so, I recited a little cheer that I had learned in little league, "2, 4, 6, 8 who do we appreciate! Caroline the 10, Caroline the 10, yay, Caroline!"

After about two hours of trying things on, we had piled 15 brand new pairs of pants and 10 blouses that did not fit onto one of the Henry VIII chairs, hoping the sheer weight of the clothes would not cause its spindly legs to collapse. Perhaps, if they held up, there was a better use for these chairs after all. The rolling rack summoned me from the far side of the closet; I knew damn well that half, if not all, of that stuff had to go back as well. Caroline confessed to me as much.

"When I get depressed, I shop, and since I have nothing to wear, I bought all this stuff to try on at home to see what I liked best."

Caroline had developed another bad habit, it seemed. She would buy things off the rack and plan to return them later. All of the clothes on this rack and the shopping bags on the floor were bought without trying them on. For someone who had lost weight and was still in the process of slimming down, this was not a great habit to have. This myriad of sizes was making her feel bad about not fitting into her latest purchases. It would have been better if she had taken the extra time to try the items on and buy them in the right size in the first place.

We painstakingly went through everything and amassed quite a return pile. The Caribbean trip was looking closer and closer.

"Do you want me to come with you to do some returns today? It might be easier with two of us," I offered.

"That would be great," she said.

She was relieved to have the company and I was relieved to have a task. We ended our trip at Saks and stopped at the café for coffee and a snack, and, more important, to review how much money we had recouped: $2,450 had been credited back to her card.

"Can we make another date to do this again? This was fun," she asked over cappuccino and biscotti.

I took out my hot pink iPad case and opened it to arrange our next appointment.

"Nice case, I love it," she commented.

"Don't get any ideas," I joked.

We agreed to meet every weekend until the bulk of the returns and closet purging would be completed.

"I just love making new friends. Now I feel like you're my new best friend—well, my best friend for hire, anyway."

"Right," I agreed.

I continued my journey on foot to the PATH train, pondering every aspect of this meeting. All I kept thinking of was what Caroline and I talked about, how much fun the session had been. How many more city girls like her needed reliable advice from someone they could trust? It was like how you ask your best friend for advice or to help you pick out an outfit, or to tell you what kind of flowers to put in your wedding bouquet. This was the stuff that a best friend would do for free, except Caroline was evidence that people would be willing to pay for this service. But what happened if you didn't have a best friend? I had just found my new calling; no longer was I Jessie De Salvo, unemployed former publishing executive. Now I was Jessie De Salvo, "Best Friend for Hire." Hear me roar.

It can be hard to sleep the night before the first day of the rest of your life. I tossed and turned most of the night thinking about the endless possibilities of my new company. I formulated logo design, stationery colors, and marketing strategies for my new venture, BFH, Best Friend for Hire. I thought about my business card and my new title, would I be president, CEO, Head Friend? When the sun finally came up, I was ready. I got dressed and headed to my makeshift desk on the counter that separated my kitchen and living room. This was not my ideal setting for the big business venture I was about to spearhead. Plus, I could not have clients at my house. That would be unprofessional. I needed a real office, a headquarters, and one worthy of my grand plan. This lofty thought process was derailed quickly when I compared what was left in my bank account to the fee of a rental office in town. My early market research indicated that something else would be needed to solve my first business challenge. Renting an office was out of the question.

Instead of mulling this heavy decision alone in my apartment, I decided to join the legions of day workers already at Starbucks, where all business ideas begin. Despite the fact that my town was only one mile square, there were three Starbuck locations: uptown, downtown and midtown. After a side-by-side comparison of each location, I chose the uptown one based on its ample seating area and particular customer demographic. My inner-market research team was working overtime.

The clientele was made up of nannies and stay-at-home moms from the nearby highrises who grabbed frappuccinos before stationing themselves at the nearby park to watch young Madison, Hudson, or Clinton play with other like-named toddlers. (All these names were adopted from the street names in town.) The downtown and midtown locations catered to worker bees who would install themselves from morning till night, hoarding the free Wi-Fi service and available electrical outlets. Finding a space there would be the very definition of insanity.

Hoboken had gone a little crazy over coffee: there were also four Dunkin' Donuts, two independent coffee houses, as well as a Panera for those who need of a lot of coffee and a panini on artisanal bread. There, they can buy a cup early in the day and fill up all day long if they chose. This was the skinny provided by a wise entrepreneur I had met during a business card exchange in Weehawken last month.

The business card exchange was designed for service people to not only swap their contact information, but also exchange the name of a client in need of service. That rarely happened. The only useful exchange I made was this piece of information about the Panera, which was located, by the way, next to a Starbucks.

Once inside the uptown location, I was lucky enough to stake claim to the best seat, the one closest to the faux gas fireplace and a handy electrical outlet. Like a lion stalking his prey, I marked my territory by spreading out an array of business magazines and sample business plans on the table. I had to let the others know that I wasn't going anywhere, a useful survival tactic in the land of coffee. Some of the aboriginals had sensed a new person disrupting the natural order of things.

The first order of business was the business plan. Putting the right image out there was important and I needed a solid plan in place to achieve that. A good business plan is essential; at least that is what it said on pages 89-99 in my copy of *Business Plans for Dummies*. *"The plan should be a road map chartering the course of the business. This document is necessary to plan for the next five years of business growth and should be aligned with the company mission."*

I wondered if there was a prequel to this book, for someone like me, at the level below "novice." Some aspect of this heady advice did sink in; the mission statement, what was my mission or more important, what was the mission of the BHF? At this point, I wished I could hire my own fully realized company to help me out of this jam and that's when it occurred to me. Sometimes people just need to bounce things off of someone else and that is what BFH would be, a sounding board, a supportive ear, someone to hear what you are saying and make a helpful suggestion.

But instead of trying to change the world, BFH would help everyday people solve everyday problems. I decided to start small, in my own backyard; after all, if I was going to gain trust and be that valued friend, that girl next door, I should probably start in a place where I actually was the girl next door.

On the chair next door to me was a copy of the *Hoboken Reporter*, the town's local paper. My quick scans of the classified section showed several listings for home improvement, but not one on self-improvement, my target. I wanted to fix people, not their houses. Putting aside the business plan for a moment, I adopted Mohammad's approach: If the mountain wouldn't come to me, then I would go to the mountain. In my case, the mountain was placing a classified ad in the local paper. I wrote:

Need an idea, stuck in a rut, need someone to lend an ear?

Because little problems are not little to us.

Call Best Friend for Hire today for a free consultation.

My Venti coffee had cooled from the nuclear boiling point at which it had been served to me, but it was still too bitter to drink; it needed another hit of *Sugar in the Raw*. At the coffee fixings bar was a man who looked familiar. It's hard to figure out where you know someone from when they're out of context. The way he was dressed ruled out all the usual places: publishing, networking, outplacement, and FOE (Friend of Emily). Nothing registered.

He was wearing faded black Diesel jeans, a Metallica shirt, and a denim jacket with the sleeves ripped off. This ensemble provided a peek-a-boo look at his heavily muscled and heavily tattooed upper arms. He was in direct contrast to the Jamaican-speaking nanny who was ordering the sweet tea in line ahead of him. I poured out half of my coffee to replace it with half-and-half and I noticed that he did the same. They never leave room for milk, I thought to myself. And as if he'd heard my thoughts, he said, "You have to ask them to leave room for milk." I nodded in agreement, giving him an even closer inspection than I had before. He studied my outfit, which was different as well.

No longer tied to the corporate suit, my new working kit consisted of jeans and a T-shirt in cobalt blue. Hair, which was usually blown out, was free to be itself, curly. Glasses had replaced contacts. Ballet flats stood in for heels. In just two weeks, I had transformed at least my physical appearance. I felt comfortable until he reached into my personal stirring space and grabbed a napkin. He tried to get a closer look at me. This was my new form of office stress.

"Hey, I thought that was you," he said, as if the proximity had triggered the proverbial light bulb.

"It's me, hi, hi, there." His closeness was making me uncomfortable. I moved back a step closer to my table before someone
else pounced on it.

"Things look better since the last time I saw you."

"Right, they are," I agreed.

Still unaware of who this person was or when the last time
we saw each other, I decided to fake it and play along until I
could place him.

"You don't remember me, do you? I served you a few
mimosas at my bar, a while ago." He moved even closer, if that
was possible. He really had no respect for personal space.

And then it all came screaming back to reality, the firing day,
the Derek and Allison betrayal day, the last day of my old life.
And most of all, the way I looked when he had seen me: disheveled, distraught, and dumped, not the greatest first impression.

"Oh, of course, I remember you. Nice to see you again. I
better get back to my table." I inched closer to my things and
farther away from this awkward reunion.

Already a realtor and client complete with listing sheets
were staging a table takeover. So preoccupied with their Old
West-style claim jumping, I left the boundary-challenged man
mid-sentence to return to my seat. He recovered quickly when
an entire Greek chorus of well-wishers swarmed him. From
a guy in jeggings who was also wearing a denim jacket with
ripped-off sleeves came a, *"Wassup brother, saw the paper"* and
a fist bump. Two giddy girls tried to manage a hug without
spilling their impossibly tall parfait-like coffee concoctions.
Even the Jamaican nanny pushed her double stroller of identical twins alongside to join the conversation.

"Dave, how are you holding it down?"

"Hey, Trana, whatever doesn't kill you makes you stronger,
right?"

"You said it, Mon, don't let it bug ya!" And off she strolled.

Dave waded through his supporters and seated himself at a table across from mine. He was challenged by the fact that I did not recognize him and respond like everyone else in the place had. He sipped his coffee meditatively, sat back and crossed his leg. Dave was one of those people who had the rare ability to be comfortable anywhere, in any venue, at any time. He had made himself right at home, which made me more even uncomfortable, bordering on awkward. As he sat in the chair across from me, he looked like a giant sitting at a dollhouse table. Why was it that when he sat he seemed taller than when he was standing? Before I could figure out this paradox, Dave was back to the questions.

"What are ya working on, anyway, the theory of relativity?" He peeked over at my notes and saw the words "business plan."

"I'm starting my own business today," I announced triumphantly. And immediately regretted my candor.

Thankfully, I was interrupted before I could cover up my embarrassment and politely tell him that I needed my "office" space, even though the opposite was true. The vest-wearing fist-bumper or, as he described himself, his "brother from another mother," had returned. Our threesome was complete when Dave made the introductions.

"This is, uh, wait, I don't know your name."

"Jessie, it's Jessie," I fumbled.

"Jess, right Jess. This is Bertram, he helps me at my bar from time to time, at least while I still have the bar."

The word "still" hung in the air over the three of us. Bertram noticeably sighed in sad disbelief.

"What's happening to your bar?" I asked, revealing that I was the only person in the room, or even the town, so preoccupied had I been with my own situation, who was unaware of what had happened.

"It's all here in the *Reporter*. My bar is closing."

I had not seen the news; I had looked through the classifieds and slipped past the front page entirely. The headline, which appeared just below the handyman listing and police blotter read, "Landmark Hoboken Bar to Close."

This was surprising news on all fronts. Not only was Dave the owner of the famed bar The Garage, and not just the bartender, as I thought, but his bar was best known for being the location for a famous Bruce Springsteen video from the mid-'80s. The article cited financial difficulties that even The Boss himself couldn't fix. That last part was cheap journalistic license, I thought.

Not many bars in town had live music. All the downtown bars that were owned by hotels or larger restaurant companies played indecipherable electronic music or had a DJ, which was cheaper than paying bands. With all the competition for bars in town, it was a survival of the fittest mentality to keep costs down and the doors open. The Garage was an expensive place to run because the big-name acts it hosted were paid top dollar.

Part of the reason that big-name acts wanted to play there was the intimate back room setting. This proved to be a two-edged sword. The bar could only hold a limited number of people, so profits were small. With rising operating costs, Dave's business model was no longer feasible.

Looked like I was not the only one grappling with a business plan that day. Dave had given up on his business challenge, but his comrade, Bertram, was not ready to throw in the towel on their plans that quickly. As manager of the club, he had a vested interest in its success and was willing to do just about anything to save it.

"Listen, I'm on my way back to the club now to work on the fundraiser lineup."

His current business plan was to gather the regulars, many of whom had moved out of town, to the event and ask them for a donation to keep the place going. This was a nice idea for a casual party when you circulate a hat around to pay the band. But this was not going to work to save this club from impending financial ruin. They would need media and a lot of it. I covertly listened to his plans while I stenciled BFH logos on the inside of my business journal over and over again, like a lovesick teenager writing the name of her beloved inside her trapper-keeper.

I couldn't help but interject, "If you want this to work, you'll need a celebrity guest list—they love a good cause—a big headliner, maybe even The Boss himself. I'd probably get some rock bloggers out there, call the mayor, and maybe even call *Rolling Stone*. Could be a good story for them," I said casually, without looking up.

"If your publicist does all that, you might just have a chance," I added.

Suddenly, they were both staring at me. I looked up and took off my glasses.

"What?" I asked.

Dave smiled.

Bertram smiled.

Dave looked at Bertram with that "are you thinking what I'm thinking look." Bertram nodded in full conspiracy mode, repeating his agreement with phrases like, "brilliant," "this could work," and "Dave, this could work...."

Dave, buoyed by Bertram's enthusiasm, moved in for the kill. He uncrossed his long legs and leaned in closer to me. It had been so long since I had any man that close to me; I was a bit overwhelmed. I fumbled for my glasses. His super-white teeth gleamed, and I detected his smell, fresh and soapy, like he had just gotten out of the shower. While staring into my eyes, he said, "My only problem is that I don't have someone smart like *you* to help me...."

Cue the finale music, the fat woman was singing somewhere. A crafty little twist of his pouty lips might have sealed the deal for me, but it was more than that, it was what he said, more than how he said it or the way he looked saying it, for that matter. The emphasis was squarely on "smart like you" that simultaneously charmed me like a schoolgirl and flattered my business acumen like he was addressing a captain of industry.

"Or do I?" he probed.

"You do still owe me...for all those free mimosas, and all..."

I giggled. I could see why those other girls had almost dropped their coffees.

When first starting a business, there is so much that is unknown. The art of business negotiation and all of its nuances were foreign to me. Up until that point, I was unaware of the many assets I had that could be useful to another businessperson. But Dave, a skilled negotiator, introduced me to an entrepreneurial staple, the barter. Sure, it would have been better to be paid money for my work that I could then apply to my mounting bills. That's how work and life balance off each other in the real business world. But I was in a new work life structure entirely. Getting something to build the business would be just as good as money. If The Electric Company and Verizon honored the barter, we might have been really on to something. Since the balance on my checking account was decreasing to warning levels, I needed to launch this business— and quickly. I was prepared to make a deal.

His logic was elegant in its simplicity. He needed a publicist and I needed an office.

"I have something you need, you have something I need," he continued.

"And what exactly do you have that I need?" I flirted back.

"I have the perfect headquarters for your new company, a fantastic office space and it's available. All you have to do is provide a little publicity help. And the best part is that, the space is totally free. A fair exchange of our assets."

It did not take too much convincing for me to leave my Starbucks pseudo-office and upgrade to his private space. And I did like the way he smiled when he mentioned my name in a familiar tone: Jess instead of Jessica or even Jessie. No one ever called me the ultra casual "Jess." I liked it a lot.

And then everything began to move in slow motion, as it tended to do when really important things happened in my life. He talked, but made no sound, and I stared at his impossibly white teeth wondering if he used Crest Whitening Strips or if he had had them professionally done.

"Jess, you can't run a real business in a Starbucks; no one will take you seriously."

The realtor and his client who were still lurking nearby waiting for a table to open overheard this comment.

"Sorry, Gerard, no offense. I didn't mean you," Dave addressed to one of the hoverers.

"None taken, man. Good luck with the bar and if it doesn't work out, it would make a great condo."

"I'll keep that in mind," Dave said, in a tone of voice that indicated he would never ever consider that option.

My confidence level was at an all-time high. I was a good publicist and I was convinced that I could help Dave save the day and maybe even the bar. It was all quite a romantic notion. I envisioned a new headline in the *Hoboken Reporter*, "Best Friend for Hire Saves the Day." The picture alongside the front-page story would show me atop Dave's broad shoulders and Bruce Springsteen would be serenading me, all the while getting major publicity for my new business. It was good for everyone, I rationalized.

Gerard and his potential client who had eavesdropped the entire conversation moved in for the kill. They sensed that Dave had this in the bag and our meeting was at an end. As we vacated my coveted spot and gathered my mobile office, Dave threw my bag over his shoulder and said, "This looks like the beginning of a beautiful friendship," even selling the line with a Humphrey Bogart lisp.

On the way over to the club, I hoped that my agreement with Dave would net clearer results than in *Casablanca*. And with that, BFH had its first pro bono client. It was all very Live Aid, I thought.

The Garage still looked like an active club on the corner of Washington Street. The door had posters for bands and a calendar for the upcoming month's events. The only difference was a sign that posted new hours—"Open on weekends only." Due to the imminent closure, Dave could not afford to keep the place open all week; instead of firing staff, he limited the bar hours and rotated his people so that everyone could still get some pay.

We entered through the back door. I felt like I had gained secret entry to the club, where the cool kids hung out. Dave was true to his word and insisted on showing me my office, to make sure I liked it, before we started work on his end of the deal. Even at that point, I was unsure that someone who looked as intimidating as Dave could be so sweet, even chivalrous.

The small upstairs office looked more like a college dorm room than a place of business. One desk was for the accountant and the other for the booker. On the walls were signed posters from bands that had appeared there: The Smithereens, The Alarm, Natalie Merchant, and even The Boss himself at the beginning of his career.

"Take your pick. The booker's work is done, no more bands to book. And well, the accountant, not sure even if he is ever coming back."

He put my bag down on the desk and looked around as if taking a survey of what was there.

"I never come up here anymore. I never liked offices, anyway."

This was made clear when he opted to sit on top of the desk that I was sitting at, instead of simply sitting in the provided guest chair. Again, he was encroaching on my personal space, but I was starting to get used to that. He told me I could redecorate, if I liked, but there was something nice about all these bands in their live-action concert glory. It seemed unfair to evict all those musicians abruptly without a fight. Besides. This was going to be a temporary office, just until I could afford a proper headquarters for BFH.

Saving the bar was a small part of my grand business plan. But the key to any good business plan is a clear mission statement. And at that point, my mission was clear: to start BFH through all necessary means, and if that meant saving a club and its owner along the way, so be it.

My lack of real employment was becoming a cause of deep concern for my family, which was one of the reasons that James and I were meeting for a check-in session. James, my brother, was waiting for me at Swift Bar on West Fourth Street in New York's Greenwich Village is where, like a good son, he was to check on my general mental condition and find out what was on the schedule for the rest of my life. Another thing about my family, they all talk behind each other's backs. To be fair, most of what they say behind one another's back is what they would say to your face anyway, so no one can get really offended. That is just the way it is. Despite my family's need to get me back on track, these first few days of inertia were seen as laziness, and it was making them uncomfortable; at least that's what they were telling one another.

I reported for my intervention of one, fully prepared to go through a verbal "to- do" list of all the things I was doing to prove that I was actually doing something. Another habit in my family, we all are constantly reporting on our activities so that we can prove our worth to one another and look for approval. The networking group and my family had many similarities. If my grandmother were to attend the networking group, she likely would have cut to the chase and tell the people wallowing in their rejection to simply "suck it up." Note to self: see if grandma has a speaker's agent.

James was sitting at the end of the bar, easily recognizable because he had not changed in years; it's a look best described as rumpled elegance. Thick, wavy black hair fringes his eyes and he has pale skin and hazel green eyes, unlike my tan skin and dark brown eyes. He is wearing his usual uniform: a black biker jacket, Levi 501s, and a graphic T-shirt with either a political statement or alternative rock band emblazoned on it. Today's choice was a longtime favorite, a faded black Joy Division shirt. Older by four years, James had always been my barometer for cool. When he dropped out of Montclair State's music department to pursue what he had hoped would be a promising solo music career, my parents were worried. But he immediately sold a punk rock-inspired jingle to Playskool and started earning money. He was actively pursuing his passion and my parents could not argue with the fact that he had supported himself from the time he was 18.

Work followed as a studio guitarist, and he happily bounced around the New York City musician scene. He even played an occasional "mercy gig" at a wedding or bar mitzvah to make his rent. I was convinced that he got work more for his cool aura than his actual talent, which, although undeniable, was probably at the same level of the thousands of unemployed guitarists all over the city. When he caught sight of me, he flipped back an errant curl and pulled me in for a nuggie. But just as the bartender served me my Heffeweisen beer, James was paying the tab and rushing me out the door.

"Jessie, I am glad you're here. And I will tell Ma that you are doing fine, which I am sure you are, right? But let's head out. I need your help with something."

Heading east toward Avenue A, James told me that his new girlfriend, Tara, would be moving in with him and they could use a little help with organizing the move. James explained that it would probably be easier for one girl to help another girl move. At the doorstep of her building, her faint voice answered the intercom and an insanely loud buzzer offered us entry to the walk-up building. The entryway and stairways of this one-time tenement building had likely not been cleaned since the building was constructed.

Tara was waiting for us at her door, which she cracked open about an inch. James gave a nod, as if to say, "She's cool," meaning me. This was my second meeting with Tara; the first had been at the very same bar that James and I had just left. People who live in New York City rarely have people over; you could know someone for years and never set foot into their apartment. This could be for some very simple reason, like your work friends prefer to meet and socialize near the office, or some people you know commute into the city and want to take advantage of all their local bars and restaurants, or people just don't have the space to entertain. All of these are acceptable reasons, but I was beginning to sense that none of these reasons were Tara's. In fact, no one at work had ever been in my apartment, mainly because it's on the wrong side of the Hudson, even though Hoboken is closer by distance to Manhattan than parts of Brooklyn, and by time faster than the Upper East Side, where it is nearly impossible to find an adjacent subway entrance to your house. Hoboken has the sad distinction of being located in the much-maligned state of New Jersey, thus making travel there by most New Yorkers unlikely.

Tara cracked the door a few more inches and said for us to come on in. This statement proved to be the first difficult transition into Tara's apartment. James pushed the door a bit more and headed in first. I wondered, not without a little bit of apprehension, what I was going to find on the other side of that door.

Entry into this apartment was not easy. The small foyer was covered with a potpourri of shopping bags of every variety. Based on what I was seeing, when asked if she wanted plastic or paper, Tara's most likely reply had been, "Yes." Several broken umbrellas sat upon an intricate recycling system consisting of twin garbage cans, one for plastic and cans and another for paper. The overflowing paper receptacle needed further investigation. Inside, it had little plastic bundles of shredded paper. They looked like little gift bags. Tara had put a ton of effort into recycling. As a late night office worker, I would often greet the evening cleaning staff. Office policy was strict: place regular garbage in bag-lined garbage cans and paper garbage in blue recycling bins. Every employee had one of each receptacle.

I watched in horror as the cleaning crew would take each receptacle and empty them into the same dumpster. This recycling thing was a hoax, I thought. Since that shocking revelation, my confidence in recycling was forever changed. In the interest of full disclosure, conspiracy theories are something that come naturally to me. Could be the Sicilian superstition gene, but both James and I had our own theories about who was behind the Kennedy assassination and who actually set foot on the moon first. We just didn't believe everything we read.

Past the bins, a stack of mail teetered above the floor, propped up by what I thought was a table, but it was so obscured I could not tell. But more than the visual distraction, all this clutter was causing a physical impediment as well; there was no easy way to get into this apartment. With all of the garbage stacked in front of the door, the door itself could only open about five inches. James had mastered entry to this secret fortress by turning sideways and sidling his way through a small path already cleared on the floor. This was not an easy maneuver for him. James is a lean six feet tall, but here he looked like a giant entering this dark crowded place. We were similar in build, but I lacked the height gene, being just a few inches above five feet tall. He waved me in, encouraging me to follow him using the same method.

What was particularly odd about this was that Tara did not think this was odd at all. She watched our side-shimmy and quickly directed our attention to where she had been packing. Usually, when someone is packing for a move, there is disarray; things are temporarily displaced before they find their even more temporary homes in moving boxes. But the designated packing area was not at all distinguishable from the rest of the crowded mess. The two-room apartment, which would have been considered roomy by Manhattan standards, was so crowded with stuff that it was nearly impossible to see what was garbage and what was worthy of packing. She couldn't possibly think that the contents of this apartment could be moved and recreated at James's small studio apartment. While I was creeping further into the space, two precariously placed boxes that were on top of the dresser caused a mini avalanche of coins, receipts, gum wrappers, and Duane Reade bags to cascade down around me. One of the boxes tumbled down, ousting in the process its resident, an oversized black cat, which landed on its feet right in front of me. He hissed at me and pounced into the corner, where a well-worn scratching post awaited more defacing. I felt like telling him, "Hey, it's not my fault."

"Mr. Felix is hard to get to know at first, but he's really quite friendly," Tara explained.

I should note that Mr. Felix was not the only feline resident here; my eyes drifted toward the two open litter boxes that blocked entry into the second room. Mr. Felix had a roommate who had yet to announce him- or herself. It looked like James was about to have three new roommates.

Like a museum visitor, I scanned the room in amazement. James shifted, moving boxes from hand to hand in an effort to appear casual. As if to say, this disarray we were standing amidst was just temporary, a function of the move. But we all knew it was not the case. Tara adopted the role of gracious hostess, offering herbal tea and a place to sit down. But I didn't want to sit. I was afraid to sit. This entire Grey Gardens scene had made me extremely uncomfortable. Not only did I not know how to help Tara, but I was also thrown off by the intimacy of knowing that she lived this way. If it were me, I would have been embarrassed, but she didn't act as though there was anything amiss.

The De Salvos are meticulously clean people. James and I grew up in a hermetically sealed environment. If Ma had known about this place, she would not only have disapproved, but she also would have encouraged James to run for the hills. With all the stuff on the dressers, the furniture, and the floors, it was obvious a good housekeeping had not taken place in many years. There is an Italian word for this, *skeeve*, which can be used as a verb or noun to show deep disgust for something providing a viscerally uncomfortable sensation that could even lead to nausea. The implication is that the offending item or items is dirty, germ-ridden.

As children, we had heard this word constantly. The dishtowel is only to be used when your hands are clean, Ma would caution, and don't sit on the bed in your street clothes, they have germs, you know. But probably the best evidence of my mother's intolerance for things she deemed "skeevy" was her inherited skills at cleaning chickens before they were cooked. To counteract her "skeeve" of birds (she thought they were filthy), every chicken that was to be eaten in our house was put through a brutal hot-water-and-salt bath. The bird was then inspected and trimmed and scrubbed further for any evidence of its "bird"-like existence. My mother, who is short on compliments, always had a good word to say about anyone who was clean. Of her own mother, one of the few nice things I ever heard her say was, *that woman sure knew how to clean a chicken.*

That world of clean chickens, pristine bed linens, and immaculate dishtowels was in direct contrast to the "thing" that I was supposed to be helping James with. How in the world James thought I could help was beyond me. But here we three stood. Moving day ahead and more junk to weed through than at a landfill. Tara, a compassionate person about other people's hardships, wanted a full update on how I was doing with the unemployment. Funny thing about people in crisis: they are always willing to shift focus to someone else's problems. Resisting the urge to smack her and say, *"You're worried about me, you're living like a homeless person,"* I thanked her for her concern and looked to James to bridge the conversational gap that was opening wider and wider.

"Jessie has always been the organized one in the family and, well, she loves packing things up, so when she offered to help...."

Throwing my drowning brother a life preserver, I began to explain my long fascination with putting things away, and how my childhood Barbie collection was still preserved in its pink carrying case in the basement of my parents' house.

"It looks like she never even played with them," James added.

How we got from my pristine doll collection to what appeared to be the home of a madwoman was beyond me, but I played along. Step one is negotiation. Tara had not created this alternate universe overnight, so what made us think that she was going to be ready to part with all of the items she had so painstakingly saved. Resistance from our patient popped up quickly with the explanation of the intricate recycling system she employed. Concern for the environment aside, this worry about things that were going to be thrown away was downright obsessive. She even removed the small plastic window out of those envelopes that carry checks, and then placed them in a separate recycling bin. All of these meticulously sorted items then received further scrutiny, which was why they were at the front door. Tara was just not sure if all of it was really garbage.

"I like to double-check everything before it goes out," she explained.

James, with hefty bag in hand, was prepared to do the heavy lifting downstairs. Our plan was to rid this apartment of trash, whether it was plastic, glass, or paper at this point. If we didn't move something out quickly, we three would have no area in which to pack, much less stand or sit. Our major negotiation revolved around the bags. She had amassed hundreds of plastic grocery bags that she insisted were "good" bags.

"They can still be used," she pleaded.

James grabbed a handful of plastic Urban Outfitters bags and started filling them with plastic bottles.

"Not those bags. Look how nice they are."

"Hon, they are really nice, but you have hundreds more in the kitchen. Can we agree that some of these can be recycled?"

"Only if you take them to the front of Trader Joe's and put them in the plastic bag recycling center."

"Okay, let's agree to do that."

"And maybe from now on, you can use the reusable canvas bags, so you don't have to deal with the plastic ones at all," I added, craning my neck to see if there really were hundreds more of these plastic bags in the kitchen.

It felt like I had just cured cancer. Tara was giddy. She opened a nearby closet to reveal a bag full of those canvas reusable bags

I had just mentioned. Apparently she had been saving those bags as well. Well, today was the day to use them. James gave me a high-five, encouraging my help. I thought the two of us were enthused about finally getting Tara to throw something, anything, out. It was a small victory, but as the ancient philosopher Lao Tzu says, "*The journey of one thousand steps begins with one step.*" At least that's what the quotation of the day had been on the MFB bulletin board at today's session.

My practical side was tempted to camp out until this job was done, but my emotional side was cautioning me to go slow. I really liked Tara. She was a kind person, a funny person; she had just gotten a little misdirected and needed some help from a best friend for hire to get back on track. Our group therapy was showing real results. The entryway was soon clear of the bag graveyard and the sad broken umbrella collection. None of the garbage that crowded the doorway had made it into the "pack" pile, but was instead dispatched downstairs to the labeled recycling bins.

"Our building is really environmentally conscious," Tara added.

Near the kitchen was a small bookcase, which was being used as a room divider. On that shelf were Tara's financial records, bank statements, credit card statements, and a good deal of personal documents. The only thing missing, for someone who wanted to steal her identity, was a sign that said "robbers welcome." For paranoid city people, identity theft is a huge concern. And for someone like Tara, the uber-recycler and separator of address labels, these obvious oversights made me wonder what other things she had overlooked.

"Do you have a paper shredder?" I asked.

"No, I usually just put all my personal papers in a bag and then do it by hand. I store the bags in the bathroom."

With a sinking feeling, we moved over to the bathroom, where, with a flip of the shower curtain, was revealed a mountain of bundled shopping bags, the "to be shredded" backlog of several months. James immediately grabbed his coat and headed to the office supply store on the corner to buy the most durable shredder he could carry. Tara and I continued to wade through the items on the floor. The way in which Tara was storing things was also peculiar. Twenty or so CVS bags of varying sizes lined every surface from dresser to desk to refrigerator to floor.

In each bag was a little time capsule from each purchase. Instead of placing the change she was given from each trip for gum or Advil or a greeting card, she simply put everything in the bag. Inside a bag could be a pack of Chiclets less one Chiclet and 36 cents or two greeting cards and $3. It would have been much easier to gather all the bags and chuck them sight unseen into the trash, but many of them had not only coins, but also dollars in them.

Each bag needed careful inspection. Go through; find money, recycle bag, place usable contents in "pack" pile. Repeat as necessary. Bag by bag, we were reconstructing Tara's last year of purchases. People could be messy, but there had to be more to this. Why would someone simply not take the time to put things back where they belonged and beyond that, why would someone throw things so carelessly around the apartment?

With James out of the apartment, it was just the two of us standing in this two-by-two-foot area, trying not only to figure out how the apartment got this way, but also the all-important why. Tara stopped and moved a pile of books and DVDS to locate a chair.

"You must be exhausted, Jessie. Maybe we should take a break."

"I'm good," I replied.

Even though my body was aching from the awkward movement of pulling things off the floor and shuffling them over to their new homes, I did not want to stop. This was a job I knew I could finish, and it was making me feel useful. Perhaps the reason the place was like this was because Tara could simply not have done this alone. She needed help from a cheerleader to spur her on. I was willing to be that person.

"How about I hand you things and you can tell me where they belong," I suggested.

As she sifted through armloads of books, magazines and mail from the floor, Tara's decisions now became pointedly clear.

"Oh, this is interesting...this is a letter from Blue Cross Blue Shield canceling my health coverage."

Now, the thing about making someone slowly come to the realization that they are losing control of their lives is to make them think that they are actually in control of their lives. Authors teach you that. Because even though we had spent $50,000 to put an author on tour and advertise in women's magazines, there was no guarantee that the book would hit *The New York Times* bestseller list. Managing expectations is key to crisis management. And this apartment situation was no different. It was just that Tara's problems were all around us. In a way, this made it easier.

"Pack, shred, or toss?" I coaxed her.

"Shred. I don't even have Blue Cross Blue Shield. And wait a minute, this envelope isn't even addressed to me, it's addressed to the person that lived here before me."

"Wow, Tara, you are even keeping other people's garbage."

The absurdity of the situation struck us both and we began to laugh. Not just a little giggle, but one of those maniacal laughs that would not end and rendered both parties helpless to do anything else but ride it out. I guess you could say that was our "icebreaker." The rest of the afternoon continued in much the same way. Tara made decisions, I dispatched the items and James ran garbage, recycling, and shredding. By the end of the day, we had cleared the entryway, the floor of the living room, most of the horizontal surfaces, and the bathtub.

There was still much to do, but we were all pleased with the start and were confident that within a day or two we would be able to pack up Tara and her now streamlined belongings. Exhausted, triumphant, and hungry, we headed downstairs to discuss our next session at a German tavern. Once seated in the large wooden booth, our blonde waitress, clad head to toe in a gunmetal gray cat suit and blond chignon, looked like she just had stepped off the fashion runway and into the bar. "The spaetzle here is awesome," she explained.

"Like she ever eats spaetzle," Tara looked at the model-thin waitress, and laughed.

Sunday dinner at my parents' house was never the relaxing, fun-filled Italian feast that you see in the movies. My family had a very different idea about what constitutes a good time. I had been avoiding this meal, for the last few weeks, since being laid off. My parents were not happy about that; they wanted me to visit more often during the months of my unemployment. And by visiting them, they meant, being at their disposal to perform endless house maintenance. They acted as if they lived on a palatial farm, instead of a small ranch-style house on a cul-de-sac in suburban Scotch Plains, New Jersey. I had preferred to call the court where I grew up a "cul-de-sac," as opposed to what my mother called it: a "dead end." I applied the law of positive thinking here and chose a more attractive spin. This attitude was in direct contrast to the overt suspicion that my mother tried to instill in her kids. She thought a healthy amount of skepticism would keep us on our toes and safe from the dangers of the world.

Providing service to my parents was expected of me. My childhood house, where my parents still lived, was a place that needed constant upkeep. Especially now that Nana had moved in since my grandfather (or as my mother referred to him, "the saint") had died. With three of them in residence, there were even more things for people to do around the house. My father did all the yard work himself, my mother cooked every day and my grandmother, in an effort to do her part, insisted on ironing anything she could get her hands on, including my father's underwear. It kept her busy and helped her feel needed. My father complained that she did such a good job that he often felt like his pants were on fire. Apparently my grandmother would go back and re-iron some of them, giving them a hot off the press feel, literally.

Sundays followed the same routine, like a well-oiled machine or factory assembly line. Every person had a role to play. My mother woke up early to start the meatballs, before heading to mass. By hand, she would mix a blend of veal, pork, and beef specially ordered from the butcher. She did not trust meat from the supermarket. "You just don't know what goes on back there," she would say as she pointed at the glassed-in meat department at the Shop Rite. I recalled the innocent butcher's wounded looks as she waved him off dismissively. While the meatballs browned, she prepared the braciole (we mispronounced it Brajoel, an Italian flank steak rolled with garlic and seasoning. Along with sausage (another special order, without fennel), the meatballs and braciole would cook to a golden brown before taking a languid dip into the tomato sauce, bath that simmered in a vat on the stovetop. We often referred to this sauce as Sunday gravy and we did not mean brown meat and potatoes gravy, but red sauce with a variety of hearty meats.

Before she grabbed her purse and her weekly mass envelopes, she told my father, who was stationed at the kitchen table, "Don't forget to stir the sauce, Ton." (Short for Tony.) She would usually whisper to me, on the side, "Please remind him to stir the sauce. You have to tell them everything, Jessica. EVERYTHING." At that point, James and I would be out of bed, with a promise that we would be at noon mass, when all we wanted to do was eat fried meatballs with a large heel of Italian bread. That was our typical Sunday breakfast.

My mom's gravy was a complicated process. She used the tomatoes that she canned the summer before, sieved them twice, added fresh basil from my father's garden, a bit of garlic, and some tomato paste before finally leaving it to simmer over a low flame all day on, Sunday. The house filled with the most spectacular tomato-potent smell you could imagine. The home-canned tomatoes were a seasonal ritual that was labor intensive and exhaustive, but netted fabulous results. In August, she called the local farm stand to find out when the tomatoes would arrive. She wanted to ensure the ripeness and the freshness of the plum tomatoes looking for just the right combination. "How do they look?" she asked. "I don't want a lot of waste." She would keep abreast of the weather reports as well, to see how rain conditions might affect the crop. Since she would need several trips to the farmer, she demanded the best of the season.

Next, she set up an appointment to see the tomatoes, hand select them, and make sure they were good enough, before purchasing several bushels. My father would haul in tens of those light, wooden round baskets and line them up all over the kitchen floor.

After being hand washed and picked through again, each pristine tomato, the chosen ones, would be laid out to dry on the dining room table, which was now covered in the same dish-towels that my mother had used for 20 years. Bunches of those tomatoes would be brought over to Nana, perched on the same kitchen stool she had taken from her house, a red metal affair that had been covered and recovered in contact paper with pictures of grapes and vines. This was one of the few items that came with her from her old house.

Like a jeweler with a loupe, she would give them one final inspection before they were to be cut and quartered, sieved, and puréed, and then finally put into Mason jars and canned in an old-style, black-and-white flecked canner that held eight quarts of the summer tomatoes at a time. The summer before, they had set a house record by doing 243 jars. And still, my mother was concerned about getting through the winter with enough.

At this particular Sunday dinner, Ma had prepared one of my favorites, eggplant parmigiana, which she made better than anyone in America or Italy. I know, because I made it a habit to order it wherever I was in a restaurant, in an effort to find one that tasted as good. I never did. The other staple was macaroni with gravy. Yes, we call pasta, macaroni. Tomato sauce with meat is gravy. Marinara sauce is plain tomato sauce. And this week, my mom had put in my favorite—bones. Bones are not for the faint of heart. Perhaps, in a recipe adopted from the Sicilian side of the family, in every Sunday sauce was an array of grisly looking parts, like neck bones, ribs, and shoulders, always pork, never with a lot of meat, but the meat that you did get off of them was the most tender meat you could hope to taste. My mother and I were the best bone eaters. When my father and his mother would eat them, they always left meat or cartilage (we also ate that; Ma said it was the best part) on the bone.

"You call that a clean bone?" Ma would say in disgust and then registered another indignation at my father's side of the family.

Since I had not been home since being laid off, I was apprehensive about the dinner. I knew I had to provide an alibi for my whereabouts and an acceptable progress report. Approval-seeking was part and parcel to being the dutiful daughter in a traditional Italian family.

As far as my father was concerned, he was still confused as to why I never became a teacher, since I had majored in English in college. Teaching was a good profession for a nice girl. "Just look at your Aunt Cookie," he would say, "she was a teacher for years." Aunt Cookie taught in the local elementary school for 20 years and had received a wonderful pension. "It's a nice job for a girl like you, a nice job for a nice respectable girl like you, nice job, nice girl. Done," he added.

I was concerned about how to explain my "not so nice" new job to my family. I knew it would be a tough sell. My mother, who was the harshest critic, was still holding out for my return to publishing and still thought that one day, any day now I would get that call from Dr. Ursula and that she would help me out. Don't hold your breath there, Ma.

Nana would be there in one of her signature blue-and-black checkered dresses complete with a broach. Her doppelganger, my father's mother, who was called Na for clarity, would also be there along with Pop, my grandfather. There was a constant competition between the two grandmothers. I could never understand why. Both had come from Italy, neither of them wore pants, English was their second language, and they both were excellent cooks. But rivalrous feelings are not to be explained, especially where my family was concerned.

It took very little for Na to get her nose out of joint, which had started when James was born and an argument ensued about which grandmother would be called Nana. They both could not be called the same name, for reasons I still don't understand. Since Sicilians always win in these types of showdowns, my mother's mother claimed "Nana," leaving my father's mother with the less elegant "Na."

Truthfully, my father's mother did not care what you called her, as long as you called her. She was the more gregarious of the two women, one of those people who was always on the phone. She loved real-life gossip as opposed to my mother's mother, who loved television gossip.

My mother frowned upon mixing both sides of the family, keeping them separate as if they were the rebel forces or the Taliban, a meeting where the outcome could never be predicted. Since Nana now lived with my parents, there was no choice but to have everyone together at all family events. Na and Pop would need to be picked up, as would the identical twin uncles, Cheech and Pep, two of her six brothers. Cheech is a nickname for Frank from the family's early days in the Bronx. Pep, I thought, was a nickname for Peter, but I recently discovered that Pep's real name is Victor, which confused the issue. People just always called him Pep.

Neither brother married, but they did live together in the same town along with the rest of their siblings. This was common among Italian immigrants. Once Italian families left their farms in southern Italy, they would choose a random New Jersey town and take over an entire page in the phone book. Once entrenched in Scotch Plains (or in their dialect, Scotcha Plain, which sounded like they were ordering a drink rather than telling somewhere where they lived) the Mastros sent for the rest of their family in the Old Country. One by one, each emigrated until the entire family was set up in a parallel American universe.

I picked up James at the PATH station, completing a routine that we had perfected in the last 10 years since both of us had moved to our respective cities. We stopped at Carlo's for pastries and grabbed six *cannoli* and six *sfogliaitelle*; which most people would know as a "lobster tail" shaped pastry, I ordered a bag of my favorite sesame cookies for the ride. We headed toward the turnpike for our familiar ride home. The prodigal daughter had returned. I still called my mom every day to talk, but this was our first in person meeting since my change in employment status, and I was anxious.

With the recent activity at the bar, our conversations had been shortened to highlight reel length. She filled me in on the "stories," asked about my interviews, and I would agree with everything she said until she finally rushed me off the phone to watch a soap opera. We rarely shared substantive information on these check-in calls anyway. And most days, I was preoccupied with Dave and our comeback so that I was only half- listening anyway. We had never gotten along better.

James hopped in my Toyota Camry with a smile and said, "Hang on, Sis, it's gonna be a bumpy ride."

"Very funny, get in, you goofball."

As we drove, James and I reviewed all the taboo subjects to be avoided. I told him about my plan to save The Garage.

"So let me get this straight, you're working upstairs from Dave's Garage?"

"Why, do you know him?"

"Of course I know him. Everyone knows him. The question is, how well do *you* know him? I mean, how does a girl go from working in a high-powered career to working for Dave Germaine. Above a bar? Oh, how the mighty have fallen."

James fell back into the old sibling dynamic of taking potshots at me. My Dudley Do-Right status in the family had always rubbed him the wrong way and he always relished the opportunity for a bit of good-natured payback. I thought we had worked through most of that petty stuff years ago, but my current situation was too much for him to resist. His description of my life made it sound even more unbelievable than it was. I wondered if I *had* strayed too far from what I knew. Was it too late for me to reinvent myself across Manhattan at another publisher? That thought sent chills racing down my spine. I couldn't go back, I had to move forward on this uncertain path. I recalled my only opportunity to reentering the publishing world, which was an interview with a friend of Daniel's who ran a literary house in Soho. He was known for romancing most of the poets he represented and was widely regarded the industry as a "kook." When I sat down to interview for a publicity manager job, which was two levels below my most recent position, he leaned back in his weathered swivel chair, looked me straight in the eye, and asked me if I were to be a cookie, what kind of cookie would I be? I stared at him, stunned, and then answered, "chocolate chip." I immediately regretted my answer as if the choice of the very popular cookie might make me seem needy. And then it hit me—if this is the kind of nonsense that a new publisher is going to offer me, they can keep it. I was ready to break out on my own. My recollection was interrupted by James, who was pushing for some explanation as to why I was going against his and everyone else's expectations.

"It's really not like that. Dave is different. Amazing, really."

"I know all about Dave and his type. He is different. He booked Nirvana for Christ's sake. NIR.VA.NA.... That makes ya different, all right. I'm not talking about him. It's you that's different."

"*Me*, I'm not different. I just have a different gig, I mean, job. Well, maybe I am changing. Dave thinks..." I sensed this conversation revealed too much about my feelings. I backtracked, telling him that this was just a temporary gig, er, job, and that Dave was really an "amazing" person to help me out too.

"Amazing? Did you just say amazing? Does that mean you 'like him' or 'like him' like him?" He winked at me.

And then, suddenly, I was transported back to fourth grade with my nose pressed against the window as I tried to get a better look at my first crush and James's best friend, Keith Muldane. Foolishly, I had told James that I was going to be Mrs. Keith Muldane. Well, I never heard the end of that one. Before James could go full force into a chorus of Jessie has a crush on Dave, I had to turn him back to the matter at hand this afternoon. It felt like I was on my way to a firing squad. James sensed my panic and proceeded to talk me down from the ledge.

"Before we get too far entrenched in your rock and roll fantasy, what are you planning to do today? If you go in there all kissy face, talking about your new tattooed boyfriend boss and his 'amazing bar,' eggplant parm isn't going to be the only thing on the menu—they are going to eat you alive."

10

With just a few minutes before we arrived at home, I had still had no idea how to explain my career choices to my family. James was right; telling my family that I had no intention of finding another corporate job, after I had led them to believe that I was diligently trying to find another, was not going to be welcomed news. Especially since the last time Ma called, she went on a tangent about applying for a job at a cooking magazine. And I told her I sent a résumé to the human resources department and things were looking good. As I thought back on that, what came to mind was the thought of Dave sitting across my desk as he drank a Heineken in the middle of our workday. That looked good. Working at *Cooking Light*, not so good. I might have said anything at that point. Those little lies were easier to tell than the truth.

"You know she thinks you've been interviewing all over the city, so you better prepare for a full rundown. Working on top of a bar. Really..."

"Okay, already, you don't have to beat me over the head with it. I get it."

Bars were not something my family had any idea about. Going to dinner, the movies, or even a concert were the kinds of dates my parents understood, but going out solely for the purpose to drink, especially to get drunk, was tawdry. While it might be okay for James, he was a boy, but it's not okay for their little girl. My mother still recoiled whenever I said I was meeting someone for a drink.

Our plan for the afternoon was avoidance, just keep busy, which should not be difficult, after all; there is always a ton of task management on Sunday, and with the extended cast of characters in attendance today, it should have been easy to deflect the conversation from me and bury myself in some meal preparation task. I could do that for a few hours, if James were going to help me. He said he would.

True to this plan: We arrived home, entered the kitchen, and were immediately put to work.

"Grab the mozzarella out of the fridge and start grating," my mother instructed.

"Hi, Ma, how are ya?" I waved, and then crossed to the counter, where she was breading the eggplant. I pecked her on the cheek.

She turned sideways to look at me and gave me a once-over from head to toe.

"You look thin. Good. But fix that blouse; whaddya think this is?"

The blouse, which I had agonized over, was opening right around the bust line. I thought it would stay in place with a little tug in the back, but my mother had detected this flaw immediately. At least she thought I looked thin. She never thought I was thin enough, actually.

I took out the metal hand grater, a bowl, and the two packages of mozzarella she had purchased from the Italian Market in town, and began my job.

"Wait—before you do that, go downstairs and grab another jar of tomatoes, a half pint and the big pot. The uncles, your other grandmother and pop are coming too," she warned, already on edge about the mixing of the two rival family factions. The War Between the States had been less contentious.

Our basement was like a supermarket, overstocked on all the important items, which were lined up on shelves down there. You could get anything from paper towels, toilet paper, and bottled water to the trove of canned tomatoes. In the second refrigerator and freezer, another family could have survived for weeks on the frozen meat alone stored in there. And, of course, like most Italians homes, another dining area was set up in the basement.

There's something about Italian people—they all eat in basements as if the dining room is to be saved for some other occasion. My mother broke away from this tradition and used the dining room for bigger, more important meals. Although my mom was a simple person really, she had the entertaining style of Queen Elizabeth. Her Drexel dining room set cost, "at that time," over $10,000. Her china was Lenox. Her solid silver tea set and flatware were by Reed & Barton.

We never used any of the china or the crystal, and based on what she thought about my father's side of the family, I was surprised that she bought it all. When she was still a newlywed, she hosted an elegant family dinner that did not go as expected. The Waterford water pitcher was passed to Uncle Cheech. Since the table was so crowded with food and serving dishes, he could not find a place to put it, so instead he placed it on the floor. That was the dinner that we affectionately called the night that "Cheech" became a "Chooch." *Chooch* is a derogatory Italian slang term for "dummy." Since that night, the beautiful china and crystal remained unused in the large china cabinet, which had been purchased to display it.

James received his first assignment as well, to pick up Na, Pop and the boys.

"Go get my keys."

Ma's keys were kept inside a series of containers like Russian nesting dolls. She claimed that if you put things in the same place you would never have trouble finding them. Her key case was one of those leather cases with a metal hook for each key; it looked more like a wallet. She tucked the case inside a zippered compartment in her purse. Her purse was inside her closet. This was all very logical to her.

I thought she had a deep-seated fear that burglars would find all of her important things, and theft could be avoided if she created intricate hiding spots. You would rarely see clutter that most homes had, like a shelf with mail or a key hook. Things were always put back where they belonged. It's a concept I grappled with, because at this point in my life, nothing was where it belonged. I was riddled with self-doubt and, in an effort to gain control, tried to manipulate the topic away from me and on to something or even better, someone else.

"Where's Nana?"

"She'll be right out; she's still getting ready."

This process was familiar to me. Nana was one of the vainest women I had ever met, even though she was nearly 80, or so we thought (she lied so much about her age that no one could figure out the year she had actually been born). She was plump and wore a large apron double-tied across her barrel waist. In the den, off the dining room, which had become her room, she fixed her lipstick and adjusted her perfect bun. Nana slid the accordion door and opened her arms to me.

"Ah, disgraziato," she said. "Disgraziato" loosely means unhappy, in Italian, but in this case, she was showing me pity. She had not seen me in weeks and the way she greeted me made me feel as lost as the day I'd been fired. She brought my head to her chest as if to comfort me, but I was in such an awkward position, because she was about one foot shorter than me. I felt as though my neck were going to break from the awkward angle in which she was holding me.

She then ran her arms across my back and down my arms and said, "She's too thin. Sest, she's too thin." (Sest, pronounced like the soap name "Zest," was my grandmother's shortened name for Celeste. No one else called my mother that. I had the feeling that she did not like that nickname very much.)

Nana had a habit of talking about me as if I were not standing in front of her. All this talk about being too thin made me feel like I deserved a taste of the cheese I'd so diligently grated. I used to sneak samples as a child, as well. Without turning around, my mother said, "Grate, don't eat. You don't look that good."

My father, who had overheard my mother's last remark, started talking on the way up the stairs.

"Whaddya sayin' that for? She looks great. She always looks great. You look great, Jessie. Great. Great. Great."

He greeted me with a hug and somewhat painful neck pinch. He also made a squeaking noise as he did this. He'd been down in the workshop fixing a perfectly good hedge clipper. He fixed anything, from electronics, to eyeglass arms, to telephones. In the workshop were ancient parts from machines that didn't even exist anymore, like tubes for television sets. A separate closet off the workshop housed a collection of vintage televisions that could rival the Smithsonian in scope and condition. Dad didn't like throwing anything away he might later find useful. He would often retrieve things that we had discarded and then later question us. "Why'd you throw that away, it's still good," he would say about a broken rubber band or a Dixie cup.

He also had a specific and personal way of storing information. Like a precursor to the Internet, he sorted items in larger categories and then put them each in a brown paper bag that he labeled in his deliberate cursive handwriting.

"Ton, grab me some more basil, would ya?" said my mother.

He winked at me and went outside with a little army salute. Dad knew not to disagree with my mother. She needed to think she was in charge at all times. They had adopted a comfortable rhythm to their banter. My mother would make extreme comments like, "I am never going to Walmart again." And my father would say, "You shouldn't, it's lousy there." The next day, my mother would say, "You know, Ton, we really should go to Walmart." And my father would say, "Yeah, I hear it's great there." He had figured out a long time ago that agreeing with this Sicilian person is the best path to his inner-happiness. Her moody disposition kept everyone guessing, so it was easier to go along to get along, especially in her kitchen, where she was clearly the commander-in-chief.

The next group of recruits arrived; the uncles were here. They were small in stature, but loud in voice. After hugs and kisses on each of identical cheeks, Uncle Cheech pulled back and stared at me as if he were about to ask me a very difficult question. My stomach dropped; was Uncle Cheech going to bring up work? But he had a more serious concern.

"Jessica, tell me why are you still living in Hoboken?" He, along with most of my family members, could not understand why I would pay so much rent for such a small old-fashioned apartment. My father had returned with a handful of basil. As he deposited it next to the counter for my mother's inspection, he threw his hands up in display of solidarity with Uncle Cheech.

"When we were your age, we were trying to get out of Hoboken, not move in, right, Cheech?" asked Uncle Pep rhetorically.

"Right, Pep."

The twins always needed immediate agreement from each other; they were big on physical, as well as verbal, reinforcement, so their conversations usually combined a verbal agreement, a hand slap, something like "Right?" Slap. "Right?" Slap.

Next in the door was Pop, who had an announcement to make.

"May I present Emma Mastro, straight from the runway in her new pantsuit." In walked Na, in a velvet Juicy Couture sweatsuit. Everyone turned to stare at the tiny 80-year-old woman who wore something that looked like she had purchased it in Macy's junior's department. James was the first to endorse this statement.

"You look amazing, Na. Right, Jessie? Wouldn't you say amazing?"

I jabbed James with my elbow to ensure his silence, but I was uncertain at that point what his plan was. He had already downed a glass of Chianti. My mother and her mother huddled together in conspiratorial horror. My father moved in to touch the fabric.

"Nice stitching," he remarked to his father, who agreed.

And then my little old grandmother turned around to reveal the word "Juicy" scrolled on her bottom. My mother gasped and managed to blurt out, "What's on the bottom of your pants?"

"Just some letters," Na explained.

"Does that say, 'Juicy'?" James asked, as he belted back another glass of wine.

"It helps her figure out which is the front and which is the back," Pop answered proudly.

In contrast to Na, Pop was dressed in pressed black trousers and a crisp white shirt with his sleeves rolled up. His shock of thick, white hair was well combed. Pop used to own a dry cleaning and tailor shop in town, and he still had the look of a properly pressed businessman. One should never play favorites in a family, but if I had to pick, I loved Pop most of all. When I was a child, he always gave me little treats on the side, and I knew that if I got into enough trouble today, he would be the one to bail me out.

James and I shared a conspiratorial grin as Cheech told Pep, "If ya got it, flaunt it, right Pep?"

"Right."

Slap.

"Right."

Slap.

At first, things looked like they might actually go my way. My new-pants-wearing grandmother and her dress-wearing doppelganger had already set a tense foundation for the dinner to build upon—and we hadn't even had the antipasto yet. As soon as Ma finished layering handfuls of mozzarella over the eggplant and adding gravy, we were given our next mission.

"Set the table and put out the antipast...," she directed.

The "antipast" was shorthand for *antipasto*, a habit that I had seem most Italians do, leaving off word endings. "Parm" for parmigiana, "mozz" for mozzarella. Maybe Italians are too busy to finish words; they are already on to the next thing, or at least my mother was. Large platters overflowed with cheese, salami, roasted peppers, and olives. Raw fennel was sliced and fanned out alongside the bruschetta; thin toasted bread was topped with a mix of fresh plum tomato and garlic. For a moment, the preparations had been completed.

Another bottle of Chianti was passed around as we lingered over the dining room table with our small appetizer plates and feasted on the pre-meal. I enjoyed a short-lived moment of silence while everyone ate instead of talked. But in my family, like on *General Hospital*, secrets don't keep for very long. There was trouble brewing, and it was on my own team. My mother felt compelled to comment on my brother's wine consumption.

"Take it easy, James, this is not a saloon."

Instead of heeding her advice, he could not resist another jab at me.

"A saloon, kind of like a bar. Right, Jessie?"

In an effort to deflect this subtle transition, I asked Ma how she made the bruschetta topping, but she brushed me off. There were more pressing matters at hand.

"Tomatoes, basil, garlic," she reeled off in a cut-to-the-chase fashion.

That was not the elaborate explanation I had hoped for. But as luck would have it, the conversation next turned to James and his girlfriend. His turn on the hot seat. My family was desperate for someone to get married, and since James had a girlfriend, he was more likely to be the first. The table needed an update. Everyone wanted to know. Marriage trumped all other conversational topics, like an accident trumped all other news stories.

"How is your sweet girl?" asked Pop.

"She's great," James answered noncommittally. Anxious to turn the conversation away from Tara and their secret cohabitation, James panicked and flipped the conversation back to me.

"How about you, Jessie, do you want to tell everyone about your new boyfriend?"

"No, James, I don't. Let's talk about Tara a little more."

"Sure, you can tell them, what's his name, the guy with the tattoos?"

Memo to self: If I ever get out of here alive, kill James.

"Tattoos? Madonna mia." Nana invoked a prayer to the Virgin Mary.

"Let's talk about how great I was to help Tara with her move," I volleyed back, not intending to reveal anything, but to win James back over to "Team Jessie."

"Why, where is she going?" asked my father innocently.

The uncles worked on a conspiracy theory, mumbling something about "dames," "cheating," "they always leave you," and "who can trust them." But my mother was not to be sidetracked; she had seen enough *Matlock* episodes to know a cover-up when she saw one.

"No one is going anywhere and no one is breaking up..." James answered in an effort to dispel the numerous erroneous theories at the table.

"Then, what?" my father asked.

James looked at me and I looked at him. It was like the gunfight at the OK Corral; someone would have to fire first. Instead of telling our own truth, like Oprah would have recommended, we each blurted out the other's secret with fingers pointed instead of revolvers.

"Tara and James are living together!"

"Jessie is working at a bar with her new boyfriend!"

The uncles dropped their forks. The grandmothers grabbed each other in a moment of pure panic and instinctively made the sign of the cross. And my mother silently stood up and left the table. James and I stared at each other, embarrassed by what we had done as my father continued to eat, seemingly unfazed by what he had just heard. He looked at both of us, but neither of us could meet his stare. We sat with our heads down and concentrated on our plates. The room was quiet for the next several moments and then Pop broke the silence and asked the only question anyone at the table really cared about:

"Is he Italian, at least?"

11

I was standing in the middle of a crowded sports bar, shoulder to shoulder with a group of rambunctious New York Islanders fans during a playoff game. Hockey is one of those sports that has a seemingly endless regular season as well as an endless playoff season. The sport seemed like it never took an off-season break. This was similar to my current problem, planning Emily's wedding, which was also showing signs of having no off-season. There are times in a person's life that make one ask, how did I get to this place? One may even inventory the events that led them to these watershed moments in their lives. This was not the case for me; I knew how I had gotten here. I had set these events in motion the moment I volunteered to help save the day, Emily's wedding day to be specific. That agreement was very much like boarding a runaway train bound for disaster.

The bar, McKenzie's, was no different than the other five or so bars on the street that looked exactly the same. There was a large screen television on every wall, tuned to every New York sports game. The décor was hand-selected by the Irish owners, who were from Dublin. They tried to replicate their neighborhood pub back home with both décor and Irish-accented staff. This amalgam of motifs and its midtown location helped attract a melting pot of patrons, from sports fans to Irish nationals, to tourists on their way to the Port Authority Bus Terminal.

Def Leppard's *Pour Some Sugar on Me* was playing as the bridal party did another round of lemon drop shots. This was maybe our third or fourth round; after that many, you begin to lose count and accountability. Feeling the effects of the last drink, I retreated from the group to observe my surroundings. I felt like an outsider, like an anthropologist studying an odd civilization's customs. In this case, the bachelorette party, that banal prelude to the formalness of a wedding. For reasons I could not figure out, a woman's most elegant event has to be preceded by this very public scene of debauchery, a necessary rite of passage. In our case, a bar crawl through Manhattan directed by Maggie, Emily's older cousin and ringleader of the bridal party, seven girls in all, including the bride. When I joked about this being a real life seven brides for seven brothers, I was met with blank stares; that was not the first indicator that I was in strange territory.

Because Maggie had an intimate knowledge of which bars had the hottest guys hanging out in them, she appointed herself as event planner for the evening. Judging by her ease at navigating the crowded bar and maintaining the attention of the bartender, I could see why. But I was not convinced about this ritual or this person as the ritual planner. When you are on a runway train, it's impossible to regain one's footing, much less one's control. And if I were more aware, I would have seen the clues that life was sending my way—I would have seen this coming when I had first met Maggie at the bridal shower, just one week earlier.

My role at Emily's bridal shower was twofold: make sure that the guests think that Emily was *surprised!*, when she had, in fact, planned the entire event months ago. Anyone who knew Emily would surely realize how staged this surprise entrance was. She would never be this composed this early on a weekend morning. Her usual routine was to sleep well past noon and stay in her Juicy Couture sweatsuit well until happy hour.

The second part of my mission was to meet with cousin Maggie to review the plans for the bachelorette party. This should have been easy since I had already planned the entire afternoon at the Peninsula Hotel Day Spa. It was all set. We would have lunch, Emily would be groomed, and the girls would chat and bond. This was a no-brainer, elegant and easy.

I should have known that easy was not exactly what Emily wanted, based on the shower, a four-hour event that itself could have been someone's wedding and which included a multi-course meal, speeches, and culminated in a gift-opening marathon. Emily's former wedding planner, in her final moments, had even planned some of those cute shower games, like the bride wearing a hat made of bows from the presents and gift bingo, where each shower member has to cross off the received gifts on her bingo card. After yelling "Bridal Bingo," the winners receive a Tiffany keychain with a tiny framed picture of the happy couple on it. I should have sent her a thank-you note for her brilliant foresight.

All games aside, one small piece of business had to be taken care of. I had to find Maggie and tell her about spa day. Thankfully, I was able to call in a favor at the hotel from my former author booking days to secure the reservation. Things were really coming together, I thought. All that was left was a quick conversation with the cousin, who undoubtedly would be relieved that the bachelorette party was not only dealt with, but also was going to be awesome.

I had received no heads up about Maggie. A simple phrase such as, "Hey, look out for that one, she will steamroll you" would have been helpful. Like a little bunny heading off to meet the wolf, I tapped Maggie on the shoulder. Maggie was a large woman with dark, shoulder-length hair and frighteningly intense blue eyes. Defiantly wearing jeans and a tank top to this elegant brunch should have been my first clue that Maggie was not going to allow herself to be handled.

"I have a plan for the bachelorette party, a spa day." As I talked, everyone at the table suddenly became engrossed in their own conversations, immediately avoiding eye contact with me. Was it something I had said? Apparently it *was* everything I had said.

"So, we finally meet." Maggie stood and sized me up as she guided me to the punch fountain, so that the two of us could have a little gangland style sitdown of our own.

"About that spa day, it ain't gonna happen. Just telling you. You might think you're in charge, but I own the bachelorette party. Just so there are no misunderstandings, 'kay fancy pants?"

I understood, and it wasn't only because my pants were indeed fancier than hers.

"Okay, good talk. Let's get some punch and get back to the gifts. Mine is next."

Maggie was a detail-oriented dictator. Her gift tied into the party's theme, a white tank top, with the words "Bride to Be" bedazzled across the front at chest height.

"That's for the bachelorette party." She hollered from the back of the room.

"It's gonna be awesome, right, Jessica?"

She elbowed me hard and I nodded in assent, scared to do anything else by that point. Being coerced into having a rollicking good time at a bachelorette party run by Tony Soprano concerned me, and for good reason.

The bridal party, at least, rode in style to the event with limousine service that I had pulled together at the last minute when Maggie said, "You know what you could do for us? You could get us a fancy car to drive us around town, that's what you could do." And so I did. I was feeling like I had gained a new boss.

We needed to pick up Emily at Brendan's apartment on the Upper East Side. He greeted us at the door wearing an Islanders jersey. I am not sure what motivates a grown man to wear this oversized shirt. Is there some repressed fantasy that he is acting out, where, in the final minutes of the game, he might be called out of the stands to play? And if that were the case, why would *he* be chosen among the hundreds of other similarly costumed men in the arena?

Much to everyone's surprise, Brendan hopped into the limo as well. Emily insisted that we drop him off at Madison Square Garden on the way downtown. Emily was also in costume in her "Bride to Be" tank top, a miniskirt that was designed like a tutu, and knee-high boots. Her look was rounded out by the requisite tiara with feathers that also said "Bride" in case anyone could not see her T-shirt, which, in her defense, was obscured by a necklace made of condoms strung-together. This look met at the unlikely intersection of Princess Avenue and Porn Street. Inside the limousine, Maggie and the rest of the girls popped open a bottle of champagne and handed out condom-inspired party favors.

Our first stop was the Bubble Lounge, a champagne lounge in Soho that had just received an excellent write-up in *New York* magazine.

"They have bottle service, which is really hot," Emily squealed in the back of the limo. This admission was greeted with high-fives among the rest of the party. Maggie told us that "this joint" would be the first of many she wanted to show her baby cousin.

"Hot," of course, was Emily's highest compliment. Emily had a liberal scope of what was hot: anything written up in *New York* magazine was hot, things that are shiny were hot and, of course, bubble gum-pink bridesmaid dresses were the hottest. There was a bubble theme developing here, the Bubble Lounge being the second installment. Bubblegum-pink was the first, which reminded me of the dress shopping, my debut event as wedding planner or, more accurately, where I had learned what exactly makes bubblegum-pink so hot.

"It's not quite powder pink, not quite rose or yucky mauve, and not really like hot pink. It's just pink, like bubblegum," Emily explained in exhausting detail.

After coordinating the six bridesmaids and Emily via text message, we had met in the heart of the garment district. Emily chose this private atelier based solely upon her having stumbled across it watching *Access Hollywood*. She also liked the idea that it was called an *atelier* rather than something "cheesy" (her word) like David's Bridal. I rang the buzzer and shouted my name over the noisy street traffic of Seventh Avenue. We were buzzed in to a nondescript entryway. These entries are prevalent in buildings all over Manhattan that house suites of different businesses, from graphic design companies, to jewelry wholesalers, to appointment-only retail shops like this one.

Past the entryway, we entered into a grand lobby area that looked like the entrance to Versailles. There, we were met by Zora, a flawlessly dressed woman in a grey, well-tailored pantsuit, accented by a long tape measure that she wore like a necklace. We followed her into a large, white dressing room that had mirrors on every wall. A large silver tray adorned with champagne flutes sat on a table to our left. Reflected in the mirror, it looked like hundreds of trays with thousands of flutes.

"Zee dresses you will like are over here," she said in an English with a put-on movie French accent. She looked at me with a smile as she sized up our group.

As a good wedding planner should, I had called Zora in advance and asked her to pull a few dresses in preparation for this mass shopping. With seven girls of varying body types, a consensus would not be easy when it came to selecting a bridesmaid dress. But these girls had no opinion either way; they were just happy to have free booze.

"Come, little angel bride, sit in the nice chair and you can zee what the girl will put on, yes?"

Zora guided Emily over to a large throne in the middle of the room. She then lined us all up against the dressing room doors. She was looking for one of us to be the guinea pig to try on the dresses first and model them for the group. One by one, she asked each girl to take a glass of champagne and sit behind Emily. Maggie, the first to sit, grabbed two glasses of champagne before she plopped down on the fluffy couch, flutes in hand. Like one of those picky judges at a dog show, Zora eliminated all the competition until I was left alone, apparently the best in show.

"Jessica, you are the closest to the sample size, you will be our model," Zora declared, handing me an honor I wasn't honestly sure I wanted.

"Oh, goody," said Emily as she positioned herself for prime viewing, ready to score the fashions like a magazine fashion editor at a runway event. Or, with all the champagne being downed, a runaway event.

The first dress was a lovely navy sheath that she deemed too "old lady." I tried not to take that one personally, as Maggie laughed from the peanut gallery. Mind you, Maggie was one year older than me. The second dress, a two-piece silver ensemble, was greeted with a simple "ick" by Emily, and the last, a tasteful black cocktail dress, was, in her jaded eyes, "boring." Truthfully, I knew that Emily wanted her bridesmaids to dress up as her real life royal court, but I thought it was my mission to guide her toward making the right decision, as I had so many times at work. That was my first mistake. Emily was getting exasperated with the process. She blew air at her bangs and began to slouch. I was losing her.

"These are just not fun," she complained as Zora poured her a second glass of champagne in an effort to maintain her buzz. "I just want something pretty...pretty and pink."

Zora reacted quickly to the pea that was irritating this princess by telling her that she had just the thing, a sample dress that had just come in. "It might be out of your price range," she warned, "but I think you must see it." Exclusive, new, and unique, I thought, were too much for Emily to handle.

"I must see it," Emily repeated. And once she started the signature handclap and began stomping her feet in perfect synchronization, I knew the fight was lost. And Zora knew it too.

"As you wish, dear angel bride." She zipped off and quickly returned with the dress in pink. The girls gasped. I gasped. Zora gasped, somewhat staged, I supposed. As if she had known this was going to happen all along, that she had deliberately withheld the pink dress in order to make a more dramatic show of it. This was not the first angel bride she had seen, nor was I the first well-meaning wedding planner she had encountered, either. There was a reason that Zora was so successful in this highly competitive business.

The dress was a strapless, skimpy-bodiced dress in full-length taffeta. It had a large bow placed on the back of the dress, to create a Scarlett O'Hara bustle effect. I worked my way into the dress from top to bottom and got a bit stuck in the middle. I then extrapolated myself by laying down on the floor. The second try was more success full as I laid the gown down and stepped into the middle and then squeezing into one side and then the other before finally hoisting the skirt below my bra band. This dress made not only a statement, it made a noisy entrance as well. The crinoline and tulle underneath caused a swishy sound as I sashayed through the dressing room. I hoped that this noise would not drown out Pachelbel's Canon in D Major that was planned for our arrival at the wedding. Note to self: Make an appointment to confab with the organist and soloist.

Based on Emily's reaction, it looked like the tradition of the bride choosing the least appealing dress for her bridesmaids was holding true to form here. "Are you sure?" I asked for a final time, feeling vulnerable now in my Pepto Bismol-colored attire. "The navy is really elegant," I said, as I tried to coax her back to reality. "It'll look very pretty in the pictures, the perfect back-drop to your white dress."

"No, no, no, pink is hot," Emily insisted and headed off to the shoe department with the peremptory manner of a mad European monarch.

With Emily gone, I pulled Zora aside to see if she could swing a deal on this exclusive dress if we were to order seven of them and pay in full. She, of course, could never discount this designer; he would not stand for it.

"Maybe I can do something on the shoes, depending on what you pick," she grinned with the secret smile of a shark moving in on its prey.

"Nice work, fancy pants," Maggie said, as she slapped me on the back before she followed the rest of the girls to the shoe department. Defeated in my pink bubble dress, I picked myself up and looked for some last hope to redeem this appointment.

Shoes would be easy; they are underneath the dress and no one would see them under all this taffeta. But nothing else about this wedding planning was coming easy. I thought about the previous wedding planner, and could well understand now why she had quit.

I arrogantly thought I could sweep in and control this wedding. A rookie mistake, for sure. Most people are not self-aware enough to realize that they may also trip over the same pitfalls that had forced the first person to quit. But if we don't have a little ego to think we can overcome these obstacles, nothing in life would ever happen. I was wondering how much I could effect change here when a glimmer of hope surfaced.

"These will be the girls' choice, I don't want to control everything," Emily said, deferring to the individual taste requirements of her bridesmaids.

This sentiment, however, was short lived. It died a quick death when Emily fell in love with shoes with a three-inch sling back heel with giant silver bows. Before I could interject my objections, Zora pulled me aside.

"Drop zee fruit, Jessica."

"Come again?"

"There is a psychological study done in Vienna with monkeys where they are given a large vase with a very skinny opening. They can get their hand into the bowl, but the fruit will never clear the small opening. Yet they try, over and over again. You, my dear girl, need to learn that lesson. Drop zee fruit."

My opportunity to drop the fruit presented itself quickly. I relinquished any idea of changing Emily's mind about anything when she insisted that we all would be wearing tiaras. Yes, we were all on our way to becoming pink princesses wearing crowns. This proliferation of girls as princesses was no doubt born out of the Disney marketing department that had co-opted every childhood girl character and transformed them into princesses. Even little Dora the intrepid explorer became Princess Dora in later episodes. Like the original Dora, I was the last holdout in this trend.

And that was not the only trend I had apparently missed out on while sitting behind my desk at work. There seemed to be this emboldened bar culture, where men and women met at bars and actually talked to one another. I was inexperienced on this front as well, and totally unprepared when a nice looking guy started up a conversation with me, bringing me out of my past recriminations into my present dilemma. He was as over-dressed as I was. But, he, at least, had made an effort by taking off his tie to make his expensive suit appear more casual. My Tory Burch pants were a bold pattern coupled with a tasteful complimentary tunic. It was kind of like a suit, I supposed, and a bold contrast to the denim and T-shirt clad crowd hanging out at the bar.

"How do you know the bride?" he asked.

"From work," I answered, adopting the attitude of a cagey witness protection character I had seen in a Lifetime movie.

"You work in fashion, right?"

"Right." My lie twofold: not only didn't I work in fashion, but I didn't work at all, for that matter.

"I always can tell a fashion girl. I'm an energy trader."

It figured, because he was coming on to me with enough energy to see the entire city through its next power emergency.

"What is that exactly?" I asked, dipping a tentative toe into the conversational waters.

"I'm on the floor at the exchange, buying energy stocks."

"Sounds interesting. So what do you think about global warming?

"I'm a fan. I mean, who wants to be cold all the time?"

I had little time to ponder this before I spotted Emily who had hopped on top of the bar and began gyrating to the rhythm of Donna Summer's *Bad Girls*, the ultimate good girl who had had too much to drink theme song. She seemed to be okay with one guy dancing around her, but when his friend who was also wearing denim with a flannel "grunge" inspired shirt, the mood suddenly shifted. Emily went from carefree bachelorette to Bambi caught in a car's headlights. Like a good mama deer, I hopped onto the bar to rescue my fawn. I looked down and saw a sea of faces looking up at us, wondering what was going to happen next. Maybe a re-creation of Magic Mike right here on this bartop.

Despite her drunken state, Emily had the presence of mind at that point to know that this little dance exhibition of hers had gone too far, and she now wanted nothing more than to come down from the bar. The crowd booed, anxious to see how this show would end. I moved past one of the flannel-shirted guys and put my arms gently around Emily, guiding her down from the bar like the mother of a child misbehaving on the playground. "Come on now, honey, one step at a time, easy does it." I reached for her hand.

But the boys would not go quietly.

"What are you, her mother?" one yelled at me and tried to grab Emily in the process.

Emily squealed. He and I started an awkward tug of war, with Emily as the rope. I pushed. He pulled. And before you could say Stanley Cup playoffs, it got worse, much worse. Emily lost her grip on both of us and tripped directly over the waitress who was serving potato skins and beer pitchers to a group of Islanders fans seated at the bar. Beer and appetizers flew everywhere. A snagged hand caused Emily's condom necklace to break, sending gold foil squares flying through the air and scattering all over the floor as they rained down.

Fortunately, my energy trader friend quickly came to our rescue, Sir Galahad in a designer suit. I helped Emily to her feet as she tried to give the flannel-shirted dancing guys a piece of her mind.

"Okay Pearl Jam, why not try to find a girl who's not getting married next time?" He interjected. Despite his convoluted syntax, I thought the dudes got the point of what he was trying to say.

Everyone now looked over at the commotion, many of them pulled away from the game on TV with the prospect of seeing a real life fight. Let's face it, most people just watch hockey for the fights anyway. But these guys didn't look like they had ever been in a fight before.

"Make me, banker boy," said one of the men.

"I will," the energy trader said with the simple confidence of a Marvel superhero facing down a bad guy.

As he lunged forward to swing, he slipped. Instead of landing a punch, he fell at the feet of two men, who decided that wrestling was more their sport of choice. They piled on top of the energy trader. And then my memory of events gets a little blurry; somehow, the three guys, in the process of wrestling, knocked into Emily, two bridesmaids, and me. We took a slow motion domino fall to the floor. After several unsuccessful attempts, I got up and reached down to help Emily, who was dazed but unharmed. Like a soldier on a reconnaissance mission, I rounded up my slippery troops, who were struggling to get up amidst the beer and condoms.

I had Emily by the arm and another bridesmaid by the shirt collar as we headed for the door, where Maggie was yelling, "Go, go, go." She had taken charge of the other girls and was rushing them into the limo. We all piled back into the back of the limo as I removed a beer-soaked condom off my Tory Burch pants. I wondered if my dry cleaner was going to be able to get this stain out, and also what I was going to tell her about how I got the stain. I looked over at Maggie, who shook her head. I braced myself for more criticism, but instead she said, to my surprise, "Nice work, fancy pants." I couldn't believe how my chest swelled with pride at the thought of this compliment from Maggie. I didn't have many friends. Scratch that, make that any friends. Maybe Maggie could help fill that gap. Stranger things had happened in my life.

In life, you are only one Google search away from finding what you need. A key word search for "entrepreneur, support retreat" provided an immediate answer to my employment malaise. Determined to continue my path to self-enlightenment, I signed up for "Finding your entrepreneurial spirit outside the cubicle," after being enticed by the advertisement.

Learn about yourself in this natural hideaway, where the trappings of corporate life will melt away. Find out what you need to succeed on your own in this soul-searching intensive workshop, which includes group sharing, individual story-telling, and light refreshments. At weekend's end, you will have the skills you need to get to the next level. Congratulations! You just signed up for the first day of the rest of your life. *Dress comfortably and bring bug spray.

The weekend promised group sharing around the campfire, nature walks to determine your animal spirit, and shamanis-tic-inspired healing circles, all of which would help participants live the life they imagined. After all, Thoreau went out to the woods, why shouldn't I? My idea of camping, however, was a Courtyard by Marriot, a hotel that, for inexplicable reasons, does not have room service. In my previous life, the Ritz Carlton was reserved for authors while Courtyard by Marriott was reserved for publicists.

I learned this the hard way in Nashville, Tennessee, after attending the Southern Bookseller Association annual trade show several years back. After the show closed, I was looking forward to room service atop a fluffy, comfy hotel bed. Much to my surprise, the phone in my room had no room service button. In disbelief, I phoned the front desk for a replacement phone. When they reassured me the phone was working, I grew impatient.

"It must be an old phone, there's no room service button."

"We don't have room service."

"There must be some sort of mistake."

"No mistake, no button, no room service."

"No way."

Roughing it was not a style I particularly enjoyed, but pushing through discomfort was, I believed, essential to my growth. The Zen Buddhists explain life as a struggle; once we push through the gift of discomfort, the true learning can begin. Struggling had now become part of my everyday existence, and if roughing it at a campground in the middle of New Jersey would provide my soul with a much-needed corporate detox, then let the healing begin, I said to myself.

But first, of course, I had to decide what to wear. A quick trip to Paragon Sports yielded new comfortable attire: cargo pants, a canteen, hiking boots, and a wide brimmed hat. I also purchased an extra-large bottle of OFF! Deep Woods (as the brochure suggested).

In the newly remodeled New Jersey Transit waiting area, the other Eastern Mountain Sports-clad New Yorkers broadcast sartorially that they were headed for the same destination I was. June Swann, our spiritual leader, corralled the troops by waving a large and somewhat noisy rain stick with a striped Hermes scarf tied onto the end. This method was usually reserved for rounding up retirees on a trip to the Vatican, but it worked just as well here in Penn Station, where we were looking for direction anywhere we could get it.

Our conspicuous rain stick-holder was a tall, tanned woman who had most likely not seen the inside off an office in many years. June was one of those people who is so comfortable with herself and her looks that she made you automatically start checking your hair, your teeth, and your newly purchased Paragon outfit for anything amiss or out of place. Her Tevas shoes and cargo pants were worn and well tested. Mine were brand new. She had been out in the woods. I was a novice. Not even one hour into my spiritual journey and already my Dolomite hiking boots were causing me painful blisters. If Zen enlightenment was measured in foot pain, then I was well on my way to the Promised Land.

The Promised Land, in our case, could be reached by a minivan. After taking an Artist's Way class at the Hoboken Adult School, I had taken up journal writing as a way to awaken my deeper passions. Now, the peaceful ride to the country would provide a picturesque backdrop to my winsome (I hoped) prose. I felt exactly as I imagined Henry David Thoreau had, heading out to Walden Pond, with the exception of my Au Bon Pain to-go box, which included a Black Forest ham-and-brie wrap, a mini chocolate croissant, and a triple-berry smoothie, iPod, designer hiking clothes, fellow travelers similarly kitted-out, and electricity. Other than that, you could hardly tell the transcendental philosopher and me apart.

Outplacement proved to be a gateway drug to the endless world of self-improvement that I had sampled over the weeks since my forced retirement. For instance, there was Iyengar yoga for downsized employees at the Integral Center in Manhattan, which involved repeating the same postures over and over again and which proved to be the exact definition of insanity. The course was devised to break down the bad habits adopted in the workplace and to bring the participants to base awareness. There was a common theme between Iyengar and the corporate workplace: in the end, both had left me feeling uncomfortable and battered.

Then there was an attraction circle event led by a dainty blonde from California who promised that whatever you focused on would come to you. Unfortunately, the law of attraction did not account for the greed of the average human being, as many of the people in the group were greedily trying to attract Rob Lowe- or David Beckham-like creatures to sweep in and rescue them (and I have to confess that I include some men who were in the group here as well). Many simply chanted "Oprah, Oprah, Oprah," to earn a spot on her couch as an expert guest without actually going through the hard work of being an expert in anything. The law of attraction might be better called the law of entitlement.

Next was a women's group focused on empowering women entrepreneurs, designed for women and only women to help one another. The website boasted the unique nature of women, uniquely qualifying them to help one another. Unfortunately, the inherent competitiveness and need for popularity that is also inherent in some women did not make for the most nurturing environment. The group was run like a high school caste system where only the "in" crowd would have successful businesses. At one of the meetings, the two women owners needed to step out of the room to have a heated discussion about who had primary ownership of the company.

It was impossible to think that there were problems lying beneath the smiling façades of these dressed-to-be-hip ladies who had been featured in *Fortune* magazine's entrepreneur issue. But something was lurking deeper within them. Just days after their magazine photo shoot, these two had ended up in court fighting over copyrights and intellectual property.

My attention was directed to the bevy of choices offered by life coaches. Life coaching is a great new way to go to therapy without the stigma of traditional therapy. A life coach plants himself or herself in your psyche with a coach's whistle providing backup for all of life's messy business. "Good for you holding the door for that elderly person," or "nice lunch choice, low cholesterol and healthy veggies," or "yup, that guy cut you off, all right."

However, what life coaches really do is encourage you to move forward, not to look back at root causes. This is in direct opposition to what all the psychiatrists on the Upper West Side have been doing for decades. They want you to go back, far back to discover that your family is really the problem of all your insanity. Made sense to me. I mention this because "Let Go of Tolerances and Negative People" was an interesting event taught by a newly certified Life Coach named Linda Best. Her seminar also included two drinks, one appetizer, and a $25 coupon for life coaching sessions, and took place in the East 30s at, of all places, a karaoke bar. Fortunately, only a few singers briefly interrupted the seminar with their renditions of "Islands in the Stream" by Kenny Rogers and Dolly Parton and "Dude Looks Like a Lady" by Aerosmith, which was held during the bar's downtime. During the latter part of the event, Linda spoke to us while dodging plates of buffalo wings and Mai Tais.

After two Mai Tais, most of the participants were ready to sign up for whatever life coaching services Linda was offering. I, on the other hand, headed over to the karaoke bar to enjoy a stunning rendition of Night Ranger's "Sister Christian" sung by a 300-pound German tourist named Klaus. Linda may have been one step away from making balloon animals, but she sure knew how to throw a counseling session.

Upon review, as I sat in the minivan, this weekend was the next logical step in my evolution, a pastoral setting with fewer people and more exclusivity. Even though my fellow minivanners and I dressed the part, it was unclear if any of us would be able to change more than our outfits over the course of one weekend. At the minimum, we all hoped to erase that shell-shocked look that revealed our feelings of displacement after being given the corporate heave-ho.

Seated next to me was a peppy woman in her mid-50s.

"Nice to meet you. Molly Jarvis," she said to me with a hefty handshake.

Molly was one of those people whom you had to call by first *and* last name, sort of like a suburban James Bond. Molly had a Midwestern accent that was immediately distinguishable when she began telling me about her job history, which began in the Twin Cities and ended up "out there to Long Island," as she put it, making it seem like she was describing a remote farming community. She had managed to ride the retail bumps of being a store manager for Target until a shiny new Walmart opened on the Sunrise Highway and put her store in the Carle Place (store number 2748) shopping center out of business.

Molly talked for most of the ride, until we hit traffic near Fort Lee, a New Jersey town legendary for traffic that backs up for miles near the entry to the George Washington Bridge. All that stopping and starting by the minivan driver lulled the portly store manager into slumber, for which I was mercifully thankful. With her head resting on my shoulder—I didn't dare jostle her less she wake up and resume talking to me all over again—I looked at the window and began to wonder if the road to fulfillment really did have to cross Route 4 in New Jersey.

We finally arrive at the camp, which was located on a rustic patch of the Palisades International Parkway, where Native Americans once lived and George Washington's troops did battle. Molly had researched the background of the camp and let me know that the family that had purchased the property in the early 1970s had run a very successful campground business until the early 1990s, when money troubles forced them to close.

As we arrive at the camp, we heard the sound of bagpipes coming from a large elevated cabin. This was likely where the campers had their big meals and meetings. The family, in an effort to recoup money, was renting the space out to whomever would pay. An elderly Scottish dance troop featuring mature men and women in kilts dancing to music played by an equally aged band had paid the $250 hall rental fee. Moving past the prancing highlanders, we were led to our accommodations, a series of small wood cabins designed to look like teepees. Molly, my unprompted tour guide, let me know that "wee people" had once inhabited the little teepees.

"In fact, the entire area is considered Midget Ville," she tediously went on. "Not many people know about this, and of course the term is way politically incorrect, but *Weird New Jersey* magazine just did a big article on it. Only a few people have actually seen them."

There were so many other weird things about New Jersey for the magazine to write about, I wondered why they had chosen an unknown village of "wee people." I made a mental note to ask James if he knew about the conspiracy theory surrounding the area. And if tiny residents still lived in the woods and no one saw them, were they really there at all?

Thoughts of mythical residents pushed aside for the moment, we unloaded from the minivan and retrieved our backpacks and received our assignments. June, in her natural element, had lost the rain stick and was relying solely on her knowledge of rough terrain to maintain the attention of the group. She led us down a rocky path to a small cabin with a sign carved out of a tree bark that said "ain Office." Most of the group was so tired that they didn't pick up on the typo. But Molly Jarvis and I shared a glance and a knowing look, giving us a bond that I felt sure I would regret as the retreat progressed.

Inside the "ain Office" was a table with a series of children's wooden blocks piled on it. Each one had our name on one side and a corresponding name on the back. We were to find our cabinmate my matching up our blocks. The names on the back of the blocks read Broken Branch, Turning Leaf, and Hidden Path, which represented the names of the corresponding teepees where we would be staying. Simply telling you who your roommate was might have been an easy way to help the group get settled, but June had chosen a more Zen Buddhist approach. I looked around and saw that the other five of our perfect six-pack of dysfunction did not mind these little games. "This is cute," and "oh, what fun," and "how clever," echoed among my new pack. My only thought was, please, God, don't let Molly be my roomie.

As the group was settling in to salutary niceties, June snapped back to business.

"You have eight minutes to get into some roomy clothing and rubber soled shoes and meet back here. Go, go!"

Before I had the opportunity to decide which roomy outfit to wear, a perky blonde woman clad in black from head to toe stood in front of me.

"Running Foot? Me, too!" she exclaimed.

Brynn Matherson shook my hand, introduced herself and mentioned that she was super-excited to be here and just all-around pleased to be out of the city and in the country. Her daddy had run a place just like this near Winston-Salem where she grew up. Before completely discounting Brynn's credibility, I realized that she was southern, which meant that she probably handled situations with politeness and grace, as opposed to her northern counterpart, who usually approached situations with skepticism and negativity. Regardless of the oddity of bunking with a complete stranger, I was, in Brynn's words, "super-excited" to have company in the middle of the woods.

You can't tell much about a room in eight minutes when you are digging for roomy clothes and need to use the ladies room. Perhaps this was a deliberate scheduling move to avoid the retreaters from taking full note of the Spartan accommodations in broad daylight. Brynn insisted on taking the top bunk and hoisted her knapsack so high that she barely missed hitting the dangling light bulb hanging from the rafters in the center of the cabin. The lighting fixture looked so old that it easily could have been taken from Edison's laboratory in nearby Menlo Park. When I was growing up, my family had been very big on day trips, and the creepy Edison excursion leaps to mind whenever I see dusty, old electrical items, which until today was, thankfully, rare.

The cabin did not have its own bathroom, but there was a large outhouse-type structure nearby, where boys went around to one side of the building and girls went the other. We had just enough time to investigate the wet concrete bathroom stalls and coin-operated showers. Brynn explained that you really only need 50 cents to get real clean.

The group convened back at the "ain Office," before being escorted down to the dock that faced the lovely lake. A few old kayaks and one canoe remained at the dock, but they were the only evidence of the "fun" that must have been had there back in the day when the grounds were overrun by campers). We were standing at the dock of the bay—literally, waiting for the inevitable icebreaker.

June went out on the dock and turned to address the group.

"I just want to congratulate you all on your bravery for standing up for yourself and to thank you in advance for trusting in me. I can promise you that this weekend will inspire you to be even greater than you already are."

June's compassion for us poor ex-corporates was bordering on the tearful, which I could see was having a healthy effect on our six-pack of refugees who, if they were not delicate pre-minivan, were feeling plenty fragile now. However, her tear was not quite out of the duct before she switched back to her other role of stern taskmaster. It was a little like being addressed, by Dr. Jekyll and Mr. Hyde at the same time.

"Please sit down in a circle. Quickly," she ordered us.

As all good business focus groups began, it was now time to get to know your neighbor. With the exception of Molly Jarvis and Brynn, this was the first time I took a good mental inventory of the others in my brave little band.

George Albertson had just been laid off from MasterCard, where he handled the company's corporate events. Last year, he had made the fatal mistake of hiring a good friend to help shoulder the heavy workload of the department. Her low-cut blouses and high-cut miniskirts were so appealing to the male management team that she was promoted over George within her first six months on the job. She returned the favor six months later and fired George.

The other man in the group was Darren Parr, a pharmaceutical sales manager who had hated his job so much that he quit it before he could get fired. His industry friend promised him a new position selling Zantac if he could regain the *joie de vivre* of his early sales career, when he was named salesman of the year for selling a fat burner pill. That same fat burner ended up being banned from the market by the FDA for wicked side effects, such as prolonged erections in men, hair loss in women, and carpal tunnel syndrome in everyone.

Cynthia had been a hardworking administrative assistant at a financial firm. At her last review, she was asked to review her boss in a company-wide, completely confidential test. The Human Resources department, in an action that was clearly resourceful, but not very humane, revealed the names of the disgruntled employees to their sub-par bosses. In corporate warfare, there are no coincidences, so Cynthia ended up being fired just days after she pressed the "send" key on the review and was told that she was being downsized. She should have just painted a bull's-eye on her back.

"Now that we know our names, ranks, and serial numbers," June said, "I would like to take you to the first phase of this natural experience. Let me introduce you to Shannon O'Connor Batnegar. She will take you through a series of meditations. Shannon and I have been in some very strange positions together," June explained as she enveloped the diminutive yogi in her arms, not realizing the double entendre many of us were misconstruing in our minds.

Shannon could easily have been the poster child for Guinness or sunscreen or both. She was simply the most-fair skinned, freckled person I had ever seen. But her attire looked like it came straight from central casting in Bollywood: Bindi, Henna tattoo, worry bead bracelet, and harem pants, which looked totally impractical given our woodsy surroundings.

After studying with her master in an ashram in Bangalore, Shannon, we later learned, had married him and brought him back to the States, where they ran a yoga studio right near the Empire State Building.

"Let's focus on the breath." She asked us to collect a blanket from the pile she had amassed under the large elm tree. After a complicated explanation on how to unfold and refold the blanket, we all managed to get it right, with the exception of Molly Jarvis, who, now clad in a lavender tracksuit, received help from June.

After ten rounds of deep breathing, we are given two more blankets, three bolsters, and two blocks. At this point, we were given another series of complicated folding maneuvers; we were encouraged to lie on our backs with our heads flat and our buttocks and legs facing straight up in the air.

"This should feel yummy," she giggled.

As she closed the session, which seemed to be more about geometry and blanket folding than anything else, she asked us to focus our intentions on spitting out the evil of corporate life by literally spitting on the ground. Each participant was to rise when tapped on the shoulder and ceremonially hock a spitball "as close to the river as you can get it." After completing this disgusting, but somehow therapeutic ritual, we received a hug from both Shannon and June. I was just grateful that the wind hadn't chosen that moment to blow in our direction.

This ancient ritual was transforming for some, but we were far from finished. As many of us were still untwining from June's embrace, she delivered our next instruction to us.

"Meet back at the large mess hall for dinner and then campfire fun!"

Seldom had the words "campfire fun" sounded so ominous in my ears.

The highlanders had vacated the premises and a small catering staff was now in the kitchen unloading supplies. Not exactly room service, but still service. My hopes were dashed when the staff left the hall, leaving us with the ingredients to make our own dinner. Each person was given a role in the pizza-making process, and together, as a team, we prepared and served veggie pizza for the group.

With dinner made, the kitchen cleaned, and the ingredients for s'mores in hand, June directed our attention to the campfire that she had been building since our arrival. The campfire was the "rest and relaxation" portion of the evening. June opened the session with her small finger bells that she'd used to signal the commencement of all sessions. As soon as those bells had rung, we knew that more discomfort was on its way.

Each of us was handed a piece of paper with another group member's name printed on it, and instead of having that awkward moment of self-assessment, we were asked to assess the others. Up until this point, the only things we knew about one another were a bit of work history and how flexible we were with our legs up over several Navajo blankets. June switched back into helpful Sherpa mode. She handed out pieces of paper and markers to each of us, then explained:

"I want you to write on this piece of paper what kind of entrée you think this person is."

Brynn was confused. "Entrée?"

"Yes, an entrée, a main course, not a side dish, not an appetizer, not an *amuse bouche*. Something substantial and fulfilling."

"Do we come with a drink?" Darren joked, making me wonder if he had a problem.

June, I could tell, was having a hard time loosening up with this crowd. Her euphoria over the cleverness of the game and the undoubted praise that would follow were being sidetracked by these little questions.

"There are no wrong answers, just feel it and write it."

For the next five minutes, we considered our entrée options, then wrote them down on the piece of paper we had been given. Then, June blew her whistle and it was time to compare notes.

Darren thought Molly Jarvis was a chicken pot pie, comforting and homey. Molly Jarvis wrote that Brynn was a garden salad with salmon and no dressing, healthy and smart. Cynthia imagined George as a big plate of nachos from Chili's, an appetizer that, in fairness, could double as an entrée. George said I was lasagna with a glass of red wine, multi-layered (for which I didn't know whether to be pleased or offended). Brynn envisioned Darren as a T-bone steak with a side of creamed spinach, strong and something a salesman would order. I thought Cynthia was chicken fried steak with waffle fries.

Each of us added the descriptive words on the end, in an effort to minimize any stigma that calling someone you hardly know a food item might carry. I scanned the faces of my peers, the interplay of the flames against roasting marshmallows and then farther into the distant tree line. And all I could think was that somewhere out there was a small person in a teepee watching us in disbelief. And I was pretty sure that he thinks *we* are weird.

Most people dread Monday mornings as it signals the end of all the good times had on the weekend. But the opposite has always been true for me; I rarely had a good time on the weekend, especially after spending the weekend in the woods with a group of strangers. That Monday, I was even more eager to get back to work, even though my career choice left my family wondering what had happened to the straightlaced business woman they were so proud of. And I was starting to see their point. My recent choice was not what they had envisioned for me. I had to agree with them on that, at least, as I walked over to my makeshift office on top of an empty bar at seven in the morning. This was not the glamorous career that I had imagined, either. As I let myself in to the downstairs bar entrance for which I now had my own key, I looked around at the soon-to-be-closed bar. The barstools flipped upside down on top of the bar, the drink glasses neatly hung after last call. The place looked all cleaned up and ready to be turned into something else.

All I could think of that morning was my family's silent disapproval at our last Sunday dinner. It might have helped if they'd yelled at me and forbade me to carry on with this unlikely and unseemly job choice, but they hadn't. They did worse. They said nothing. The only conversation that took place after my mother's abrupt departure was getting the elderly family members up to speed on what exactly had transpired at the table.

Nana joined my mother in the speechless category, but managed to utter some indecipherable Italian phrases while she shook her head. My Juicy Couture-wearing grandmother had somehow watched enough of *Access Hollywood* and MTV to be curious about the tattooed boyfriend she had just heard about.

"Does he look like Steven Tyler?" she asked.

The fact that she knew Steven Tyler at all left me to wonder about the effects of excessive television watching on the elderly. Without knowing what to do, I decided to answer the best I could and not keep the little old lady in suspense.

"Actually, Na, he does look a bit like Steven Tyler. But not as many scarves," I added.

"Not that many tattoos!" James added, as if coming to my aid, finally.

I assured them that my "boss" was not my new boyfriend, an admission not entirely false, but the denial made me feel like a fourth grader, too embarrassed to reveal her true feelings. In their eyes, I might always appear to be a fourth grader struggling with a schoolgirl crush. I wished that my only problem was dealing with unrequited love, but my problems were much worse.

"I am just using the office space, really. Strictly business until I get my own space to rent. Temporary. No biggie," I assured them.

James, on the other hand, turned his unfortunate admission to pure gold, as he was prone to do. He told the grandparents exactly what they wanted to hear. With Tara moving in and sharing the expenses, he was getting one step closer to the perfect engagement ring. The mention of marriage sidetracked all of them for a few moments while I squandered the only opportunity I had to stand up to my family, to explain that I believed in what I was doing. But, my inner-fourth grader won out; I remained mute.

The meal continued with no further talk, the eggplant and macaroni served, the pastry sampled, and the demitasse cups collected. All in a quiet and polite fashion, completely unlike any of our family meals; it was as though we had assumed the formality of the meals my mother had hoped to host when she first got married. James and I moved on from our altercation with no adverse effects and got back into the car as if nothing had happened. We simply carried on as if the nasty words had never been spoken. Deep down, we knew we didn't mean them. We ultimately knew that apologizing was unnecessary and made us both feel uncomfortable. My mother had opted to show her supreme disapproval with her silence. It was when she was quiet that you truly had to worry. Her words symbolized attention, caring, regardless of how perverse the message. And the silence sent a cavalcade of doubts into my already fragile mind. My family stationed themselves as the executive committee of my new company that was already having trouble getting off the ground. At that point, I felt like I had people to answer to. I had hoped a weekend with like-minded corporate outcasts would add more than just company to my misery, but it only made me more doubtful about what to do next.

Regaining any career confidence without my former job title and corporation was already precarious; just when I thought I had my footing, another rung was taken out from under me. So when Dave and Bertram arrived in my life with all their hopes and dreams of saving the bar riding on me, I thought this might be what I needed to turn the tables, maybe even set a *karmic* shift into motion. Besides kindred spirits, they were becoming my friends, which made me even more vested in helping them. All I could think of was my father's advice as I left the house; he pulled me aside and said, "Just try to wrap this up quickly and don't tell your mother any more about it. It's best to leave her out of these kinds of things."

And as much as I wanted the approval of my family, my new life promised something different, something heroic. My plan of the moment was to save the bar from early extinction and to do that I would need to muster all of my public relations know-how. The goal was to use the media to create a story about the bar, the bar's owner, and the community that needed it so badly. At least that's what I decided to pitch the *Daily News* metro reporter when I spoke to him that morning.

"The Garage is more than a bar, it's a community space, historic really," I bragged. The reporter on the phone was sympathetic; he had seen REM play there when he was in college at Stevens Technical Institute, which was located just two blocks away. He agreed to write an article and include the list of famous artists who had received their start there.

I assigned Bertram to conduct a social media campaign, tweeting information about the fundraiser attendees. Patti Smith and Richard Hell had both agreed to attend. Our YouTube channel received some noteworthy buzz as well. Dave had a ton of video that he had compiled over the years, and his job was to get all of his admiring fans in town to share the feeds on Facebook. The virtual community "liked" us and the journalistic community was supportive. That looked good but I wondered if that would really amount to anything substantial. What I needed was a great headliner to make the show. If we had a big star to support the bar, maybe a media-hungry benefactor or politician might step forward with enough money and influence to turn the tide.

I even called the local historical society to have the bar listed on the national registry of historic landmarks, but the historian answered my request by saying that across the street from the bar were the Elysian Fields, the site of the first organized baseball game, which was played in 1845.

"That is a historic landmark. A bar that opened in the early 1980s is not really the kind of history we're looking for," he told me. I would have to create from scratch a new place in history for the bar.

The bar's demise landed smack in the middle of the mayoral election in town. I contacted both candidates to make a statement, but each was reluctant to say anything about saving a bar. They were both more comfortable with a ribbon-cutting at a charter school. I would have to wait out the candidates, who were reluctant to lend their support without gaining a political advantage. I was going to need divine intervention, but it looked like it would take someone big to make this into a political issue, rather than a business one. I stared at the poster of Bruce Springsteen hanging over my head when Bertram came in to the office.

He had stopped for coffee and had three in his hand, expecting the third part of our office group to be assembled. He was exhausted from staying up late to tweet, re-tweet, and tweet again. The impulsive immediacy of it all was a dream for insomniacs, but made it impossible to get sleep.

"I always think I'm going to miss something," he explained.

"I thought Dave would be here, by now," he added.

"Nope, just me," I said.

Bertram handed me my coffee and a few extra "Sugar in the Raw" packets.

"Not that you need any more sweetness. You are sweet enough, girl," he added.

"Corny, but effective," I remarked back.

Dave had been making a last effort to fend off Schmidt, the landlord. His big renovation plan was to make the place into a large daycare center, the latest franchise called Tot Land, which his daughter would run. The entire building would be repurposed for its new small residents, complete with a bouncy house and a jungle gym where the littlest Hobokenites would live out their playground fantasies. Ironically, this was the place that people had come to live out their rock and roll fantasies.

Schmidt's daughter would be here at any moment to look over the office, which *she* planned to renovate into a luxury penthouse space for her and her daughter to live in. Schmidt was an older German man who owned the oldest and only German pub in town, and most of the block on which The Garage was located. He had bought up the block, building by building, in the 1980s when the town was experiencing a down-turn. It was Hoboken's "before" picture. Nobody was coming to town to hang out due to an upturn in crime.

This was the time in New York City following the famous Bernard Goetz subway shootings. Cities were perceived as more dangerous than ever. Most Jerseyans headed for the suburbs, to large warehouse-like dance clubs instead of risking theft and shooting in New York or even, Hoboken. Real estate followed this flight trend and prices decreased. Just as Uncle Pep thought, people were always trying to get out of Hoboken. This was another grand exodus from town, not seen since the rough and tumble days of the 1950s as depicted in *On the Waterfront*, which had been filmed in Hoboken. People were trying to get out and get out fast. For someone with forethought and capital, this was a place to invest. Enter Andres Schmidt, a first-generation Hoboken resident with vision. He had inherited his family's beer garden across the street from The Garage. And with a careful eye on the uptick of his bank account and the downtick of the real estate market, he scooped up properties on upper Washington Street faster than you can say *weinershnitzel*.

Earlier that morning, I felt nostalgic as well, but about my personal history and not the neighborhood. I thought about Daniel and Emily hard at work at Smith & Drake. I knew they would be at the biannual meeting, where the editors pitched the next season of books. There, each publicist would learn his or her fate as to which authors they would be stuck with all year; this was rarely news that anyone welcomed. But the fickle hand of fate was to intercede once again and this time it was Mr. Freud. There are no coincidences. I learned this via text, which is where all important information is shared these days. Daniel sent me four words that were to change the course of my life; well, at least my morning. "We got The Boss."

After years of persuasion from the CEO of Smith & Drake, a huge Springsteen fan (despite his staunch Republican ways, which seemed to be in direct contrast with everything Bruce stood for), the publisher finally had the financial backing to get The Boss to sign. The picture book of Bruce's early days at the Jersey Shore was to be packaged with the release of his early, never recorded songs. All this was to be a fundraiser for the rejuvenation of his hometown, Asbury Park, which, not unlike Hoboken, was experiencing a resurgence. The book had not been announced yet, but Daniel had already planned a social media campaign of his own; the regular media would pick up a carefully worded tweet from Bruce.

The book deal was in no doubt put together along with the backing of the French media conglomerate that had acquired Smith & Drake. The media company owned several record labels, magazines, and other international publishers and was always looking for company synergies across their various holdings.

These acquisitions were so common that many of us joked that we would all be working for one giant publishing company, instead of the several independent houses all over New York. But with the changing digital landscape, the traditional publishing model was not as profitable or as feasible. Besides, just about anyone could publish a book from his or her iPhone.

Immediately deeming this information way too important to await words coming over my screen, I speed-dialed Daniel. I wanted to leave no room for misinterpretation, like those suspicious of those emoticons and shorthand phrases. He was expecting my call.

"Hi, Jessie, before you say anything, I already got us in," he preempted me.

Daniel, with his new super-status as Bruce's book publicist, was to meet "The Boss" at a benefit concert, and he was allowed to have a "plus one" guest. I was to be his "plus one," for these kinds of events which real spouses never wanted to attend. This would be perfect; what's one more benefit concert? It's in New Jersey, plus the video was made right here at The Garage. It was all too good to be true. This had to happen; I would make it my life mission to make this happen. I said as much to Daniel, within earshot of the curious, but skeptical Bertram.

Bruce had been the soundtrack for my childhood. I even had a button that said "Bruce Juice" on it, which I wore to sixth grade every day. It was his face on an orange juice label and the pin was shaped like a bottle. I still had that pin somewhere in my parents' basement. Sidetracked by the button's whereabouts momentarily, I may have jumped too quickly. Bertram was watching me relay all of the juicy and not so juicy details to Daniel. As soon as I hung up, he cautioned me to take a breath.

"Move slowly, Jessie, don't count your chickens before they're hatched."

This advice was not taken, because when Dave came in looking dejected, sad and out of hope, I grasped for whatever I could do to make him happy.

"I think I can get Bruce," I blurted out. Instead of cautiously considering my remarks, which I had done for my entire career, I had turned into a person who leaps before the net appears. At least that was my working philosophy at that point, courtesy of a greeting card Caroline had sent with that Zen Buddhism statement on it, just last week. That card was the only personal thing in my workspace.

I told Dave all about my uber-connections. My still best friend Daniel worked for my former publisher, he was Bruce's publicist, Daniel would do anything for me, and that, in turn, meant that Bruce would do anything for you. Somehow it all seemed logical.

Dave jumped over the desk and gave me a spinning hug that lifted me off my chair. I think I was overwhelmed by the closeness. Something I had only fantasized about, a hundred times since meeting him at Starbucks. But I was so slightly weak with the excitement of it all that I may have overpromised, just a smidge. I looked over Dave's shoulder to see Bertram nodding his head.

"Or you could go a different route entirely," he quipped.

But I did not want to hear from any more detractors. I was happy in Dave's arms and, for one moment, I had his attention. And he seemed happy too; at least, that is what he said.

"I knew you could do it. And to think for a moment, I thought I might sell out entirely and have you start one of those crowd sourcing websites, like some kid who has real problems like he needs a kidney or bone marrow or something. I want The Garage to make it back because it's important and people need it, not because we are a charity case."

But that moment was to be cut short, when Andres Schmidt's daughter, Lively, arrived at the door, tape measure in one hand and Hermès bag in the other.

"Do you mind if we have a look, privately?" she asked. As Bertram and I gathered our things, Dave was about to follow, when suddenly, as if by second thought, Lively said to Dave, "You...can stay." Dave hunched in his shoulders in one of those "go figure" motions.

But we both knew even a stuffy, spoiled good girl like Lively could not resist the irresistible charms of someone who looked like Steven Tyler.

I had made the promise and broken the cardinal rule of publicity, underpromise and overdeliver. And Bertram knew that I had confused the order of that mantra as well.

"Be careful with what you tell Dave. It's hard to break a promise once you make it."

"I know, but this is Bruce. It just has to happen."

"It might all look good now, but it's like Jerry warned. 'When life looks like easy street, there is danger at the door.'" At that point, the double entendre of Lively at the door had not quite registered.

Bertram, a devoted Grateful Dead fan, had a habit of bringing Jerry Garcia's philosophies into every conversation. But, I, as much as Dave, needed some good news. Bertram was going to have to come up with a less foreboding Jerry lyric to suit my mood that morning.

At that point, I should have promised that I could get an invitation to The Boss, not that he would ultimately accept it. Promising that he would be there was an entirely different story. But Dave was so happy, and when someone is that happy, it's hard to take that away.

The next night, Daniel and I headed down the Jersey Shore to the event. Before I could even think about meeting Bruce, there was the concert. A Bruce Springsteen concert is much more than a concert. He has his band, which is more like his family, all so well meshed, that it's hard to imagine these people any place except on stage. I often wondered about performers, what did they do when they were not on stage? Did they do laundry, shop for produce, clean the bathroom? Did they perform any of the functions of real people or let others do that for them? I mean, at some point, doesn't Little Steven just take out his own garbage?

I felt like I could speak for Bruce. His life story was in his music; even his wife was in the band. As he played all of my favorite songs, I believed that he was singing the soundtrack to my comeback as well. He has a way of making you think you could get out of any situation in New Jersey, or anywhere else, for that matter. But for some reason, I was thinking that a lot of bad situations do happen in New Jersey, so he had plenty of material to work with.

Bruce is great at depicting that angst and struggle, bringing together an overwhelming wave of hope that you can get yourself out of your current station in life. And after seeing him in concert, I believed that he would singlehandedly pull me out of my current malaise. But, as I knew from my brief experience with self-help, the answers are always within. And most Bruce songs help you recognize the difficulties. The path you take after that is of your own choosing.

After the music ended, we were given large placard badges and led backstage to the meet and greet along with 30 other non-groupie looking VIPs. The placards we wore made us feel special, but a casual observer would have witnessed how out of place they made us look. We were not a cool-looking bunch.

One by one, we were led to the couch where Bruce sat drying off from his performance. Daniel's editor and Bruce's editor had already talked on the phone, so this meeting was more of a technicality than a real business event. These things are strictly perks for the minions who would be putting in countless hours to ensure the success of the book. But the event serves its purpose by putting those who work on the book in complete awe of the artist. The show guarantees their servitude. For a short time, anyway, the publicists, the editors, and the publisher, as low as they are on the media food chain, have that one moment where they think that they can publish the best book ever. And celebrities, whether they are aging Broadway stars, retired baseball players, or former talk show hosts, all romanticize the idea of writing a book, as if it's the last piece of the puzzle that finally gives them the credibility they long for. They all want to be an author, which is odd, because we all want to be rock stars or celebrity athletes or models. But the obvious irony aside, we had one shot to get Bruce to the bar and I was not going to blow it. After all, I had met countless celebrities, I had been in Oprah's green room, and I had met Katie Couric *and* Matt Lauer. I once rode in an elevator with Bill Clinton. Celebrities did not scare me.

When it was our turn to meet and genuflect. Bruce said in that signature raspy, almost Southern cadence:

"Hi, it's nice to meet you." He shook my hand and the realization hit me. Bruce touched my hand. So overwhelmed was I with that notion, I stared at our joined hands in amazement.

"I'm Bruce and you are?" he prompted, indicating that this was not the first time an adoring fan went mute in his presence.

I said nothing, I just stared at him, his hoop earrings jingled, and his dark tight T-shirt was still a bit moist from the encore of "Rosalita." The way he sat on the couch, so casually as if he had not just changed the life of everyone in the arena. The sheer god-like nature of the rock star. He sipped from a bottle of Evian.

Daniel released my hand from Bruce's and nudged me, hoping to break me out of my stalker-like trance.

"Wow," was all I could manage to say. Daniel jumped in, worried that our few minutes of greatness was coming to a close. The list of well-wishers behind us needed their moment of praise as well.

"This is Jessie, she's the publicist for The Garage. They're having a little event; they thought you might drop by."

"The Garage, I did a video there." He looked over to George, his manager, and said, "What was that video?"

"Glory Days," said George.

"Yes! Video!" I echoed, now only able to use one word at a time, incapable of putting a coherent sentence together in front of my hero. Daniel interjected once again, "They're shutting the place down, but there's one last hope, a fundraiser later this month," Daniel explained.

"Fundraiser!" I blurted.

"That's a shame, that's a shame. If there's anything I can do, let me know," The Boss added, but he was already being introduced to the next group of VIPs that stood behind us. I hoped that theirs would go better than mine, but I was doubtful.

"Come to our fundraiser," I squeaked out just as I was being ushered off.

"George," Bruce motioned to his manager, "take the information and see what I'm doing. If it can be done, then it can be done." He looked at me and winked.

And that was that. I met The Boss and gave him an invitation. The rest would have to be left to chance. If it can be done, it can be done.

Nobu was not my usual place for lunch, especially in my weakened financial state. But, when Mark Feist, the tech mogul turned philanthropist, accepts your invite, you have no choice but to accept his terms, regardless of what financial straits that puts you in. My "page-a-day" calendar of inspirational quotes for that day was, "Lack of money is no obstacle, lack of an idea is an obstacle." I hoped that Mark felt the same way. Mark and I had met outside the backstage door at the Springsteen concert. I had no idea who he was at the time. Daniel thought he was hitting on me as he flipped his business card and jumped into a hummer that waited for him on Ocean Avenue. "Let's do Nobu back on the island." "The island," of course, could only refer to one location: Manhattan. As if this New Jersey side trip had disoriented him so much that he needed to ground himself back on the terra firma of New York City.

Calling his office to set up our Nobu lunch felt more like running the gauntlet. His officious assistant was trained to separate the real from the charlatan, a skill refined by all good gatekeepers. I had had some experience with gatekeeping of my own. You only have to run into one kook at a bookstore to know how important a position this is. I once had a fan try to lick one of my authors at a Barnes & Noble. I also knew that you have to befriend the gatekeeper, as it may be your only chance to gain entrance. But this gatekeeper wanted only to ask me a series of pointed questions, Gallup Poll-style. She took down my name, my company, and the place where her boss and I had met, and then finally she asked me which celebrity I most looked like. That was strange, but without another option I told her Drew Barrymore. That was not the first time I had played the celebrity lookalike game either, which made me more or less prepared with an answer. Apparently my credentials checked out enough for Mark to merit calling back to set up the lunch.

I got my research department immediately on the case. My Chief Information Officer, Bertram, conducted a thorough Google search that netted over 500 images of Mark with a host of rock and roll stars, captains of industry, and political figures, which included the obvious you would expect: Bono, Elton, and Madonna. He had even started a foundation company called Rock and Roll Feels, which was meant to be a clever tease, but begged the question, what exactly does rock and roll feel— happy, sad, angry? Despite his rock and roll pedigree, his look belied the image he wanted to project. At first glance, he looked more like someone who worked at the Geek Squad at Best Buy, maybe even the manager; he had the years of experience to pull off that responsibility. Mark was a cross between the Count from *Sesame Street* and Jeff Goldblum, just a few degrees off good looking. But those few degrees can make all the difference. No amount of designer clothing and personal training sessions would ever make this man good-looking.

When we first met, he came at Daniel and I so strongly that we both recoiled at his presence. He had a lumbering gait and a shocked look on his face as if always in a state of being taken by surprise. I suspected this might have been the result of a bad eyebrow waxing. I tried not to focus too much on his unattractive looks, but more on his attractive wallet, which had the potential to save us all. In that regard, he was the man of my dreams.

"This guy is made of money," said Bertram, succinctly summoning up the man.

At 35, Feist had sold a data retrieval system to Sony for $5 billion. It was a tiny but essential technology that would change the way people used touch screens. It was likely these two companies were the only ones advanced enough to understand the full impact of this microscopic breakthrough. This research would enable upgrade-happy people to scroll even faster on their tablets and iPads. And God forbid we lose a nanosecond when searching for important information on our Facebook pages. How privileged we have become, so totally reliant on ultra-fast convenience to help us through our day. The sad part was that once this was introduced, we would likely not be able to live without it, at least until the next iteration came along.

"Oh, look, here's a picture of him with Naomi Campbell. He must like it crazy," Bertram editorialized.

Mark's assistant called back to give me a special set of instructions. He lunched at Nobu at noon, in his usual corner booth. "You can discuss your business there. And please, no PowerPoint presentations, he hates those." (I did, too, by the way.) She went on to explain his philosophy on work; he would just prefer to have a casual meeting where people talked and made eye contact rather than getting into the formality of a business plan or anything crude, say, like talking about money. He hated talking about money. He must have thought that I was an insider, based on our elite backstage status. I was no insider, but he didn't need to know that. I agreed to the lunch at Nobu, refusing to let my lack of money get in the way of my great idea. I had no clue how I would pay the bill. But I would worry about that later.

"He and Naomi officially called it quits, so this could be your opening," Bertram joked, still fixated on the love lives of the rich and famous.

"So, if I make him think this is a date, maybe he'll pay?" I offered weakly.

"Be prepared to pay for this in one way or another. The rich are different, they don't even carry wallets," he shared, as if he were telling me about an odd species found in the Himalayas rather than a fellow human being. And as if to emphasize further, he made his finger into quotation marks and said, "Different."

I was the first to arrive at the restaurant and was ushered back to Mark's signature corner booth by the hostess, who had the look of an Amazonian warrior, clad in a Vivienne Westwood dress.

"Geraldine told me you were coming," she said. "She always calls ahead when Mark has a guest at his table." She emphasized the word "guest" as if to give it some special significance. She then gave me a cursory look up and down, as though sizing me up for some future purpose, and told me to "wait here, for his arrival." She pointed to the corner seat, left a menu, and turned quickly to return to her station.

I scanned the menu and, much to my astonishment, there were no prices listed. This was even worse than I had expected. My three credit cards were maxed out, so I planned to skip food entirely and use my debit card, hoping that my unemployment check would hit my account in time to pay the bill. I was cutting it close. If the bill exceeded $112 or if the unemployment check was late, I had no way to pay.

When Mark arrived, 30 minutes later, the Amazon-like hostess was all smiles and warmth as she escorted him arm-in-arm to the table. He winked at the two women at a nearby table, who had dropped their chopsticks long enough to wonder and whisper who "that man" was. He received such four-star treatment, they just naturally assumed he must be a somebody. I overheard one of them say, "That's not Jeff Gold-blum, is it? He looks so much shorter in person." Mark had perfected the self-congratulatory strut of someone famous. He scanned the restaurant over his aviator Ray-Bans, in an effort to get more people looking at him. But all the other patrons seemed engaged in their own personal dramas, not his. He would have to settle for the two tackily attired housewives from Long Island with orange press-on nails and an overt mixture of designer knock-offs that they had no doubt picked off the Loehmann's clearance rack. They were his groupies, which seemed to be fitting, since his appearance was more accountant than rock star.

I stood up to formally introduce myself. Instead of shaking my hand, he gave me a kiss on both cheeks and then again, three times in total, French-style. He then stepped back and formally bowed, as if to fit in with his Asian surroundings. I, in turn, bowed as well, which caused him to bow again. I hesitated and tried to bow again and then he bowed again. What? A little dizzy and tired from all that kissing and bowing, I finally just gave up and clumsily plopped down in the banquette. Whatever happened to a simple handshake?

His grand and foreign greeting was as much for the effect of those around us as serving any meaningful exchange between us. It was weird, but I sensed that he thought it was cool and necessary to cement his image, making me think this was a spiritual meeting of the minds. His entire body language and demeanor was all "we are just here to hang, baby," as if he were Sting and not a short Jewish man originally from Islip, Long Island, which Bertram later discovered on Gawker.

He slid into the booth and sat next to me, instead of opting to sit across the banquette at the chair provided for normal conversation to take place. I always wondered about those people who sit on the same side of a dining table instead of across from their companion, but my wonderment was cut short because I had just become one of those people. And as I'd suspected, it felt decidedly odd.

Before he ordered, he was presented with green tea and two cups. "This is organic and the best in the city, you have to try it," he explained and poured. People like Mark Feist are always looking for things to deem the "best in the city."

"Bono drinks this," he added.

"Of course he does," I agreed, half sarcastically.

I thought about how I would be identified on the bottom of the TV screen when people are interviewed and a few choice words are used to define each person, such as, "Linda, wife of the accused gunman." Or, "Trina, the last ousted Bachelorette." Mine would read, "Jessie, the destitute publicist, unable to pay the restaurant bill."

Okay, tea, that should not be too expensive, maybe $10, I tallied the bill so far in my head, calculating that I was left with just over $100 until unemployment came through.

Thinking that less would be consumed over a short meal, I decided to cut right to the chase. "Thank you so much for meeting me, Mr. Feist. I wanted to talk with you about..." But before I could get any further, he was distracted. He was fixated on something and asked, "Turquoise or lapis?" He moved closer, if that was possible, and I thought he must be looking at something over my head or behind me, so I began a veritable "I Spy" of items above, around and behind me. Then he motioned at my necklace and flicked the charm with his pinkie finger, a move I felt was slightly invasive and an intrusion of my personal space.

"You know," he said informatively, "Jim Morrison always wore lapis, not turquoise, that's a huge misconception about him."

I wondered if this misconception was really the most important thing to note about Jim Morrison. After seeing that Oliver Stone movie, I thought that Jim's problems went far deeper than his selection of jewelry.

"Is that Kendra Scott?" he asked. So, he was still focused on my jewelry. "I had her make me a belt buckle, just like Jim's." And he slid back an inch in his seat so he could lift his paunchy belly off his waistband to reveal a silver-buckled cowboy belt. I tilted my head and awaited an explanation.

"Oh, man, I don't have that one on today, my bad," he apologized.

He let out what would be the first of several loud guffaws. It was the kind of laugh that everyone hears and everyone wonders about. I mean, who laughs that hard in public? I had a great sense of humor—with my family I needed one—but I never laughed like that, in public or really any place, for that matter. I tried to turn us away from that laugh and back to the common quieter ground of jewelry design.

"Um, I don't think it is Kendra Scott," I blurted, uncomfortably, "I think it's H&M."

"Oh yeah, H&M, I've heard of them, they do nice stuff, nice stuff." He sipped his tea and repeated his last statement as if in meditation. As he sipped, my text alert came on; a techno rap beat that had come with my phone and which I had never bothered to change.

"I made that." He said in recognition and guffawed again. Could this one have been even louder? Once he calmed down long enough, he continued in a strained voice, "I made that text ring. For Jay-Z." But he did not say "Jayzee" like everyone else does, he said "Jazy," like lazy, which led me to believe that he could have possibly been talking about someone else entirely. People with affectations do this a lot too; they mispronounce the obvious pronunciations, as if their life is on such a higher plane of living that they have no time to wallow in the everyday trivia, like learning people's names. I apologized and put the phone on mute.

"No need to apologize, people need to reach others, it's the great paradox of our connected society." This non-observation was followed by a small guffaw, for which I was grateful. This lunch felt like it had its own laugh track.

I noticed that the message was from Citibank alerting me that I had insufficient funds in my checking account. That unemployment check would need to clear and soon. No doubt this technology was more of the kind of stuff that Mark's former company, InfoBase, had perfected. There is such a thing as too much information, for sure.

The waitress came over and made a big deal of seeing "Mr. Mark." When you go to lunch in the same place every day, this is the kind of service you are bound to receive. This was his personal Cheers bar, where everyone knew his name. He placed his usual high maintenance order.

"Two Hamachi rolls, with no Hamachi." Mr. Mark didn't do fish, which begged the question of why he ate at Nobu at all, if all he planned to do was order cucumber and rice. The obvious answer was to see and be seen by the equally high maintenance patrons who regularly ate there.

"Oh, and how about that awesome green salad, but no dressing and some edamame without salt and not cooked?" I could only imagine what I would be paying for all this naked produce. At my local Korean deli, this order would probably have totaled $3 to $4, max.

"We can share, right, Jenn?" he said. Somewhere in the Nobu kitchen I knew was an angry sushi chef flipping Mark the bird. And I might have actually done the same, because I thought he had called me Jenn. Carrying on, nevertheless, I pep talked myself back to the reason I had asked him to lunch. At that point, I was willing to have him call me anything, as long as he could write a check to save the bar.

"It's Jessica," I gently corrected him.

"That's what I said," he answered.

"So, Mr. Feist," I continued, but he put his finger on my lip, to quiet me, which worked, because at that point I had no idea what else to say during this conversation. I felt like I was in the middle of a Fellini film and I had no idea what the subtitles meant.

"Let's take a gratitude moment for this meal we are about to enjoy." He closed his eyes, put his hands together in prayer and kissed his small sushi plate. I wondered if I was supposed to follow his lead and cringed in expectation of what the other patrons might make of my display. But with a slick whip of his napkin, he covered his thigh and my thigh, and then leaned in.

"What were you saying, baby?" he asked. Now all of this would have been charming if Mark didn't look like someone who used to get beat up in high school. At that moment, I wanted to kick his ass myself. While he was crafting his entire new age Jim Morrison persona, I was watching my chances of landing the capital I needed to save the bar dwindle away. I had real business to take care of and he was not taking me seriously. If this is how business is done, I resolved, then I would beat him at his own crazy head game.

"That wasn't the first time you met Bruce, right? I got the distinct impression that you and he were longtime friends." I flattered him with proper hero worship.

"Oh, yeah, we go way back," he beamed with fake modesty.

"I thought so, that's why he told me to contact you about a little project that has Mark Feist written all over it." I billboarded his name with my hands.

"Bruce said that?"

"Oh, yeah, he said that, and more. He said if you want a cool guy to help save the day, you need Mark Feist." Again, I used my hand gesture to add a special touch. I could see from the flattered look on his face that I had him right where I wanted him. It was all going so well, when through the front door I saw a familiar face enter the restaurant. It was Dr. Ursula. She did not see me at first; so quick-thinking me dropped my napkin on the floor before diving directly under the table, to hide from her as she made her way through the dining room.

When I leaned down under the table, Mark thought he was getting a bit more than lunch.

"Take it easy baby, we just met," he half-joked and then looked around to see if anyone else had noticed. I had lost count of his laughs at this point, but he had worked himself up into a healthy new one by the time Dr. Ursula made her angry promenade over to us. Damn, I hadn't ducked under the table in enough time for her not to notice me.

In all my coolness to be inconspicuous, I knocked my head on the table, which sent the entire tea service crashing to the floor. All heads turned, including Dr. Ursula's, who, once she realized what I was doing, picked up her pace a notch to angry commando on a revenge mission.

"Jessica," she teased in a "come out, come out, wherever, you are" tone of voice.

And then I began my slow motion rise from the floor. I noticed every expensive accessory she had on as I made my way back up to the banquette. Bowing at the good doctor's feet was something that had not changed since I'd been fired.

"Jessica, stand up this instant. There is something I have to say to you. You left my tour in ruins. This new publicist is unimaginable; she has no idea what she is doing. You had a lot of nerve leaving me."

I lurched back into the banquette, next to Mark. He and most of the restaurant were listening. Instead of letting everyone know that I had been laid off, I just sat there and let her continue. Mark sensed that as well and had taken the role of spectator at the U.S. Open tennis match waiting for one of the Williams sister to deliver a final smash.

"All that woman does is tell me that I am amazing. Well, I know I'm amazing, but you, Jessica, I needed you. You were hired to serve me."

The two women from Long Island caught the tail end of the conversation and said to each other:

"Oh, no, she did not."

"Oh, yes, she went there."

"Doctor, please calm down, it can't be that bad," I cut in mid-tirade. "You still have two books on *The New York Times* bestseller list."

"This is heavy," Mark said, rapt at the notion of a public girl fight that could or could not be over him. From a distance, even this bad publicity was good for the image he wanted so desperately to create for himself.

"Who is this person?" Mark Feist wanted to know.

"She is like, killing my green tea buzz with her total negativity," he added.

The good doctor turned to look at Mark and she recognized him, as most highly moneyed people are apt to recognize one another, like they all belonged to the same private club, which, come to think of it, they all did. She composed herself, realizing her celebrityhood and, finally, her manners. She extended her hand.

"I am Dr. Ursula," she announced.

"This is Mark Feist," I introduced. I could see her eyes light up.

"Did you say Mark Feist as in InfoBase Mark Feist?"

"Guilty, as charged," he admitted with mock humility.

"Well, I am happy to meet you, even under these circumstances. Good day to you both." And with that, she stormed off.

"She is hot. I dig cougars," said Mark.

I tried to fight down my nausea and redirect the conversation back to Bruce, back to The Garage, but the opportunity had passed, because, before I knew it, Mark looked at his watch and got up to go. I could only imagine what was next on his agenda, hot yoga, and a massage, a meeting with the Dali Lama?

And then, in a flash, he took my face in his hands and placed a wet, messy kiss on my mouth, before sliding out of the booth and heading toward the door.

"This was fun, baby. Let's do it again," he said as he made his way toward the door. The hostess, as if to scold him, pointed him back to the table, where there was quite a mess, myself not included. He nodded and, like a scolded child, reached into his pocket, grabbed a few $100 bills and, to my immense relief and the eternal thanks of my checking account, tossed them on the table.

"That's for the housekeeper," he said loudly. Then he strutted out of the restaurant, in an effort to make himself look like a naughty rock star taking reluctant responsibility for a trashed hotel room.

I used to be a "go to" person, someone who people rely on to help them out of life's sticky situations. In my former position, people were constantly coming to me, to resolve their travel issues, get them an interview with Charlie Rose or manage the expectations of jittery first time authors. I prided myself on being able to solve these problems with ease. I rarely even asked Saint Anthony for help when something went missing unless it was a total emergency. But times had changed. I had landed squarely in my discomfort zone as the asker, a role that required asking people for help, mostly people I hardly knew, for colossal favors. Paramount on that list was Mark Feist with his lofty bank account and connections, which, despite high hopes, had netted nothing from our meeting at Nobu. After suffering the humiliation of explaining and re-explaining the celebrity I looked like to his nonresponsive assistant, I pretty much realized that Mark helping anyone but Mark was a long shot. Sure, it would have been easier to simply stick my head in the sand (Jersey shore sand, in this case) and assume that Bruce would rise like a savior from the streets to save the day, just like he sang about in so many of his anthems. But my business side knew that I had to get practical and follow the money, regardless of how many times listening to "Born to Run" convinced me otherwise.

Dave, on the other hand was quite good at asking for help, specifically my help and often. In my fantasy life Bruce calls to say he is coming to the fundraiser, Mark Feist lines the streets of Hoboken with money, and Dave asks me to pose as his wife to secure a bank loan. This fantasy was much better than Dave's actual ask, which in signature Dave fashion was vague yet somehow irresistible.

"Listen, I gotta a meeting at TD Bank North and, well, I was thinking it might look better if someone is with me, like a girl, they might even think we are married and cut us a break. Besides, all those suits make me nervous."

With an unlikely combination of confusion and flattery, I happily accepted this open invitation. I was ready to redeem myself in everyone's eyes, to prove that my life in the business world could be put to good use in the real world. Taking meetings is something I should be good at; I'd sat through enough of them in my publishing days. In those meetings, I was in my former and more comfortable role as favor granter, but my new role as favor asker was off to a shaky start. My meeting with Bruce rendered me mute and my Mark Feist meeting featured me crawling under the table at a five-star restaurant. But hope springs eternal.

We arrived at the bank for our scheduled meeting and were immediately met with a cheery hello from the bank greeter, who opened the glass double doors for us. Door greeters are everywhere lately, whether you are buying a new camisole at Victoria's Secret or trying to procure large sums of money; these gatekeepers want to know what you are doing in their establishment. Their melodic inquiries are designed to be customer service-oriented, but instead alienate people who are just trying to enter the building.

"How can we help the two of you today?" a smartly suited twenty-something chirpily asked us. Dave stared at her blankly. Perhaps women wearing suits intimidated him as much as men wearing suits, or perhaps he saw his own reflection in the glass that surrounded him. All that pristine clean glass and banking efficiency. His reflection was all black and white, his skin somehow paler and his black attire somehow darker, kind of like a film negative. He looked out of place here.

Feeling his awkwardness, I overcompensated by being overly formal, letting the bank greeter know that we would like to see someone about a real estate matter. I even donned a slight British accent for which I make no excuse. We confused the bank greeter, the pale speechless rock star shunning the light and his uptight companion with Jane Austen affectation.

"Right...Why don't you come down here, our mortgage broker is with someone now, but you can wait over here until he's done."

We were seated outside a glass-cubed office, where the banker was talking to a smartly dressed woman who appeared to have been delivered some excellent news. They seemed to have had a very happy outcome and I was feeling momentarily at ease. As he ushered out his satisfied client with a "have a great one!" he waved us in. His initial excitement wavered slightly upon a head to toe inspection. In his line of work, sizing people up was a necessary skill. I thought he already thinks that we are out of place, but he had also been taught not to judge people solely on their appearances, so he steamrolled ahead with his pitch.

"Hello, I am Benjamin Huntley. Come on in, let's get this show on the road."

Dave shook his hand and managed to blurt out his name, before Benjamin Huntley interjected.

"And who is your better half?"

"Jessica De Salvo, an associate." I suddenly donned the office-like behavior that is needed at a meeting like this.

"Nice to meet you, Benjamin."

"Okay, first let's set a few ground rules. You can call me Benji, you know, like the little doggy. Benjamin is okay, but a little too formal, but fine. And not Benj, never call me Benj. Benj, no good. Okay, let's get started."

Dave was fiddling with the long chain that was connected from his back pocket to front pocket and shifting his weight uncomfortably in his chair, his heavy Durango- booted leg crossed in front of him, hitting the shiny uncluttered desk of the young banker. Benji had taken notice of this, perhaps because Dave had about a foot on him in height or perhaps because Dave was making so much noise with this rattling and kicking that Benji was distracted. At one point, I took my hand and settled it on Dave's leg to steady the rhythmic tapping that was increasing in volume.

My mind then drifted to that little dog, Benji, who was so popular in the 1970s. His cute puppy face was all over posters and lunchboxes and no doubt where his mother got the inspiration for his cutesy nickname.

"Okay, Dave and Jessica, first things first. Let me set you up with some coffee, water? Nothing? Come on, it's the only thing that's free in here." He laughed loudly. Before we accept or refuse, he is up and out, bringing back with him two Styrofoam cups containing scalding hot black coffee, each with a stirrer.

"Okay, so what brings you to the bank today?"

Dave was struggling, overwhelmed, all those suits creeping in on him as he gulped down the first sip of that nuclear liquid.

"Benj, what I really want to say is…"

"I am going to have to stop you right there…. It's Benji, not Benj. I am sorry, maybe I wasn't clear. Okay, now that we have that cleared up." Benji was at ease, again. "I want to buy the building I rent. It's The Garage...uptown...it's a club. Do you know it?"

"Okay, sounds easy enough. Let's get started with your rank, file, and serial number. Do you have an account with us? Account number? Any other holdings? CDs? Money markets? Annuity? Credit line?"

He began to rapid-fire keystrokes into his monstrous computer. Perhaps the machine was equipped with some omniscient program that could tell if a loan applicant was really to be trusted, if their dream had enough merit, or if they were just not the type. After a flurry of data entry, he swiveled the monitor around and asked Dave if it "all checks out." Dave nodded, sheepishly, retreating into his chair as if the proximity to the suited Benji might suddenly whip out a stake and drive it into his heart.

"And you don't have any other holdings? Stocks? Bonds? Vanguard accounts?

"Well now, let me tell you something about what we do. We take all this information and we powwow. We will run it up the flagpole, see if anyone salutes, we spitball it, hash it out, and see if that dog will hunt. Let me go kick this around with my manager. Okey-dokey, does anyone want more coffee? Great, make yourself at home, these things usually take a while."

I was preparing a Tony Robbins-like speech in anticipation of filling the enormous void that Benji's leaving would cause. But we both knew before Benji even leapt out of his chair that no amount of running it up the flagpole was going to make Dave the right kind of guy to get a huge sum of money from a guy like Benji. Guys like Benji just don't hook up guys like Dave.

I could see that even more clearly, not because I am psychic, but because I could see the reflection of Benji and his manager in the window behind Dave. Dave might have seen it, too, had he not given up completely and tucked his head in his hands on his lap in some sort of crash position. If he had been on a flight, the oxygen mask surely would have dropped by now. Benji made a good show of it; he took Dave's application to the manager. The manager looked at the application and then looked out at Dave. Then she looked back at Benji as if questioning his judgment. Benji shrugged his shoulders up and down as if to absolve him of any responsibility for the matter. The manager took one more look at Dave before the two bankers broke out in laughter. They paused for a moment, before Benji composed himself and returned to our glassed humiliation station to break the news. But I already knew that Dave's dog did not hunt.

16

Running the world's greatest wedding that the earth has ever seen and saving a landmark rock club from extinction can really take a lot out of a girl. And with all that on my plate, I had devoted too little time to building my new business. There is an adage that says if you want something done, give it to a busy person. I had always been that busy person, one that I now embraced in my two new roles as wedding planner and community activist, but those jobs were temporary; my business was my future. All that bartering for business may have gotten me an office space, but I was getting very concerned about how I was going to pay the bills. I was also quite sure that a bank loan was not in my future either, after Dave's TD Bank North meeting went south. I needed to bring in some paying clients and quickly. Balancing all of my new roles was challenging. Especially since I was already backlogged on client requests.

Between talking with the wedding venue and managing the guest list for the fundraiser, I managed to squeeze in time for some of my original clients. I donned my superhero cape and resolved to solve everybody's problems. This was a decent, even feasible, idea if I had not tried to jam all of it into one weekend, but I was so desperate to make money that I had to take the work when it was offered.

I stayed up late and created posts for Craigslist, but most of those responses turned out to be people looking for complicated money laundering schemes that involved banks in Africa or Guam. Those exchanges would begin by a professionally worded e-mail asking if my services were still available. I would answer yes until I gradually figured out that these first vague e-mails were designed to identify willing targets. These kinds of shorthand responses are common on Craigslist, which, for some reason, encourages people to ignore standard rules of etiquette and simply treat each other like prey. It is like the Wild West of communication, with no rules or boundaries. Appointments are made and broken, requests are offered and rescinded, salutations dropped; just about anything goes. I thought my successful eBay experience would translate to Craigslist. I had sold an entire collection of Lilly Pulitzer resort wear that I foolishly bought during an author tour in Miami. But that did not help when dealing with the exceedingly odd world of Craigslist. When receiving a vague message like, "I am eager to hire you for a big job if you provide services to my area," I would respond immediately, politely and acknowledge my interest. The follow-up e-mail was the one that would confuse me. Something like, my assistant tells me that you are a professional working in the {insert city} area, I would like to retain your services, please provide an e-mail address and bank account number so that I can begin the wire transfer. I didn't need too much more life experience to see that scam coming from a mile away.

The ads in the newspaper provided more legitimate leads. One of my first respondents was Grace, a holistic counselor intrigued by my "clever" ad. This was exactly the person I wanted to work for, someone who made my initial outlay of $145 to pay for the ad worthwhile and, of course, someone who thought I was clever. I was so happy to find a client that I was able to squeeze her in the next day. In an effort to appear busy, I placed her on hold for a minute before saying, "This might be a bit soon, but I had a cancellation tomorrow morning at 10. Are you free then, by chance?"

My tactic worked like a charm. I grabbed a handful of news releases to write on the train and headed into the city. As I left Hoboken, I received a call from the florist regarding the unavailability of peonies for Emily's bridal bouquet. Sensing an impending crisis, I quickly texted the manic bride, and she texted me back in all caps. I NEED PINK PEONIES. ROSES ARE SO LAST YEAR. I called the florist back and asked her what the options were and she said simply and succinctly, "Dead peonies or live roses." That was pretty clear. I texted Emily from Grace's lobby and told her the bad news. I suggested a substitute like hydrangeas and, for the moment, she was momentarily silent, which concerned me. I knew a larger storm was brewing, but I had a client to service, so I would deal with that fallout later.

Grace's luxury apartment on Park Avenue was not exactly where I thought a holistic health counselor would live. Actually, up until that point, I had no idea that holistic health counselors even existed, much less had any preconceived notion of where they lived. Apparently, holistic health counselors make a ton of money. Maybe having your own business *can* be profitable, I thought.

My client greeted me at the door, barefoot in printed flowy pants and a tunic top. She looked like she had just come from an ashram rather than a luxury apartment that looked more like a modern furniture showroom. Chanting yoga studio music played softly in the background. I got the feeling that she had just finished her morning meditation, because the apartment was dark, lit only by candles, which surrounded her yoga mat. At the head of the yoga mat was a large statue of young Buddha.

(Not the fat Chinese restaurant Buddha, but the boyish, hungry Buddha.)

Grace, as her name indicated, was totally gracious. When I put my hand out to shake hers, she grabbed me and hugged me instead.

"I am a bit of a hugger," she shared.

She continued to talk, from the moment the door opened, across the threshold and down the hallway with a familiarity and ease that suggested we had been in the middle of a conversation that was continuing rather than meeting for the first time.

She motioned me to follow her through the spartanly decorated foyer, which had only a glass top table and no other clutter, no coat rack, nothing, just a simple Aztec bowl that housed her keys. The look of the apartment was in contrast to how she had adorned herself, in colorful prints and an armful of bangle bracelets, several anklets, and toe rings. She jingled her way into the living room, and told me an ancient proverb about entering into one's house as strangers and then leaving as friends, although I think she might have combined a few proverbs to suit her needs. In any case, I only caught half of it, because as I was formulating my response she had already moved on to the next topic.

I noted the sterile white-and-silver chrome design theme, which carried through to every room of the house. A recent "stock up" trip to Whole Foods was evidenced on the kitchen island. She apologized for the mess as she waved at the two lone bags of groceries that had yet to be dispatched into a stainless steel refrigerator that was buffed to such a high shine that light bounced off of it and made the room seem as bright as the sun.

"Please sit." She directed me to a heavily cushioned white couch, which was so thick that when I sat, my feet were elevated off the floor. It was early in the morning and I hoped she would offer coffee, which I needed since I had been in such a hurry to get to her apartment that I had skipped breakfast entirely.

"Tea? I just got this new chakra tea. You can pick which chakra you want," she said as she fanned out my choices of teas, which corresponded to the chakras on my body.

"Oh, okay, sure, thanks," I said, with a puzzled look. My knowledge of tea was limited to iced Lipton, or green, if I felt adventurous.

"You look confused. Let me pick one for you. How about 'Sacral?' That helps us be open to new experiences."

"That sounds nice, thank you."

"And would you like an agave nectar stick?"

"Absolutely." And I did. I have always loved any food served on a stick—corn dogs, popsicles, lollipops. My track record here was good. When I sipped the tea, I was glad that I had taken a sweetening stick to doctor it. If this was how you open yourself up to new experiences, I was not sure that I had the taste buds to be that open. Happily, she had turned her back so she could not see me spit the tea back into the cup. It tasted more like liquid backyard.

"I really liked your ad," Grace said between sips of tea. "A friend of mine who lives in Hoboken sent it to me and she thought that we would be a good fit."

I was a bit distracted as she talked because she had given me a large pottery mug that was unwieldy to handle. Since it had no handle, the agave stick kept poking me in the eye every time I brought the mug to the vicinity of my mouth.

"Do you like the mugs? I bought those in the most adorable place in Queens, a West Indian store," she called out from the kitchen.

From the look of the slanted mug that seemed the result of a beginner pottery class, I had expected her to say that she had received them as a gift from a toddler relative, but I guess you can find anything, even faux tribal goods, in Queens, if you know where to shop.

I searched for a place to put the teacup sculpture down. In that split second, she found her way back on to my side of the couch, where she sat in lotus position next to me. I repositioned myself a bit so that I could face her as we spoke. Balancing the tea, her closeness and the ultra-fluffy couch beneath me was not easy. In fact, as I moved my crossed legs to make room for her, I knocked over the only object on the large glass coffee table in front of us. It was a coffee table book about Buddha, the four-color companion series volume that went along with the PBS special. Viewers who identified with the life of Buddha could go one step further by purchasing a $100 limited edition coffee table book that showed his life in four-color gatefolds.

"Oh, I am sorry, let me get that." I fumbled for the book and placed it back on the table.

"Did you watch?" She awaited my answer for a nanosecond, before resuming her monologue.

"The Buddha. Did you watch the Buddha special?"

"No, I missed it. I was working," I lied. I had a habit of telling people that I was working all the time, which had some truth to it. I tried to project the image of a busy bee to make clients think that I was in demand. I was busy creating my own myth, just like Joseph Campbell, the subject of another PBS miniseries that I had also missed watching.

"It was awesome, he gave up everything, until he was down to one grain of rice per day, that was all."

As she explained his diet plan, I looked quizzically at the two bags of Whole Foods groceries, whose contents probably would have fed the young Buddha for the rest of his life.

"Was he your motivation to start..." But before I could continue my thought, Grace interrupted.

"Yes, yes, yes...Buddha, Jesus, Krishna, they are all inspirations to me. I have had conversations with all of them. What would Buddha do? What would Krishna do? I realized that I had to start asking more questions in my life, mostly spiritual ones. I was pretty hungry for enlightenment back then. Working with lawyers can do that to you." She laughed.

I laughed as well and sensed I finally had my moment to speak. Usually when you meet with people who like to speak about themselves, the best thing to do is to continue the conversation centered on them. I liked this idea, because, in my state of mind, I did not want to talk about myself; I found comfort in asking others questions. And I knew that, at the same time, my phone was piling up with ignored texts from Emily. To be in this tranquil environment, knowing the storm of unanswered texts that would soon rain down on me, made me anxious.

But interrupting the flow of Grace's monologue was proving to be difficult, simply because there were so few conversational breaks. She was like the Energizer Bunny of conversations. She just kept going and going and going and going...

"How did you get started in holistic healing and wellness, exactly?" I managed to squeeze in as she paused to take a breath. This was the story she was dying to tell. And I had the feeling that she had rehearsed this script before.

"I quit my job and saw the light. I worked in 'the law.'" It was a job change she had made after 12 years in the "corporate blood-sucking division."

Now it made sense. Her digs were courtesy of her old life, where she billed corporations $500 an hour, not her new life, where she helped wayward dieters get on the right track with high-priced supplements from designer food stores. She went on to tell me that she had left her firm almost by accident, like a divine intervention had taken place. Becoming partner at her firm had taken a toll on her health. The hours, the stress, the bad eating habits were her body's way of telling her that she needed a change.

One morning in her local coffee shop, she had eyed a New Age publication and picked it up. There she saw an ad for a spa and retreat center in New England. The power of that ad really spoke to her, she told me.

"I knew the hand of something larger was at play in my life," she explained and leaned in, just like they do on the Barbara Walters special when the celebrity is just about to cry.

After attending the expensive retreat, she had revamped her diet, her outlook, and her career choice. She reported back to work that following Monday and handed in her resignation. That afternoon she signed up for training in her new career as a holistic health counselor and wellness expert, a double major, if you will.

I had heard about this kind of transformation before, where you get so immersed in another experience, like a good vacation, that you think life is meant to be better. I was not convinced that life could be anything like a vacation, especially my life. But Grace did. In just a few short weeks she had her certification through an online course. And had rounded out her new education with some added study at a yoga center in lower Manhattan. She received an additional degree in Thai Yoga Bodywork. With those new certifications under her belt, she hung out her new shingle. She was ready to counsel other unhealthy corporate people who had abused their bodies through too much work.

Grace appeared to be unaware of her wealth. It had come so easily to her that now she wanted to distance herself from it to find deeper meaning in her life. After leaving the law, she started doing pro bono work at a women's shelter. I couldn't help but wonder which of her clients was more high-maintenance: a moneyed corporate raider who needed to hide money in the Cayman Islands or a homeless person who needed shoes but would prefer to spend her last dollar on a fifth of Popov vodka instead. Somehow, her first experience gave her the confidence to handle the second experience. Talk about extremes. But sometimes people go there when they are looking for a change. I knew that firsthand.

She sat drinking her spiritual tea as she discussed her working philosophy of nutrition and how she had seen this awesome "TED Talk," about the globalization of food and how artisanal preparation was going to change the world.

"Did you know that there is a large part of the Iowa corn fields that is being grown just to make high fructose corn syrup? And they put that stuff in everything, even cough syrup for kids..." she explained. "I am just not going to eat that garbage anymore. That is why I decided to become an educator and advocate for this kind of food." She had now adopted a spokesperson-at-a-dais approach to show me what she was talking about.

"Come over here and try this organic, gluten-free, wheat berry muffin with boysenberries. This is such a better breakfast than what the packaged stuff is." She waved her hand over the Whole Foods bounty.

"It sure beats a Pop-Tart!" I added enthusiastically.

"This is what Jesus would eat, before there were any preservatives," she boasted. She paused and waited for me to react. This was her big moment.

I had the feeling that a professional litigator was schooling me. Needless to say, she already had me convinced. But then again, I couldn't argue because the wheat berries made my mouth so dry I had trouble breaking them down and swallowing them. Mental note: if she needed a name for her company, I thought, "What Would Jesus eat?" would be perfect and kind of Book of Genesis cool.

My practical side was anxious for conversation more practical, maybe looking at a business plan or news release, but she just wanted to talk about odd foods and have me sample the stuff she was mashing up in her very professional-looking juicer. She followed up the backyard tea with lemonade that contained no actual lemons; it was pretty good, actually, although I questioned why she would need to find a better substitute for lemons. At that point, I was questioning so many things that the danger of eating a real lemon was the least of my worries.

But like a good BFH, I was not there to ask questions, but to support, listen, and, in this case, taste and praise. And in turn, I was being paid for my service. Then suddenly she looked at her watch.

"Oh my goodness!" she said. "I am going to be late for my monthly colonic! Can we continue our conversation another time?" I was relieved that she hadn't asked me to accompany her to the colonic in order to continue our conversation.

She got up and led me to the door, scooped a check out of her Aztec bowl, and handed it over to me. She gave me a "Jesus" muffin to go, gave me a quick hug and rushed me out the door. I did not have a chance to present an invoice, discuss my rate, or even make sure the check was made out properly. Our session was over. I slowly unfolded the check and was thrilled to see the amount.

I had little time to savor my success before the next emergency had presented itself.

I had missed eleven calls from Emily and the twelfth text had come in just as I turned my phone back on. It read, GET

ME THE PEONIES, IT IS ESSENTAL. She, of course, had spelled essential wrong. I left a voice mail for the florist. I had turned into one of those people who ask the same question over and over again, until I got the answer I wanted. And if that weren't enough, I got a callback for the fundraiser RSVP line letting me know that Cyndi Lauper would not attend, after her publicist had promised that she would. Needless to say this girl was just not having fun at the moment.

When I left Grace's apartment, I needed to stop by another one of my recent clients, Gary, just to check in. I had met Gary during my publishing days. He used to date Andrea Koslowitz, an editor from Smith & Drake with whom I had briefly worked. The two had been dating for a number of years after she had acquired his book about weapons of mass destruction. I think I met him at the book's release party at Housing Works, but I couldn't really be sure.

Gary and Andrea were one of those couples that found love after trying several times with everyone else on the island of Manhattan. Andrea had serial-dated her way through most of her authors, most journalists she had worked with, and the few male producers who were straight in the television industry. Actually, she had also dated a few gay ones, in the hopes that she could turn them. That never worked, for reasons obvious to everyone but Andrea. She had met Gary before he was divorced, and the ink dried on his separation agreement, she already had a strategy in place to snare him. Just a few months later, they were ready to make it official and signed a lease on a new apartment that they would share.

Combining households had proved to be a bit more difficult than they had expected. They needed an objective third party to help them. The move was more complicated, since Gary's children would be moving into the apartment as well, at least part of the time. Gary shared custody with his recently divorced wife, a child psychologist who opted to stay in Old Lyme, Connecticut, where, until recently, they had lived together. The kids would stay on alternate weekends and holidays, and Gary wanted them each to have their own room so they could feel at home there as well.

At our first meeting, we discussed room placement and choosing a moving company. But the hidden agenda (in my business, there is always a hidden agenda) was what to do with all the things from Gary's first marriage. He wanted to take as many of his things with him to the new apartment. Andrea was not interested in taking all this furniture of his first marriage into their future world. They fought. They were "in front of people" fighters. I am not really a shy person or unfamiliar with conflict. But the openness in which these two went at it made me uncomfortable. They wanted me to be the referee to their verbal sparring. Take, for instance, the subject of plates.

"These are just plates, pretty nice plates, if you ask me," Gary argued.

"But I don't want to use somebody else's plates," Andrea pleaded.

"Why buy new plates, these plates are good."

"They are HERS. And I don't want HER stuff in MY house."

"Oh come on, Andy, do you think you're going to catch something, like a bad attitude off these plates?"

"You never know. I'm already going to be raising her kids on the weekends, why should I also have to do it on her plates?"

"Do you believe this?" Gary looked to me for comfort.

In most arguments, one of the parties involved gets to a breaking point and simply gives in, but not these two stubborn mules. Instead, Gary stormed out and slammed the front door. He then came back in, grabbed the box of plates, and took them with him. Only he didn't take the plates, he took a different box instead. When he realized this, he came back in one more time and switched boxes, and then slammed the door for the third time. This would have been a good time for them to realize that this was a silly fight.

"I mean, really," Andrea said. She was one of those people who used those catchy phrases that I describe as conversation fillers. Terms like, "have you ever," "and there you have it," and "really, right," all of which were usually part of larger declarative sentences, but used by Andrea as standalone fragments, begging for approval and acceptance.

And that is how session one ended. Andrea and I stared at each other and wondered what to do to fill in the awkward gap left by one of the parties leaving mid-session.

"Right, so, here we go," I said in an effort to show support. It was hard to be totally honest with her, but I got the sense that the plates were not the real issue here.

I read in *Self* magazine that people get frustrated when their needs are not met, so it is important to communicate those needs to others. Then, and only then, do you have a chance for those needs to be met. I explained this philosophy to Andrea as I left her apartment that afternoon. I was not sure if I was giving her the advice or advising myself at the point, since we both could have benefitted from that wise counsel.

Two days later, Gary e-mailed me to set up another meeting. I should have known from his e-mails, which were more "I" focused than "we" focused, that there was a deeper problem here. I arrived at his new apartment and found it nearly empty, save for his bedroom and the two bedrooms for the kids.

"Let's sit down and talk for a moment," Gary said. And I said to myself, "Uh-oh."

I took a seat in his bright empty apartment and settled in for the long story.

"She told me that if I could not let go of the plates, then I was not ready to move on with our life," he confessed.

And while I thought there was some truth to this, I was skeptical that the plates had anything to do with the underlying problem here.

"I am so sorry, Gary. Do you think there is any way she would come back?"

"No, she said it's either me or the plates. And I guess I picked the plates."

With that handy yet cold piece of information, I sat on the couch with Gary, sipped Dunkin' Donuts coffee and again wondered how in the world I could help him. I was still a friend in training myself. Trying to employ that sage *Self* magazine advice, I went directly at the target.

"What can I help you with?" I asked. I needed an activity, something to ground me back to work, to productivity. Gary answered that he just needed someone to sit with him and had thought of me.

"You can't get what you want until you know what you want," I said authoritatively, not immediately aware of the fact that I had serendipitously quoted one of my favorite Joe Jackson songs from my childhood.

"I did get my yoga instructor to come up for a few hours the other day by bribing her with a smoothie. But I doubt that I could do that again," he shared, embarrassed that he had revealed that much about himself.

He was lonely. In one year, he had divorced his wife, broken up with his new girlfriend, and moved to a new city where he didn't know many people. He needed a best friend, even if he had to hire one. So I did what any friend or girlfriend would do—I hung out with him for a typical Saturday. Gary made breakfast, read the paper, and watched a little tennis on television. Eventually, we took a walk to the Fairway and prepared for the visit of his children, who would be staying that weekend. Together, we unpacked some of the things from his old marriage and I convinced him to let go of some of the things that held him back. And he did. Who knows, maybe he would now have more room for Andrea in his life without all those stored memories. I left as the kids arrived, happy that I was able to fill up his alone time.

In between calming down my budding bridezilla and chasing down publicity leads, I hunted down any other possible clients for BFH. I was overcome by my monthly expenses, which I had listed on a spreadsheet, and since my time away from a steady paycheck I had made a significant dent in my savings account. I feared that borrowing money from my parents would give them even more control over my life's choices. In truth, my parents were not the kind of people who would do that. This was more about my fear of failure. I doubted that my mother or father would want me to go without anything that I needed, but I had too much pride to ask.

In the meantime, I took some small clients to help out on the side. These clients could best be described as people who needed help with the mundane things in life. Late one Saturday night, I came up with a new ad to cater this particular client; I called it the Gal Friday Special. It included an hourly fee for running errands, picking up dry cleaning, shopping, and picking up takeout. Essentially, I offered to do all the stuff that no one feels like doing. I made up a flyer with those tiny little contact tabs at the bottom that you see at bus stops and train stations so that interested clients could pull a little tab of your information off of it on their way through the terminal. That's how I found my target audience—a woman named Marcy.

Marcy liked all the latest trends, but hated to shop for them. Since I had a car and she did not, she hired me to travel to stores that she could not get to. Mostly, she wanted decorative items for her apartment, like throw pillows, curtains, and kitchen utensils. I would arrive at her apartment on a Monday morning, where she had my shopping binder prepared. It was a classic three-ring binder with plastic sleeves divided by each room of the house. I no longer wondered who the audience was for all those sections in magazines that do a roundup of the new things for each season. Marcy would tinker with the binder throughout the week, shuffling the order of the pages, to make sure she had just the right items. But even with her obsession over the binder selections, she often was unhappy with the items once they were in her hands. So I also had to return unwanted items that she had wanted so decisively the week before.

The NJ Transit bus ad also helped me to find Lois, who owned a family-run real estate business in Hoboken. She pulled my name off the tab on her way back from the new Guggenheim exhibit. Lois was super-connected and enjoyed recommending people she liked to others who needed help, like her son, who needed assistance at the real estate office. My superior office skills and genius filing helped those realtors keep all the house keys and clients straight. I would run down Washington Street from the bar to the real estate office on Tuesday and Thursday while I juggled calls from Emily. As soon as I got back to the bar, I put on my fundraising and PR hats before hopping across the Hudson to the clientele that I had built in New York. My day planner looked like an intricate puzzle of double-booked calls and appointments. With all the recommendations from Lois, my client list grew and grew. This was good for business, but bad for Emily, who sensed that I was not as devoted to her wedding and became even harder to manage. On a personal level, I was out of touch with my family entirely, and I feared another day of reckoning would be in my near future. I couldn't hide from their scrutiny much longer.

I thought about Grace and her never-ending litany of questions: "What would Jesus do?" "What would Krishna do?" "What would Buddha do?" I was not sure how any of those people would be able answer my current questions. The only thing I knew for sure was that no amount of backyard tea and agave nectar sweets were going to get me through this career nightmare. I was going to need something a lot stronger.

I had no idea what to wear. I stood in my hallway in a pair of shorts and a ski sweater utterly and completely confused about what to do. I was so freaked that I called Maggie to help me out of my self-imposed inertia. Maggie had proven herself to be good at a lot of things, rounding up unruly drunk people, putting aggressive line cutters in place and, my personal favorite, becoming an advocate for those she called friends, but a fashion consultation was not the obvious role that sprang to mind. I needed just the right outfit, nothing too dressy, nothing too casual, the perfect combination of clothes that suggested I was ready to be asked out, spur of the moment. The outfit should outwardly say cool, calm, and casual, which was, of course, the exact opposite of how I felt, which was stressed out, scared and insecure. I was not getting dressed for an ordinary night out; I was getting dressed for a night out with my boss, well, with Dave. When Maggie got to my apartment, she immediately sized me up and remarked, "You look like a slutty coed. You clearly have never done this before."

"I'm a mess, help me," I whined and dragged her into to the apartment.

Maggie asked a few basic questions that confused me even further.

"It's just the two of you, right?"

"As far as I know. He was really vague, almost like he didn't know all the details himself. I think his exact words were, 'Are you free tomorrow night?'"

"So, it could actually be a work thing, but on a Friday night, no chance. He's definitely asking you out."

"Well, it could be a work thing. We're going to meet at work and then walk over, so it's not like he's picking me up or anything."

"But a babe like Dave Germain isn't going to work on a Friday night, no offense, but he's probably pretty booked up with girls. I mean, they must just line up down the block for him."

"Are you trying to make me feel better here? Because you kind of suck at it." And now the image of scantily-clad groupies who looked like they just appeared in a White Snake video was seared into my mind's eye, which made me feel even more inadequate. I had nothing in my wardrobe to compete with that.

I picked my first three outfits, outcasted separates from my work days that even paired cleverly with good jeans still looked more Junior League than effortless date night cool. It takes a lot of effort to look effortless. I was determined to find the perfect outfit, even though I had no idea where we were going, why we were going there, and what we were going to do when we got there. This made getting dressed very nearly impossible. The only thing I knew for sure was that Dave would be there. Since I was a little out of practice—I had not had a date in almost a year—Maggie was my Sherpa to navigate the tricky terrain of being invited to dinner under cloudy terms by a guy she deemed as "hot tuna."

"You need something like an Abercrombie ad, but with some clothes," Maggie bellowed as she leafed through an old *InStyle* magazine she had found on my couch.

"Oh, boy," I said as I looked down at my outfit and realized that I was nowhere near the look that reproached me from the magazine page. I marched out slowly and braced for her reaction.

Maggie termed the first of the three outfits as "too old lady." The second choice was "too retirement village." And the third was "too middle-aged," which she explained was getting warmer. After those disastrous choices, she took matters into her own hands and joined me in my closet, where she finally approved a pair of dark washed denim jeans and a fitted, black v-neck top that I usually wore under a suit, because it was a bit flimsy. Maggie insisted that it was fine, as it was. As I was ready to leave, I grabbed my trench coat, at which point, Maggie put her foot down once again.

"Hold up, Columbo, you are not heading out to solve a mystery. Don't you have a regular jacket?" she said as she hunted through my coat closet and eventually dug out a leather jacket that I had had since college.

"Here, this is cool. Wear this," she said as she tossed the jacket to me. My new, unassuming cool look could go just about anywhere, she assured me.

"What if he takes me somewhere really nice?" I asked.

"A babe like Dave Germain is not going to take you somewhere fancies schmancy."

"Um, do you think you can dial back the 'babe' talk a few notches? And it's fancy schmancy, one fancy, not plural."

"Take it 'EAZ,' looks like someone is testy about their new boyfriend."

"He is not my boyfriend," I insisted, even though I really wanted him to be my boyfriend. It was going to take more than Maggie's belief to convince me that he could think of me as more than just a girl he worked with. The more people asked me about our relationship, the more awkward I became. If he were my boyfriend, no one would ask, it would be clear. But, as in so many other things in my life at that point, this one, too, seemed up for debate. The only silver lining might have been that I had something else to feel insecure about besides work.

If someone were going to ask you out, you should know that you were being asked out. I had no idea what Dave asked me out for, his "ask" was so vague. He had simply leaned over my desk and wanted to know if I was available Friday night. That was it. He didn't tell me why or what we were doing. Since Bertram was in the room, I said, "I was," casually without looking up. And although he pretended not to notice, I saw Bertram look over his horn-rimmed glasses at me, with a worried look on his face. But this was expected since after meeting Dave, I had become the "yes" girl. Pretty much anything he asked me to do, I did. He just had that sway over me.

"Okay, then, meet me here at seven," Dave said and then he left, creating an awkward void, which I attempted to fill by overtalking.

"He probably just wants to go over fundraising stuff. You know, so much to do, so much to do. We really should get some more hours in on this. Some more hours in…on this…" I repeated.

But Bertram had already formed his opinion and, of course, let the wisdom of Jerry Garcia speak for him.

"The wheel is turning and you can't slow down, You can't let go and you can't hold on, You can't go back and you can't stand still, If the thunder don't get you then the lightning will."

"Jerry, right?"

"You got it, sister," Bertram said.

Bertram's advice via the Grateful Dead was no more helpful than Dave's *Mission: Impossible*-like instructions for the date. Like Tom Cruise in those movies, I was on a need-to-know basis.

At the appointed time, I waited for Dave, under The Garage sign, feeling conspicuously alone. The feeling of being in the wrong place at the wrong time always crept in during those moments of being the first to arrive. There is no comforting reward for the punctuality, just a gnawing feeling of getting something wrong, which you fill by double-checking your watch, your address, your hair—a nonverbal checklist that you run through over and over again to reassure yourself that you *are* in the right place at the right time. None of these moments of doubt is part of the late person's routine. There is probably more comfort in the hurriedness of being late; at least you know someone is waiting on you. Waiting on others is angst-producing.

He was late, 15 minutes late. As I stood there, a car pulled over to the corner and waited. I looked and then looked again, and it was not until the window of the teal green Honda Civic rolled down to reveal Dave as the driver that I knew it was him. But there he was, cool Dave, in one of the most uncool cars I could imagine. He should have been on a motorcycle or in a Jeep Sahara. He leaned across the front seat and cranked open the manual window. "Hop in," he said. And then he put on his blinker and entered traffic. It was not exactly the dream pickup for a first date, more like a parental pickup from school or practice. I took a moment to acclimate myself in Dave's car and picked up on the small details. Your car says a lot about who you are, and Dave's screamed suburban dad: AM radio and cassette deck, the evergreen vanilla-scented car freshener, a used travel coffee mug. And to make matters more confusing, he was dressed differently; he had swapped his rock and roll look to match his car. He wore khakis and a polo shirt of, all things, looking like a Dockers ad. I was officially thrown off.

"I wanted to take you somewhere special," he said with a smile, his arm slung cavalierly over the steering wheel, as if he were driving a fancy sports car rather than a fuel-efficient carpool sedan.

We drove out of Hoboken and he told me he had to make one stop at the mall. The mall, I thought to myself, I couldn't imagine this guy at the mall. But he seemed to know exactly where he was going, into the heart of mall country—Bergen County, New Jersey, where, along Route 17, there are malls on either side of the highway, and not strip malls, but big malls with big anchor stores, the big New Jersey malls synonymous with the state. He chose the swankiest of the bunch, the Riverside Square Mall, where the anchor store is Bloomingdales, and the retailers include high-rollers like Hermès and Salvatore Ferragamo. Our final destination, of all places, was Brooks Brothers, where he needed to pick up something "different" to wear. Different may have been an understatement.

"Well, I got an interview in the city for a job with my brother-in-law," he explained. "And I was hoping you could help me pick something out to wear." I pondered what kind of interview he would be going on for which he needed a suit.

For someone who was constantly scrutinized for what she wore, I seemed to be consulted constantly about what other people should wear. Even though I was thrilled that he had asked for my help, I was saddened by the fact that he had given up on the bar; it was as if he were on to the next thing.

"What about the bar?" I asked. "You don't think it's going to make it?"

"Let's just consider this a backup plan, if things don't work out for us."

Work out for us, I thought. What does that mean, exactly? Was our fate linked to the fate of the bar, and if he thinks the bar is sinking fast, then why did he chose me to help him with his future, a future I would have no part of if the bar closed? Maybe I was reading too much into this, but given the sketchy clues I needed to investigate further. Maybe I should have left the Columbo jacket on after all.

Clearly, he could have taken someone else to get this task done based on what I knew about his appeal. We entered Brooks Brothers and were immediately greeted by the quintessential men's suit salesman. They are bred in a special place and then kept in a time capsule, where pocket squares and inseams are always essential. All the Brooks Brother men are dapper gentlemen who clearly never work in an office, but are attired as if they did.

He sized up Dave easily as a 42 long and directed him to a dressing room, where he had placed a navy blue pinstriped classic with a white shirt and red tie. This was the exact outfit the salesman was wearing. In fact, this was the same outfit that most of the salespeople in the store had on, whether they were male or female. I had a hard time telling which side of the store was for men and which was for women, the looks were so similar, the only giveaway being a slightly more pronounced cinch in the waist of the woman's suits and of, course, that some of the women's suits were pinstriped skirt suits. I searched the mannequins for something different for Dave to wear, disappointed to see him join the ranks of this uniform-wearing sales force. The thought of him giving up on his dream to become a corporate clone was almost too much to bear, so when he came out of the dressing room with that outfit on that looked more Halloween costume than business executive, I was moved to action. My anxiety escalated as I viewed him in the three-way mirror. I snapped to action.

"Please, God, no. Take it off, I can't deal." I had three different thoughts running through my head, so I wasn't sure which one I had actually said out loud. I shepherded him back into the dressing room and ordered him to change back and quickly. I could not bear the idea of him getting a real job, getting into the shark tank that I had just escaped from, especially since he, in some way, had helped me escape from that boring pinstriped fate. He changed and headed for the door without another word. The dapper salesman followed him, confused. But I intercepted him with my hand up like a traffic cop.

"Don't go, no thanks," I muttered.

Dave continued to walk ahead of me directly to the guardrail and then finally turned dramatically and said, "Okay, now I know that you're serious about our commitment."

This was another confusing comment. Our commitment might have been our fledgling attraction or our intertwined fates of the club's success. In any case, I felt like I had passed a test there at Brooks Brothers, that perhaps he was trying to see how deeply I was committed to our union, personal as well as professional. And then, as if the ghost of Christmas Future had been completely exorcised, he turned and said," Are you up for something to eat? They have an awesome Cheesecake Factory here."

"Really? Awesome? Cheesecake Factory? Well, those are some words I never thought I would hear from your lips," I said.

"Lighten up, Jess, it's just a meal, you have three a day."

I laughed. He was pretty funny.

"You know I grew up in Ridgewood, right?"

And then it started making sense to me; he was from New Jersey, not Williamsburg or even an obscure upstate New York town that sounded cool, like Rochester. He was a Jersey kid, just like me. I should have known by the way he took the back exit to the mall. Not many people know that entryway.

Happily we strolled through the mall, past the Sunglass Hut, Brookstone, and L'Occitane, all the familiar places that had served as a backdrop to my afternoons of hanging out in the malls of New Jersey. It was like coming home again. That familiar walk comforted me. And I sensed that Dave was familiar with this terrain, as well.

We made our way to the Cheesecake Factory, a chain restaurant designed around a dessert I never ate. How they even come up with that as the driving force behind a restaurant remained a mystery to me. But that mystery was secondary to round two of our evening. At the front of the restaurant, the hostess, a perky high school student, welcomed us with a peppy smile and a quick once-over. Here we go again, I thought. She looked at Dave and then at me and then at Dave again, as if to say, how did *you* get with this guy? Dave, garbed in his traditional outfit, still had a touch of the bad boy tattoo that peeked out of his polo shirt sleeve enough to let people know that something darker lurked beneath his Dockers preppy exterior.

"How about a nice booth for you guys?" she asked.

"A booth would be nice, wouldn't it, dear?" Dave waited for my reaction.

"Yes. Booth. Nice." I had once again regressed to monosyllabic speech. I usually fell victim to this cavewoman speech pattern whenever I was overwhelmed with circumstances beyond my control, like people calling me "dear" in public.

"We have some 'business' to discuss," he said with a wink to the giddy hostess, who led us to the table and let out a little giggle as she told us to have an "awesome dinner." They seemed to share a moment of understanding, like they were in on a secret that I had yet to discover. What exactly was going on here? How did we suddenly turn into a couple that eats at a cozy booth on a Friday night in a mall in Hackensack, New Jersey? The waitress who served us made no mystery of her attraction to Dave and directed all of her questions to him as if I were not there. I think she was so smitten with him that she reverted to some old school, let-the-man-order thing, but I couldn't be sure. The only thing I was not sure of was how out of place I felt at that moment. And in true patriarchal fashion, Dave took control.

"Hi, uh, what's your name again?"

"Helen," the portly waitress answered.

"Helen, Helen," he repeated, as if to make sure he would remember her name. "Um, okay Helen, let's start with a drink, something frozen, like a Piña Colada? Make it two Piña Coladas and a starter and we will have the roadside sliders, the lettuce wraps, and the crab and artichoke dip to start," he shared.

I was speechless with this order as well as impressed by his menu knowledge. I was even more confused when the extraordinarily large drinks and our potpourri of "starters," appeared. Everything was super-sized here. I questioned how people actually saved enough room for the actual cheesecake. Dave sipped his drink, which came accessorized with a large piece of pineapple, a cherry and an umbrella.

"So, let's talk about the bar," he said, turning directly to business. "Tell me what you've done to save the place." And with a sharp turn in tone and conversation, he waited as I gave him a complete rundown of the activities that I had done on behalf of the bar, and while he looked impressed, he seemed unsure that it was enough.

"I still think I need to take that job in the city," he said. "I mean, we really have no guarantee that we're going to make it, do we?" And there he was again with the "we" language that he used so carelessly, so effortlessly that it made me think that there was an actual "we" here.

"I am still holding on to hope the fundraiser will help us. More money, more time, a hero to save the day," I offered. But the way he was talking had eroded any confidence I had built up about saving the bar. It suddenly seemed impractical.

"Listen, I appreciate everything that you've done, but honestly, if I'm out on the street, so are you. What are you going to do then?" He delivered this hard news by reaching across the table and placing his hand over mine. I reciprocated his appreciation, but his odd behavior made me question where I stood. Whatever I thought I knew about him was being questioned, first by a test of commitment outside of Brooks Brothers, and now a test of emotional fortitude at The Cheesecake Factory.

The waitress returned to clean up the remains of our starters and to serve a second round of drinks. He already looked and sounded drunk, and I worried that he would not be able to drive home.

"Um, do you want me to drive home?" And instead of doing the responsible thing, like not ordering another drink, he went right ahead and ordered and said," Yes, if you could drive home, that'd be super." My recent bachelorette party experience had made me skilled with belligerent drunk people. While drinking the festive Piña Colada drinks, Dave had become both, belligerent and drunk.

"I could use another, Helen, thanks so much," he smiled and winked at the adoring waitress, who had him backed up with another drink. I think she thought he said, "I could use another Helen," which somehow charmed her. And in the meantime, he reached over the table and finished my drink as well. After downing it in one gulp, he gasped a little and then put his head into his hands and leaned on the table. I thought he might start to cry, but instead he motioned to his head and then managed to say:

"Brain freeze."

"Here, have some water. And just put your tongue on the roof of your mouth, it'll help get the nerves warm again," I explained. After a few minutes of recovery, he was back at his Pina Colada and ready to talk.

"Jessie, I'm a 30-something, unskilled, tattooed dude with no direction. People think these tattoos are cool, so I keep getting 'em. Look at this one," he said as he rolled up his sleeve. "I don't even know what this means. I am just a character, a figment of everyone else's imagination. And while I'm on the topic, what is with all these tattoos that are sentences? What is that all about, I mean, is it a reminder, like, don't forget to be a good person all the time? Like you need that? Can't you just remember to be a good person; you have to write it out? What the hell ever happened to someone just getting an American eagle? A good old-fashioned American eagle."

As he rambled, I pieced together his story. He was no different than me, a kid who grew up in the suburbs of New Jersey, so anxious to get away from his normal past that he had created a new city persona for himself. I had done the same thing to some degree. I understood.

And then as abruptly and forcefully as the rant began, it ended. He paid the check, thanked Helen, and then said," Okay, I'm ready to go now."

Standing up proved to be a little harder than Dave had expected, so I helped him up and guided him back through the mall to where we had parked in the Bloomingdales parking lot. He needed a little help walking at that point, but I managed to offload him into the passenger seat, where he slurred one last request.

"Can we make one more stop on the way back?" he asked. He stared out the window dreamily and asked if we could stop by the Teterboro Airport, which was a short drive from the mall and turned out to be a special childhood memory for Dave.

"When I was little, my grandfather used to take me here to watch the planes take off. We would pick up an ice cream cone and just watch them go. Life was easier, no big deal, just a plane and some ice cream."

We pulled up to the side of one of the runways and watched a few planes take off and a few land. We sat there quietly for about 20 minutes or so. And then we silently got back into his car and drove back to the city. I walked him to his apartment, which turned out to be just a few blocks from mine. I opened his door for him, said good night, and shut the door behind me. And then I walked home.

Roddy's of Springfield is known for two things: its Wednesday Night All You Can Eat Clam Bar and its elaborate weddings. Among New Jerseyans in the know, Roddy's of Springfield is widely considered to be the top New Jersey wedding factory. It is impossible to get in there on a Wednesday night and even harder to book a wedding without at least two year's notice. Luckily, my erudite and bipolar bride Emily had secured the coveted Saturday spot long before Brendan had proposed. She knew that a place like Roddy's of Springfield was bound to be triple booked for Saturday night events and for her wedding she wanted to have the biggest and best room, "The Camelot," which had all the amenities modern brides wanted and included a dramatic entrance for the newlyweds.

The celebration complex, as I had referred to it, was located on the not so scenic Route 22 in Springfield, New Jersey, sandwiched between a Toyota dealer and a Pier 1. This particular stretch of Route 22 has the unique distinction of being one of the country's most dangerous, largely because it is four lanes wide and jam-packed with retail, big retail. And if all of that retail on either side of the highway were not enough, smack down the middle of the road was a median with more retail, which served as a divider between the eastbound and westbound lanes. Without notice, a driver might cross two lanes of traffic to pull into a newly opened Party City store in the middle area. For this reason, as a child, my father would caution me to avoid "the highway" whenever possible.

I am the first to admit that the highways in New Jersey have as bad a rap as the state itself, but Route 22, with its unpredictable jug handles and U-turns, can cause even the most responsive driver to give in to impulse and cut someone off without a blinker. But who can blame these people when so many retail choices surrounded them?

Roddy's of Springfield had been in business for more than 40 years and was a staple for proms, weddings, and office parties. Despite the changing of times it had maintained its original themed rooms, which mimicked those found in old-time England or Scotland. In addition to the prestigious "Camelot," there was also The Sherwood Forest, The Maid Marion, The Pirates of Penzance (where my junior prom was held), and the lesser-used Round Table, which was used for business meetings, like a business card exchange, for example. The themes of the room were in direct contrast to its catering style, which leaned toward down-market Italian fare that was more likely to be found at a Super Bowl party, like fried calamari, meatball hoagies, and baked ziti.

There had been a growing trend to "Italianize" everything for weddings, whether or not the bride or the groom was Italian. I guessed you could thank Olive Garden for that, which was also located on Route 22, in the westbound lane, across from Chuck E. Cheese.

This notion of Italian-American had nothing to do with either Italians from Italy or Italians from America. Those two groups differ as well and I'm not talking about just the difference between eating pizza formally with a fork and knife or casually, folded in half on a paper plate. That's minor. What I refer to goes deeper. It's the perception that all Italian Americans are connected to criminal activity, just like every New Jersey Italian portrayed on television.

I recalled educating a coworker about my own family connections. He could not believe that no one in my family was a gangster or knew one.

"Really? You don't have an uncle who's in waste management?" He used his hands to put air quotes around "waste management" and winked to drive home his point.

"No, although I did cheer with a girl in high school whose father was a garbage man."

"You just proved my point. No one is really a garbage man." And then for emphasis, he added a hand gesture to show he knew the lingo.

"Come on."

"I never thought about what Gina Fellonica's father did. I just thought she was pretty," I offered. Based on that conversation, I was careful not to tell too many people at work about my New Jersey roots.

Emily wanted her wedding to include everything, literally. She was an equal opportunity bride who embraced the traditions of all ethnic groups regardless of her own nationality. In the planning stages, I was concerned that her ceremony would come across more like the opening ceremony of the Olympics rather than the elegant affair that most imagine. I tried very hard to limit the campiness of the event, but failed most of the time. And I know that she had the suspicion that I had failed her as well, but I suspected my disappointment in her choices might have been misinterpreted. Because the more I tried to push her toward tasteful choices, the more she demanded the audacious.

She called me hourly to "touch bases" and to "check in" to see if I was "okay," using corporate catchphrases that she had learned at work and often used incorrectly. The teacher had become the master and her tone had become patronizing and, at times, even insulting. Even with our recent role reversal, I believed that the bridezilla would eventually transform back into the person I once knew and liked. Bridesmaids and wedding planners tend to acquiesce on most things, with the hope that it would all be over soon. Emily's expectations were hard to predict and even harder to keep up with as they were subject to any media event, like something she saw on a E! Network special on celebrity brides. She would immediately want Victoria Beckham's hair or Eva Longoria's veil, even though, as late as the week before the wedding, all of these decisions had been made, everything had been ordered and it was too late to make a change. Any good event planner knows that, at a certain point, the event happens, warts and all.

I had read an article on theknot.com that said, "It is not avoiding the disaster of a wedding day snafu, but how you fix it that matters." I had made the plans the best I could, but all events that involve humans are subject to variation. And this cast of characters were more human than most and likely more subject to disaster. Add in a bride who is not only hyper, but also crazy, and little things could add up to big things in no time.

The perfect example was the wedding favors, which were ordered weeks in advance. At each place setting, on top of the specially ordered pink charger plate and white dinner plate, which was sprinkled with silver "dust" that would emulate the pixie dust that helped Peter Pan and Tinkerbell to fly, would be the favor. After an exhaustive review of our favor options, from customized bags of coffee, to silver-plated corkscrews, to golf balls, she decided on a personalized shot glass. When we received the glasses, Emily conducted a thorough inspection of the artwork, which featured a tiny bride and groom. She threw a temper tantrum after she deemed the bride pictured looked fat.

"Everyone is going to think that is me on the shot glass. And I am not fat." In her defense, that was true. In the months that preceded the wedding, Emily went to great lengths to lose weight, an unnatural amount of weight, which she achieved by eating only meat and drinking grapefruit juice. The results on her body were significant, but I sensed that the carnivore diet made her act even more aggressive and, well, crazy.

I assured her that the tiny bride on a small shot glass could not possibly look fat. And that no one would notice or make the correlation. "She is smaller than the size of a button." I reasoned. Plus, half the glass was taken up with the customized messaging, which said *Happily Ever After, Emily and Brendan* and the date. Emily loved the idea of having her name on a shot glass. But when they arrived, it was worse than the spoiled bride-to-be thought; not only was she "fat," but "super fat." Immediately, I called the online vendor to upgrade the traditional glass to a taller tequila popper-sized glass, which magically elongated the squat appearance of the bride.

Emily and I reviewed a redesign on Skype the day of the rehearsal dinner one final time. And once she was satisfied, the printer was given the "okay." I drove to the factory in Fresh Meadows, Queens, that, despite its name, had no meadow and did not smell fresh at all, and picked them up in person. I dropped them off to the stressed-out staff at Roddy's of Springfield who, in 40 years, had never seen a more bridezilla bride than Emily. Forty years. When I arrived, they were trying to figure out how to clear the pixie dust off of the dinner plates before meal service would begin. I overheard the chef yell, "Fucking pixie dust, is this bitch nuts?" before he slammed the kitchen door.

Her all-is-best philosophy continued through the nations, with America exemplified by Ken and Barbie centerpieces. Bridal Barbie and Groom Ken were a special order (naturally), with the strawberry blond hair to mimic the real life Barbie and Ken. The two dolls sat on top of a bouquet of baby pink roses. Next stop was Scotland, where a bagpiper would play a recessional of "Danny Boy," since Brendan was Irish. I tried to tell her that bagpipes are actually from Scotland, but she did not want to hear that. Her tour of nations was multidenominational as well. She wanted the bride and groom to be lifted on chairs on the dance floor like at a Jewish wedding, regardless of the confusion this might present to the guests who just sat through a one-hour Catholic mass. Neither the bride nor the groom went to church ever, but that was beside the point. Emily's mother was Catholic and a member of the church and managed to secure the date by dropping off a hefty check to the priest before another couple did.

Italy was represented with *Ave Maria* and *Con Te Partiro* being sung by an opera singer I found on Craigslist. At least Emily was half-Italian, so I could not put up too much resistance there. To be fair, I did not expect my mild-mannered assistant to be such a prima donna, but like a pod person in *Invasion of the Body Snatchers*, by the time the wedding came, Emily was almost completely unrecognizable as the person I thought I knew.

The manic princess called me as I finalized the hotel arrangements where guests and the bridal party were to stay. Emily was frantic over Brendan's speech at the rehearsal dinner, to be held at Dave's Famous Ribs later that night. She wanted *Sonnets from the Portuguese* to be read. This was met with resistance from Brendan, who, in his defense, was not the obvious choice to embody Elizabeth Barrett Browning's sentiments. He was, however, the perfect Famous Dave's Ribs customer, a burly junk food-eating fraternity boy who talked with his mouth full and interjected phrases like "you do the math" into just about every conversation he had. Getting through the tame, *"How do I love Thee"* sonnet was not easy for him to pull off. Especially, given the condition of the groom as he sampled the "all you can drink" open bar at dinner.

But deal making had become essential to my survival. To get the *Sonnets* reading done, I convinced Emily to let Brendan add "one thing only" to the hotel gift bags. He chose a large box of Cheez-Its. That was one of the easier deals I negotiated. The other deals included pink neckties for the groomsmen in exchange for a vodka ice slide at the reception. Honeymoon in Hawaii for the bachelor party. It might have been easier for a Hatfield and a McCoy to get married, at the rate these two were going. But all that negotiation was excellent practice for the compromise of marriage, I reasoned.

Despite the casual, all-you-can atmosphere of Famous Dave's Ribs, the family and friends behaved well. I was encouraged. Brendan's reading received great response from the elderly members of the family as well as some unexpected high fives from his ushers. But all that pent-up anger and compromise had eaten him up inside. He was like a time bomb about to blow by the time the rehearsal dinner ended. He gave a respectful kiss on the cheek to each and every family member as he and Emily hosted a receiving line near the salad bar as guests left.

Unfortunately, what they say in theater about a bad dress rehearsal before a great show should have been enough fore-shadowing. Brendan could not wait for the bachelor party; this was the one time "for him."

"We are going to read to the blind," was his clever cover phrase for the activities that would follow that evening. He adopted the "don't ask, don't tell" philosophy to his last night of bachelorhood. I was concerned about the bachelor party being planned the night before the wedding, but it was the only time, Pierce, the best man, was able to get away from work. He had been training for his new job in Omaha, Nebraska, and was able to get a few days off for the wedding. "It's the first time he has, like, been out of the Jersey, like ever. You do the math," Brendan explained.

To ensure everyone's safety and the bridal party's safe delivery back to the hotel, I had to take extra precautions. I arranged for a special escort to drive the boys door to door. The escort needed to be someone trustworthy, but with muscle. Instead of a retired police officer or bouncer, I opted for someone even better, Maggie. I capitalized on the fact that everyone was afraid of her and everyone listened to her, including a bunch of "lightweight frat boys." She said, "I partied in Daytona in '87 with the Hell's Angels, you little shit," she warned Brendan. "You kids are nothin...." She laughed maniacally.

Brendan looked at me and hunched his shoulders, a move he had perfected after being pushed around by his fiancée and now his fiancée's brawny cousin. Maggie relished her new duty.

"It would be my pleasure to serve the groom, my dear," she said in a mock British accent that still came off as trashy, more Cockney than posh.

I even bought her a little chauffer cap to complete her ensemble. Check, check, and check.

After the rehearsal dinner ended, the invited guests and bridal party were shuttled back via minivan to the Hampton Inn on the Garden State Parkway, where they were treated to a discount room rate and a large amenity bag. Emily selected a large shiny pink metallic gift bag that looked like it could have housed a VCR rather than snacks. Emblazoned on the outside was *Emily and Brendan, Happily Ever After*, scrolled on them by hand, my hand, to be specific. All of this labeling was a helpful reminder to those guests who may have attended so many weddings that they might have forgotten which they were attending. Inside were a host of inedible pink snacks, including Hostess Snowballs, pink jelly beans, pink Jordan almonds, and an Evian bottle with a customized label. And of course, right on top of all that pink, sat a large box of Cheez-Its.

Maggie rounded up her crew for their appointed rounds and was instructed to return by midnight, no later. I cautioned Maggie to stay close. I even stocked the minivan with water, snacks and aspirin to help, but I knew that would make little difference. I didn't mind if Brendan was hungover, that was a given, but I didn't want any vomiting. That would send Emily into a clinic.

Emily stayed in my room, so we could have "a slumber party," as she put it, but I suspected that she wanted to torture me with her mood swings and last-minute jitters until the bitter end. Maggie texted me at 11:30 to tell me she was leaving the last club and would be back to the "robin's nest" soon. She had adopted using odd code language in her new capacity, as if she were guarding the president. Her ward she called "Dodo." I expected "Dodo" and the boys to be tucked into their rooms, so I was surprised to get a text from her minutes later that said:

"Hotel bar. Stragglers. Backup. Stat."

I popped into the bathroom, out of earshot of my captor. Emily pounded on the door, demanded to know what I was doing in there, without her.

"Location confirmed. I am on it," I texted.

"Where are you going? You can't leave me," Emily stamped.

"Just a last-minute little surprise for our little princess bride." My lie had the desired affect and Emily's mood suddenly swung back.

"Yay, this is so fun. I wish I could get married every day!" she exclaimed as she clapped her hands. After I had her settled back in bed with her bunny slippers and a large pink grapefruit juice, I headed downstairs in yoga pants and flip flops, anxious to clean up whatever disaster awaited me in the hotel bar. When I arrived, I found Brendan sitting on the lap of a scantily-clad woman in a nurse's outfit who introduced herself as "Candy Stripper."

"You see. We were reading to the blind." He laughed.

19

Any thought of getting sleep the night before the momentous day
was swept away, since I spent most of the night trying to locate
the ushers and, one by one, extricate them from their chosen
professional dancer. Brendan, who had decided he had enough
of the bride getting all the attention, made a late-night bid of
his own and carried on at the hotel bar until hotel security
finally persuaded him to go up to his room. His stunning rendition of "It's My Party and I'll Cry if I Want to" was forever seared
into my mind's eye. At 4 a.m., I was back in my room, unable to
sleep; I paced the floor waiting for the next breakdown to occur.
I went through a mental checklist of all the events that would
follow that morning, which, at that point, was just a few hours
away. The hairdressing team of three was scheduled to "up do" all
the girls at 7 a.m. The makeup team would come in 30 minutes
later to do makeup for all the girls. Food would be delivered to
the bachelor suite. Food would be delivered to the bridal suite. I
adjusted the boys' order to double the pancakes and bacon in an
effort to soak up the alcohol each had ingested last night. The
photographer and videographer also had early morning report
times to begin the documentation. Emily did not want to miss
a moment and asked that a camera crew be assigned to film the
bride and groom in various stages of getting ready. Emily felt it
important to have video as well as photos shot of her getting

made up, getting her hair done, drinking her morning meal, checking her nail polish and then, finally, donning her dress, tiara, and veil. The video in length would likely rival that of a made-for-television miniseries, the only difference being that people actually want to watch made-for-television movies. With the exception of these video stars, I was doubtful that anyone would endure watching this epic.

The lobby of the Hampton Inn was swarming with people, Emily's people. The bride had gotten her desired effect of becoming the center of attention; there was simply so much staff on hand to get her ready for this day. The florist delivered all the girls' bouquets. "Those look nice," Emily noted. "Nicer and bigger than mine." She then sent the florist back to readjust the size. To do that, a few flowers were taken from each girl's bouquet so that Emily had the biggest and best one. The girls were gathered in the bridal suite getting ready and each was given an audience with the bride on camera to appear as if it were candid. The result was an awkward conversation with each girl, some of whom were so frightened of saying the wrong thing that they just bowed, smiled and left. By 8 a.m., we were posed for those awkward group pictures, like all the girls fanning their dresses around the bride to look like a huge pink flower. Maggie and I had donned Madonna-like headsets to keep in touch throughout the morning. As the wrangler of the boys, she had become essential to the process. And I needed her help to make sure that the groom was still standing.

The makeup artist pulled double duty and headed over to the groomsmen for makeup as well. Normally this is not a necessary thing that happens on a wedding day. But the "stripper event," as I referred to it, in the hotel bar had gotten a little out of hand. Pierce, the best man, had sustained some physical damage when he went to lift Candy Stripper over his head and smacked his face into the bar. The result was a black-and-blue mark that went straight across his cheek. The makeup artist used cover-up to make sure that he would appear as normal as possible in pictures. The groom, after a cathartic night of singing karaoke and screaming his lungs out about the impossibility of getting married, had fared almost as well as his best man. He got a few hours of sleep and was ill most of the night. I hoped that he had exorcised all of his digestive demons by the time the morning came. But the results of all that drinking and all that soul-baring rendered the groom with no voice at all. And no amount of Swiss cough drops was going to bring it back. The wedding vows, which were custom written by Emily, would have to be improvised unless he could regain his voice quickly.

Another problem popped out literally with bridesmaid number six, Emily's sorority sister, Rachel, or, as I called her, "Baby Mama." Unknown to anyone, she was pregnant and not newly pregnant, either, but having-a-baby-any-minute pregnant. The dress that she had tried on had to be retrofitted to take into account her growing stomach. At the original dress fitting, she hadn't "popped," so to speak, so she didn't see the point in telling anybody. Her logic defied the very notion of pregnancy itself; she didn't expect to get any bigger. Two weeks before the wedding, she had a dressmaker secretly build a panel into the back of the dress to camouflage her growing belly, but the dress was still too small. I stuffed a pink Pashmina scarf into the back to cover as much skin as possible. We would be fine as long as she didn't go into labor. I warned the photographer and videographer to shoot Rachel at a distance and only from the front, not the side. Once the girls were dressed and deposited into their Hummer limo to go to the church, I awaited the father of the bride, who would escort Emily in their own separate Hummer. Emily's father was a wealthy man who had made his money in the pharmaceutical business, like many in New Jersey had. He ran Merck, or some other large company in the late 1990s and then bailed out on a golden parachute and took his secretary with him for the next chapter of life. The two had been carrying on a secret affair for 10 years. Post-retirement, he spent most of his time golfing and smoking cigars and relished the fact that all of his hard work had netted a great wedding day for his "only baby girl." But he'd divorced wife number one and upgraded to the newer model, so naturally, Emily hated the new wife, blaming her for "stealing Daddy" and shattering her perfect image of her parents' storybook marriage. When the couple arrived at the bridal suite to see Emily, she ran into the bathroom and told me to "get rid of *her*."

Deidre, the quintessential trophy wife, was probably around my age. She left without causing a scene, making me think that she had been in that position before. And my position of being good cop to Emily's terrible cop was also familiar. It was like one of those episodes of *Law and Order* when one of the cops is too emotionally invested in the case and the other, more logical, cop has to talk his partner down and get the convicted person to confess.

After depositing everyone in their Hummer limos, I checked on "Dodo" and the groomsmen. Pierce looked adequate enough, if not slightly pink. The rest of the party was in working condition. But "Dodo," unfortunately, was not well. The lack of sleep and dehydration had wreaked havoc on his body. In his weakened state, he was being held up by two groomsmen, who were giving him tiny increments of Gatorade that he fought to keep down. With assistance, he joined his men in their Hummer.

The horse and carriage, looking for all the world like the one that had carried Cinderella to the ball, awaited in the parking lot. Emily wanted to make a grand entrance. The plan was to exit the Hummer and slip into the carriage with her father to enter and exit the church that way. I tried to explain to her that no one would see her arrive as the guests would already be seated inside, but she insisted on getting into the carriage nonetheless and going for a little ride with Daddy. It seemed impractical to have a horse and carriage drive around a parking lot and then load up the horse into a horse trailer that would travel down Route 22 back to the reception hall, where the horse again would be walked around another parking lot. And then, after the reception, be loaded up once again and walked around the Hampton Inn parking lot. I thought it was an NSPCA violation, but the horse trainer assured me that "Sugar," the horse, did this kind of gig all the time. Apparently, the horse needed the money as well, backing up my growing skepticism that the wedding industry defies morality and ethics if the pay is good enough. I was taking a head count of all seven brides and seven brothers when bridesmaid six let out a shout.

"This can't be labor, right?" I pleaded with Rachel.

"No, my due date is not until next week," she assured me.

"Next week? Seriously?" I couldn't believe what I had heard.

"I'm fine, these little pains happen all the time. I'll be fine," she tried to assure me.

I believed her. What other choice did I have? The only thing I knew less about than weddings was childbirth. In the meantime, the creative cameraman interviewed each bridesmaid. He took his job a bit too seriously, as he asked each girl how they met and what their hopes and dreams were for the bride. And then off camera, he asked them if they were single and if they had ever done any other kind of film work. I noticed this and, while I thought it was weird, I let it go. I could only handle the top-level crisis at that point.

When he got to interview the cousin, she let out a holler and screamed, "Oh shit, the baby is here," just as Emily and her father entered the church. An enraged bride yelled, "Get yourself together, this is my day, not your day." And as if by divine intervention, the labor pains immediately subsided. "False alarm!" smiled Rachel. Somehow, Emily had scared that baby back into the womb. Who could blame him?

On the groom's side, Maggie, who opted for a tuxedo rather than a dress for the wedding, had become the leader of the pack, something she had only dreamed about. She had no easy time with the groom, as the ushers continued to feed Brendan a combination of Gatorade and Ricola cough drops. Maggie organized the boys for their interviews. On the side, I asked the priest what to do about the vows if Brendan was still speechless. He joked that this would be good training for marriage, right? I didn't smile; I had no time. He offered me his guarantee that it would all be fine. He had a plan. Meanwhile, on camera one was Pierce, who shared his euphoria about being back in New Jersey.

"I've never left the state for more than two weeks, ever, and that's counting vacations. I always take one week." He described his two-week business trip to Omaha as "scary." "I mean, don't you think that New Jersey is just getting better than ever? The roads look great. The beaches look great. It's just even better than I remember it." It was as if he had just done two tours in Afghanistan and was back from years suppressing the rebel forces rather than being put up in a Comfort Inn in an office park to be trained on special banking software. He also knew that he, too, would turn into a pumpkin in just a matter of hours. His flight back to Omaha boarded at 9 o'clock the next morning. With that ringing endorsement of the Garden State, the videographer moved to the groom, who had doused himself in the baptismal fountain in order to keep himself awake and refreshed. He stood and gave the cameraman a weak thumbs-up as he shook out the water from his head, like an Irish setter after a bath might.

As the guests arrived, they were supposed to be treated to a stunning rendition of musical selections, but the church was quiet, the singer nowhere to be found. That mystery was solved quickly when I received a text from the aspiring singer letting me know that she'd gotten a big break in an off-Broadway musical. She had been called to replace "the girl" in the matinee of *The Fantastiks*. I had to find a quick substitute, and then I remembered that Daniel's partner, Patrick, was a theater director. He could stand in. Patrick quickly found the lyrics on his iPad and up they went to the balcony to rehearse.

Just as soon as I remedied that musical crisis, another was on the horizon and came in the form of Jimmy Fleming, the bagpiper, who embodied the modern day cliché. He was drunk beyond recognition when he had arrived at the church. He was to play the exit music of "Danny Boy" as everyone got into his or her respective cars to go to the reception and he would also perform a rendition of "Wonderwall" by Oasis that he had been practicing. Since he had about an hour before his performance, I put him to nap in one of the confessionals and assigned Daniel to help with waking him and getting him coffee before he had to straighten out and pipe right.

Meanwhile, inside the church, another storm brewed. Two ushers ran into some difficulty as they attempted to seat the mother of the bride. When she got to the front of the church, someone was already seated in her seat. Deidre had taken the seat next to her husband. They both wanted to sit in the front row, but Emily's mother would not have that "gold digging tramp" sitting next to her. Emily's mother squeezed in between the pew and Deidre, causing a wrestling match between the two. They scrambled to get the front seat and each knocked their bottoms together as they tried to squeeze into the front aisle. The priest finally had to come to the front and separate the two. Emily's mother won out and ousted the trophy wife to the end of the aisle, where she would sit next to the bridesmaids, who would be fanned in front of the altar and asked to stand throughout the entire mass. Deidre looked like a bridesmaid understudy instead of the respected position of wife of the bride's father that she so desperately wanted to be. But she was luckier than the bridesmaids; at least she got a seat. The bridal party was asked to stand for the entire mass facing the audience, even the sitting and genuflecting portions of the mass. The bride and groom would also face the congregation, a late change that Emily had insisted upon.

"I don't want everyone to just see my back!" Emily added.

The wedding was set to begin. The processional cued. Emily and her father walked down the rose petal-lined aisle with her cathedral-length train, two videographers hitting the floor in front of her commando-style to get interesting footage of the bride. The pink bridesmaids were in waiting. The Princess escorted down the aisle by her dashing father into the arms of her gallant Prince Charming. This, of course, was how it was supposed to play out. But when Emily hit the white runway, her eyes darted around her, taking a mental inventory of all the things that looked off. The flower girls were too slow and were making a mess of the rose petals, the singer sounded like a boy not a girl, the best man was wearing more makeup than she was, and her Prince Charming was being propped up by a lectern, unable to stand on his own. Her bridal glow began to darken. She glared at me from under her veil and I knew that this would be the final revolution of my slow descent into madness.

Emily's bouquet, now weighed down by additional flowers and a solid silver flower holder, was just too heavy to carry. Upon reaching the altar, she was so aggravated by the terrible conditions of the church that instead of handing the flowers to her petite maid of honor and sorority sister, she flung them at her. Surprised, the petite attendee screamed and then flung the hot potato backwards, where it bounced off the head of Deidre, who had become accustomed to public humiliation. She held the bouquet and shook it with a little smile, becoming an unlikely seventh bridesmaid.

The rose petals on the runway were plentiful as the bride had instructed but the result of the 3-year-old flower girl, who took an entire basket and emptied them at the end of the aisle, which proved to be a little too dense for the father of the groom. On his last step to hand the bride over to the groom, he lost his footing and knocked into Brendan, who was unable to steady himself, much less Emily's father, and toppled over. The father of the bride landed squarely on his bottom before making his way to the nearest seat available. Emily's mother, after fighting for that coveted seat, was once again abandoned by her husband.

The priest was what you would call a progressive priest, one of those people who gives solid advice on topics he has no idea about, which, in this case, included holy matrimony. He compared the struggles of Jesus carrying a cross as a parallel to the kinds of hardships that a married couple would have to struggle through. He likened the doubt and betrayal that Jesus faced to be par for the course when you lived with someone day in and day out for the rest of your life. And then, to add levity to this monologue, he added, "Eternity and forever are a pretty long time, ya think?" I had seen this kind of priest before—at one moment he is damning you to the flames of hell if you miss confession, and then suddenly is your best friend, offering a funny, inappropriate quip to humanize himself.

Such is the paradox of being Catholic in today's society. Most of us know it's not practical, but we try anyway. This combination of shame and acceptance seemed to work for Dr. Phil, but this crowd was a little harder to win over. I was holding my breath for the vow portion of the ceremony, but the priest had a surprise that only he and Brendan knew about. Surprises? Emily hates surprises. And since she hated them, I, by extension, really hated them. The priest turned to the congregation and cued the organist. And then, in the most unlikely scenario I could have ever imagined, he told a little story about two kids who met when they heard this song playing in the background. "This is a little gift from the groom to the bride on their special day," and then he invited the congregation to join in singing "What is Love?" by Haddaway. The stripped down version of this techno-dance song did not translate with strictly an organ accompanist.

It was as if the priest deemed this moment as his perfect opportunity to try out new material. After the priest had regained his composure, he invited everyone to take communion, followed by *Ave Maria* and then the vows. At that point, Emily had no idea that Brendan had no voice, so she was asked to say her vows, which she did with just the right combination of humility and sincerity, an Academy Award-wining performance based on her recent personality transplant. When Brendan was ready to read, the priest jumped in once again and Emily shot him a look of terror and disbelief, or was it just pure anger?

"The groom is so choked up about the event, that he has asked me to read his vows, and he will agree by nodding his head." Emily, so confused as to whom to look at, Brendan or the priest, had too little time to formulate an adequate angry response. And that is how Brendan entered marriage, by being told what to do, and not being able to say anything.

Next was my favorite part of all weddings, when the priest asks if there are any objections to the joining of these two in holy matrimony and the immediate silence that follows. Unless of course, it's a soap opera on a Friday afternoon, leaving an open-ended cliffhanger for viewers to ponder all weekend. But that would have been quicker; instead, a deafening, piercing noise stunned the crowd. Emily's grandmother's oxygen tank bleeped red alert as the tube became suddenly disconnected. Thankfully, the tube was reconnected quickly and we were able to move on. Momentarily.

The priest repeated the question. Brendan's mother, who was allergic to flowers, finally succumbed to the fragrance around her and had a coughing fit. Brendan tossed her a cough drop and the fit subsided. "Three times's the charm," the priest joked as he repeated the text for a third time. And then, without an ability to stand in waiting any longer, Rachel's water broke, which caused alarm at the end of the bridesmaid line. The baby was on the way.

"Is there a doctor in the house?" yelled Pierce from the altar. In minutes, Rachel was in labor, big labor, the kind of messy painful labor you see in the movies. She sat where she stood, simply unable to hold out any longer. The "baby daddy," also known as Groomsman number 4, was quick to her side, holding her head as Deidre dialed 911 on her phone. Brendan, unable to hold it back any longer, ducked behind the lectern to vomit once again. In minutes, the rescue squad was outside with sirens blaring. Upon entering the church, they didn't know who needed assistance, and immediately started to cart out the grandmother and her oxygen tank. Instead of thanking them for their help, she pelted them on top of the head with her purse. They turned and looked at the bride, who was hyperventilating to the point that she was red in the face, looking as if she were about to go into cardiac arrest.

"Try again," I said and motioned to the screaming woman sprawled in pink taffeta on the altar. In all the excitement and heavy breathing, Rachel's dress finally gave way, the Pashmina inched its way out of the back of the dress, causing the skimpy bodice, which had been hanging on by a thread, to fall completely. The result was a half-naked woman trying desperately not to make a scene as she was awkwardly plunked on a stretcher. The stretcher was then rolled out the center aisle trampling flowers, rose petals, and the white carpet as well.

The priest cued the organist once again, who could be heard asking Patrick what songs he knew. Patrick relished the unexpected stardom and landed on something familiar. "Cue Sondheim in D!" he instructed and then broke into highlights from *West Side Story*, beginning with a lovely rendition of "Tonight." Amid the splendor of arguably Sondheim's best musical, I asked the priest to make an announcement.

"We will take a quick break to help the mother and pray for the child," said the priest. The crowd chatted as the bridal party tried to tidy up the altar and comfort Emily. I guided the fragile Emily into the back so she could lose her mind in private, rather than in front of everyone. But that really didn't matter; she was so inconsolable at that point, no one would be able to get through to her. By the time we returned to the altar, relative peace had returned. The screaming Rachel had been escorted out on a stretcher. The crowd had been treated to most of *West Side Story*. The grandmother's oxygen bottle had been replaced. Emily's father resumed his place between Emily's mother and Deidre, who seemed to have come to a temporary truce. And the bagpiper was finally awake. It looked like everyone would be on their best behavior at least long enough to get through the "I dos," which they did or, more accurately, Emily did. The priest had to do Brendan's part, since all Brendan could do was mime a thumbs-up to show his consent.

Once inside Roddy's of Springfield there was much to check on pre-arrival of the bride and groom. First, the bagpiper needed to be propped up once again and led to the cocktail hour room, where he would do an encore presentation of the only two songs he knew. He was set. The shot glass wedding favor and the pixie dust were all in place. But Barbie, with her knowing smile, housed a deeper secret. Her station was precarious; if the centerpiece moved at all, her head would come off, and I feared that was not the only head that would roll today. I went to each table and made sure that the Barbie heads were secured, but many were beyond help. At some tables, she simply lay in Ken's arms, her head propped up in his armpit as if she had taken ill. Even though the florist had put them on good footing, the unreasonable request to have the two dolls swimming in roses had the effect of making them sink into their pink flowery grave. As the guests entered, they picked up their table assignments. In keeping with the theme, Emily wanted every table to represent a Disney Princess: Mulan, Ariel, Cinderella, Snow White, and Sleeping Beauty were all natural choices. But it got a little harder to come up with 25 different princesses, so we extended the theme to all Disney movies, which included *101 Dalmatians/Wreck-It Ralph,* and *The Hunchback of Notre Dame.* Daniel and Patrick were seated at the *Dumbo* table.

The DJ arrived and he was not alone; he had company, and it was bad company. As part of the super wedding package, one that ensures everyone has fun, our DJ had hired additional professional staff to get everyone on the dance floor. The dancers in this case were hard-bodied blondes wearing small black cocktail dresses. They looked like professionals, all right. But there was something more to these working girls; they looked familiar. One of them in particular danced with the bride's father, much to the encouragement of Emily's mother and the disdain of wife number two, Deidre. Emily's mother stood next to wife number two with a look of "now you know how it feels" as she watched the already inebriated father of the bride get his groove on to "We Are Family." This was not my greatest concern, however. My concern was that this dancer looked more professional than the others, I knew her from somewhere, but before I could piece the two together, I was summoned to the bottom floor of the hall, where there was operating difficulty.

One of the hallmarks of the Roddy's of Springfield "Camelot Wedding Package" is the entrance of the bride and groom. Instead of traditional, and dare I say, classy or normal style, Roddy's of Springfield had a state-of-the-art entry from the floor. The bride and groom would appear as if by magic on an elevated platform in a cloud of smoke and then be raised above the wedding party. Emily, who had proven herself unable to rise to any occasion, had the floor operator pinned to the wall when I arrived downstairs to remedy the problem. The elevated platform was working, but "there is not enough smoke!" yelled Emily. As he turned to crank the smoke machine, the sleeve of his jacket got caught on the lever. He was so aggravated that he snapped his arm back, taking the on switch clean off the base. Without the switch, there was no way to turn the machine off or to stop the smoke from billowing upward. At that moment, only he knew the impact of what had happened. We exchanged a look and I ran up the stairs to the Camelot room to see how the entrance panned out.

The bride and groom began their slow ascent. At first the trapdoors opened halfway, shut and then opened again. The happy couple peered out at eye level, viewing their wedding party's feet. Finally, smoke billowed out, causing the woozy groom to begin a hack and then a gag, followed by a hack and a gag. Emily, in full panic mode, decided to scare Brendan into sobriety by pinching him on the ear so hard that he lost his breath and the ability to cough as well. The crowd, some unfamiliar with the smoky trapdoor entrance, misinterpreted the peek-a-boo effect of the doors opening and closing. Many thought it was supposed to be that way and applauded. But those in the know understood that Roddy's of Springfield could do better than that. I heard one woman say to her husband, "They should ask for their money back, those doors are supposed to open, period, end of story." As the bride and groom continued to pop up and down, the billowing pink smoke made the room so cloudy that it was hard to see anything but pink. Finally, the trapdoors clanked open fully and the platform began to rise as the DJ announced, "For the first time anywhere—Mr. and Mrs. Brendan Connolly!" The crowd cheered as they watched the platform rise and rise. At some point, it was supposed to stop. But it didn't. It went higher and higher, until it finally stopped right below the ceiling and then so abruptly that both the bride and groom were knocked on their bottoms.

They were sitting on top of the world, or the Camelot room, to be more accurate. But instead of feeling the effects of a grand entrance, they feared for their own safety. The fast-thinking staff reacted immediately with a ladder, but it was not tall enough to reach the couple. Without any other option, the Scotch Plains Fire Department was summoned with an inflatable cushion like the ones stunt men use. The couple would blindly leap, hand in hand and land safely on the soft mat. All of this was recorded on video to be viewed for a later lawsuit or, better yet, to be sold to

America's Funniest Videos, the wedding edition. This installment no doubt to be entitled, "Leap of Faith Weddings."

The DJ played Lionel Ritchie's "Dancing on the Ceiling" in an effort to provide some levity to the disaster. But no song was going to provide relief. The entire wedding needed to be moved to another room. I grabbed the microphone from the DJ and instructed the wedding party to stay calm and, though we were experiencing operating difficulties, we were still here to celebrate the happy couple.

"If you don't mind taking your place setting and moving down to the Sherwood Forest room, we can all get back to the fun," I enthusiastically told them. The DJ continued the crowd control efforts.

"You heard the lady, grab your Barbie and Ken and head back to fairy tale village, just down the hallway, past the clam bar," he said. And as if to add insult to injury, the DJ repeated his instructions, but all I heard was "past the clam bar, on your left," being said over and over again. I was unsure if the real-life Barbie or the centerpiece Barbie would be able to make it through this transition. The centerpiece Barbie had more of a chance. The real-life Barbie had come completely unglued. She searched the room to find me. Instead of going to her side, I opted for a diversion and had the DJ cue up the first portion of the video presentation early to quiet the impending riot.

"Cue Paul Anka," I whispered into my headset.

"The Times of Our Life" came blaring from the DJ booth as the backdrop to a photomontage of the happy couple, which took them from birth to present day and every rite of passage in between—the baby years, Emily at a dance recital, Brendan at tee ball, and, finally, the awkward teens, the high school graduation, and then the college years. As Emily stalked me from across the room, she was swarmed with well-wishers, which gave me a brief reprieve before the next problem arose.

Over my headset, Maggie radioed in that there was "a buzz kill at Lake Placid, I repeat, buzz kill at Lake Placid." It took me a minute to figure out that Maggie's code words meant the ice shot block. "What now?" I said out loud within ear shot of Emily's grandmother, who took her finger and circled it around the outside of her ear and pointed to Emily as if to indicate, this child is crazy. Disturbed by that motion, I turned around and backed right into one of the hired dancers, and then it clicked.

"Hey, you look a little better than last night," she said. I took her by the arm and pretended that I knew her. It was Candy Stripper. I recognized her face immediately after trying to coax her off Brendan's lap last night.

"Listen, can you just keep your recent involvement with the groom a bit of secret? I would hate for the bride to put two and two together." But it was a little late for that as Pierce and another fraternity brother swooped her up arm and arm and led her to the vodka ice bar.

"Might be a little late for that, don't ya think?" she said as she "electric slided" her way off the dance floor.

At the vodka ice bar, guests were encouraged to squat down in their formal wear, with their mouths open at the bottom of an ice block to meet vodka shots that were propelled from the top by the ice block bartender.

"What flavor would you like sir? Madam?" The ice tender was uber-polite as he rolled the flavored vodka down the ice luge. An elegant request for something more suited for a fraternity party. Apparently, Emily's Uncle Bob was stuck to the bottom of the ice luge and needed assistance. He had a wicked ice burn after lingering too long on a Pomegranate martini shot. His overreaching tongue had stuck to a part of the mechanism. In ice block shots, you are not really supposed to touch the ice at all with your tongue for this very reason. But he didn't know that. By the time Candy Stripper and her merry men were at the ice block, I had already shut it down.

"You really don't know how to have a good time, do you?" Candy said as she danced off.

In the meantime, I took Pierce by the arm.

"Do me a favor, keep Candy away from Brendan. And another thing, you need to powder your nose." I left him adjusting his makeup in the reflection of the now unusable ice block.

To say that Emily was outraged was putting it mildly. No sooner did I turn around then she was in my face, grabbing me by the arm and displaying superhuman strength to drag me into her private dressing room.

"This wedding is a disaster," she cried.

"Well, some things have gone wrong, but I think the crowd is handling it well."

"I wanted it to be perfect and it sucks, the whole thing sucks. The floor almost ate us, my bridesmaid went into labor, the ice luge injured my uncle Bob, Brendan is mute, and some trampy lady is stalking my husband!" I had to admit that was a pretty impressive list of problems, but I couldn't let her know that.

"Hey it's not over, it can still be great, let's get out there and see that video presentation, cut that cake, have a wedding."

"Do you think it sucks?" she asked, adopting a bit of the girl that I once knew and liked.

"Not at all, now let's get out there and maybe even have some fun."

"If I don't have fun soon, I am never talking to you again," she said and stormed off. That notion was okay by me. We entered the room and I softly cued the video presentation through my Madonna headset. "Cue the video and 3...2...1..."

"Through the Years" by Kenny Rogers played for Part Two, a photojournalism- style interview where an off-camera voice asked the white buttondown-shirted and jean- clad couple searing questions like, "When did you first know that you loved each other?" The camera went in tight on the happy fiancée with the ring on her finger, brushing away her strawberry blonde hair behind her ear. "I just always knew that I would marry my best friend and that is what Brendan is. He has always been there for me and now we are beginning a new life together, just like I dreamed about when I was a little girl." Brendan, when asked the same question, was less philosophical. "I knew she was the one when she walked into my frat house and was able to hold her own. A partner should be there for me. I mean us. You know each other." The 40-minute video recounted the proposal story and a short stroll through Times Square before wrapping up in a heart-shaped graphic reminiscent of *Love American Style*. With that, the bride and groom went to the center of the dance floor to the "oohs" and "aaahs" from the crowd. Things looked like they might work out after all. And just as we were about to have a nice moment of wedding bliss, over my headphone came the final nail in the coffin. "Jessie, we have a dead horse in the parking lot."

I have always hated roller coasters, even as a child. The unpredictable ups and downs always made me feel nervous and unsafe. I could never anticipate all the turns and sudden drops, which is why I have always chosen the safer routes in life, like book publishing, where things have remained the same for more than 100 years, despite whatever is happening in the rest of the world. I had come to rely on certain things being constant, like my employment. But these last few months of career-searching had eroded my confidence and made me wonder if I was really any good at anything. All of my recent attempts had been epic failures. It might have been a different scenario had the wedding gone well, or if the relationship with Dave made any sense at all, but I was batting zero on both fronts. The fundraiser was my last chance at redemption. And I was not the only one fixated on its success.

The event had gotten a considerable amount of media attention, thanks to my efforts. The celebrity event has a strange effect on the people in my world, as if my proximity to the celebrities made me more important somehow. If I hadn't been such a basket case about recent events, I might have let all this attention give me power, but I had so little confidence in my abilities that people demanding things from me made me feel even worse, even less important. It was like suddenly having more people to prove myself to.

If the fundraiser went well, I might have a chance at regaining my career footing, but my focus was Dave, whose attention and gratitude I craved more than anything else. Saving the bar meant saving Dave. In a traditional role reversal, I was the princess on the white horse sweeping in to rescue Dave, the unskilled laborer, from an uncertain fate in corporate America. After I delivered him to his apartment after his hopeless ramble that night, I felt like not only was he not interested in me romantically, but also that if I didn't make this fundraiser work he would never talk to me again. So far, my career had a short list of people who were not talking to me, starting with Emily, who, since her return from her honeymoon in Hawaii, had texted to tell me that she would never text me again. Now would not be a good time for me to ask for a customer testimonial from her, I figured. I wanted desperately to turn this sad state of affairs around, but I was still shell-shocked from the debacle of the wedding, Emily's rejection and Dave's disinterest. This was not an overwhelming amount of support, to say the least.

I gained new supporters in Derek and Allison, who were obsessed with the event. After the unsettling news of their status change, I had not been anxious to spend time with them, either individually or together as a couple. I had avoided every possible opportunity to mend fences, which was not easy since Allison lived in my building. But when you spend virtually no time at your apartment and all your time at your new office, that can be easy. Nonetheless, Allison cornered me long enough to secure a job at the event. Derek had the ulterior motive of talking up his screenplay to anyone remotely connected with the entertainment industry, and Allison, like every other girl who grew up in the suburbs of New Jersey, wanted to meet The

Boss himself. Since I needed all the help I could get, I put aside any personal feelings I had about either of them and put them to work. They followed Bertram's orders to bus tables and help manage the line outside. They were utility players, out of their element but happy to pitch in. Every once in a while, I looked over at them as they danced or posed for selfies. At least they were happy.

The media, which I had relied on to make this event, turned out to be the catalyst for ruining this evening. And it all began to come apart like a pulled thread on a crocheted sweater that you simply watch unravel as the yarn is stretched further and further. Media professionals know that anything you say to a reporter is on the record. The concept of "off the record" is pure myth. I knew this better than anybody, but I made that rookie mistake, and it ended up costing me.

Journalists and celebrities share the same bloodthirst for publicity, any publicity, and both are about as predictable as toddlers. When I had mentioned (off the record) to Chris Knoll, the reporter from nj.com, that there was an outside chance that Bruce could show up, I knew it was dangerous, but I never thought that he would print it. I never actually said he was coming. But then again, I never said he wouldn't. Maybe it was because I had just met Bruce and I thought there was a chance. Bruce is not your typical celebrity. He was known for showing up at these kinds of events unannounced. And maybe he might surprise us. My first surprise of the day came via text message from Bertram, which I picked up as I headed to the bar. *"Want to see The Boss? Head over to The Garage finale in Hoboken before the doors close for good."*

The tweet had been from nj.com, one of the feeds that Bertram followed. He quickly followed up with another text that was simply, *"trouble ahead, trouble behind."* Bertram even texted in Grateful Dead speak.

This veiled message from nj.com was as unpredictable as the final, stomach-lurching backwards loop on Lightning Loops at Great Adventure. But just like my decision to go on that ride when I was 12 years old, I was damned if I wasn't going to ride this roller coaster to its uncertain end. I could only hope that, at the end of the ride, I would get off unscathed. That seemed unlikely once those 140 characters hit the twittersphere. I was completely out of control and no one could hear my screams.

#Nightmare.

"I never said that he would come to the event, I said he was invited," I reasoned with the reporter.

"Neither did I. But he might show up and that's good enough for me."

Even though I secretly shared Chris' optimism for a good outcome, I knew it would be irresponsible to keep up with this charade that was only going to disappoint a ton of people and perhaps put the final nail in the coffin of The Garage.

James and Tara arrived just as I hung up with the reporter. James had volunteered to use his musician expertise to wrangle the talent, namely local artists who had appeared at the club, Marshall Crenshaw, Mike Peters of the Alarm, and a few others that only James, as a musician, would recognize. When I told him about what had happened on nj.com, he immediately had an idea of how to fix the problem.

"Well, if you can't get The Boss, maybe a substitute will do," he suggested.

"Like who?" I asked, as I looked outside at the gathering crowd.

"There are 254 Bruce cover bands in New Jersey alone, but only two in this zip code," James explained.

"Who told you that?"

"Steve Hartman."

"And who, may I ask, is Steve Hartman."

And just as I said his name, Steve Hartman appeared at my side, a fifty-something slender man wearing black denims and a Born in the USA T-shirt.

"I am your savior to rise from these streets."

"Oh, boy," I sighed.

"It's perfect," said James. "If you can't have Bruce Springsteen and the E Street Band, than you can have Steve Hartman and the F Street Band."

"We are actually called Badlands," Steven corrected.

How I would explain to the crowd that the F Street Band would be performing in place of the E Street Band was not going to be easy news to break. But it was something. Before I could come up with that awkward introduction, another issue was taking place outside the bar. Police cars had blocked off Washington Street, and Hoboken's finest mounted on horseback had isolated the crowd to the sidewalk. The group was being rounded up as if they were protesters at a New Jersey toxic dump site rather than happy concertgoers. Instead of a call and response protest, the jovial mob was singing "Glory Days" over and over. I thought about grabbing one of the megaphones from the person leading the choir to tell them that Bruce might not come at all, until I noticed that the song leader was Allison. I knew she couldn't be trusted.

As the policeman set up the wooden sawhorses around the singing mob, another emergency erupted, and this time it was an emergency vehicle. Two of the early bird drinkers who had been downing shots of absinthe before Bertram cut them off had left the bar in dramatic fashion. They were on their way out to a "real bar," when the first girl tripped on one of her platform heels and fell face first on the sidewalk in front of the bar. The girl screamed as blood ran down her face and all over her gunmetal gray sequined tank top. The ambulance parted the crowd and loaded the girl, who wasn't too hurt to scream out threats of lawsuits, onto a stretcher and off to the hospital. I hoped that she would be the only casualty of the day, but that was wishful thinking.

I made my way back inside the bar to find Maggie, who had the CBS reporter by the collar. She yanked him from the media pit where she had an obedient group of media professionals in check, save one. As I walked through the door, she almost knocked me off balance as she picked him up by his collar and the waistband of his pants and tossed him out onto the sidewalk.

"And stay out," she yelled after him.

The media pit grew quiet, even the "stringer" photographers who never settle down. The stringer photographer is an unusual breed, perhaps considered to be the bottom rung on the media hierarchy. They are rarely on assignment, rarely credentialed, but show up to snap photos of whomever they can, wherever they can. As soon as they get the photo, they shop it around to the highest bidder. This is how they make their living; they are the plankton of the media pit. Usually the most rowdy, they grew surprisingly quiet after Maggie's act of aggression toward one of their kind.

"Who wants to be next?" she shouted at the sheepish crowd. They all avoided eye contact as if they were the sane ones dealing with a crazy person.

"Do I want to know what happened there?" I asked.

"The less you know the better," she answered back.

So wrapped up in the emergency vehicles, the police lines and the raucous media was I that I was paying little attention to Dave, who had been treating me with a cool, businesslike demeanor all day. It was as though I had learned too much about him on our pseudo-date and now he had to put distance between us. When I finally located him at the end of the bar, he was leaning against it with a beer in his hand as Lively Schmidt leaned in to talk to him.

How she could show her face here when her father had bought the place for her I could not understand. In essence her future depended on the demise of Dave's bar. This was odd. But jealousy aside, I needed to put on my big girl pants and greet the mayor. Where was she, I wondered? That was about a nano-second of doubt, because when I returned to the door to check and see if she had checked in, I noticed that the mayor was being turned away at the door.

She may have been led right in if she had been wearing her usual business attire, but instead she wore a pair of outdated jeans and a double-breasted blazer that made her look even more out of place. Daniel, confused by her look, thought that she might be looking for Tot Land, which would be open next month if tonight's efforts were a bust. He whispered that she should come back later when the daycare was fully operational. I looked at him in disbelief, not only because he seemed to think we were doomed to fail, but also because he was about to boot our town's mayor out into the street.

"Oh, Mrs. Gallagher, Mrs. Mayor, come right this way," I interjected and led her by the arm into the foyer.

"That man was very rude," she noted as she puller her blouse collar outside of her stiff blazer.

"Yeah, it's part of his charm. He's from New York, you know."

She nodded in agreement, as if being from New York explained his rude behavior, like it was a psychological malady rather than a geographic custom.

The mayor wanted to greet some of the younger residents in town. She was a big music fan, too, and told me about her heyday standing in line to see Barry Manilow.

"I get it," she told me with a knowing wink.

Linda Gallagher had been in office for the past four years and was the mother of three Ivy League daughters and a former Wall Street banker who took on the civic duty of reforming Hoboken, kind of like Bloomberg had in New York City. She was pretty effective at balancing the budget and ridding city hall of high-salaried workers, but she was low on compassion and was often criticized for being out of touch with the young residents in town. This appearance was an attempt to bridge that gap, to become more "relatable."

Her assistant now strong-armed me into letting the mayor give a small speech to make up for the "disaster" at the door. I knew this was a minor thing; besides, the crowd would probably not even notice her between set breaks. She would be slotted in to go before The Presidents of the United States of America, which would have an apt political tie-in. Her challenger, Robb Robinson, was already in the bar; he was an obese man who showed up in a Bruce Springsteen T-shirt under his portly custom-made suit. Despite his very right wing conservative stance, he was a longtime Bruce fan. I'm not sure that I think there is a less conflicted person than the Republican Bruce fan. Did they ever really listen to his lyrics, and what the heck did they do at concerts when Bruce makes a political statement? It just made no sense. Regardless of his political affiliations, he had made himself right at home at the bar, deciding not to make a political statement but to accost every rock star-looking person for a photo opportunity. When I looked over, he was posing for a shot with my brother and Tara. On second glance, he had cornered the guitarist from Badlands, who was dressed up to look exactly like Steve Van Zandt, bandana and all.

Meanwhile, the mayor took the podium and made an effort to quiet the crowd, but no one was listening. She became upset and began to use tactics a sixth grade teacher might employ to hush up a classroom full of disobedient children.

"Settle down for a few announcements, guys," she pleaded.

"Mommy, isn't it time to put your kiddies to bed?" someone yelled from the back of the crowd.

She stopped for a moment, reconsidered getting back to the podium before she thought better of it, then cut her losses and left the stage. But not before she gave me a good dressing down.

"I shut down Fake St Patrick's Day, so closing this place will be child's play for me, missy," she warned.

"All it takes is one call to the Fire Chief and you are over.... Don't try me, I will do it," she continued.

Needless to say, she did not win over any votes that day, mine included.

The mayor had a precedent for curtailing public spectacles. She had recently shut down the Fake St Patrick's Day Parade, a must go-to event for young drinkers across the tri-state area. Every year, the town throws a St. Patrick's Day Parade, which is never actually held on St. Patrick's Day. Due to the demand of marching bands, each New Jersey town (Newark, Belmar, Kearney) rotates a Saturday in March to host St. Patrick's Day. In Hoboken, this is enough reason to pack the bars early and carry on like the world is ending. It's a boon for local businesses, but comes with a price for public safety, and stretches the resources of the order keepers in the city. But fake Bruce Springsteen day was turning out to be even more raucous and costly. Business may have looked good, but crowd management had proven to be difficult, despite the fact that the summons for drinking an open container in public might have made some extra money for the town. But the mayor's threat weighed heavily on me: what if I had destroyed the last chance to save this New Jersey institution? I prayed that she would not close us down.

Before I could ponder this further, I was given false hope when screams from the crowd erupted outside. A limousine had pulled up slowly and parked. After about five minutes, the door opened, only to reveal—to everyone's colossal disappointment—the emergence of the unattractive Mark Feist. I, like the crowd, would have been happy to have never seen this poser again, but there he was. He waved to the crowd, assuming that they were gathered to see him and his companion, a leggy supermodel type. He spotted me and planted his customary three kisses on my cheeks and then said, "Jen, can you show us our table and get us some Cristal?"

"You got it, Mark. Let me get someone right on that." I quickly motioned to Tara to come over and help me with these VIPs. As Mark walked away, I heard his companion say, "So is Bruce here yet?" She was not the only one who'd be in for a surprise.

There was, however, one bright spot. After weeks of convincing, the Hoboken Historical Society had finally agreed to make a special decree for The Garage, making it a memorable landmark of the town, not exactly a historic landmark but a memorable one nonetheless. They had even created a plaque to present to Dave. This took place right after Mike Peters of The Alarm gave a stunning rendition of "The Stand," which got the crowd happy again after the mayor's brief reprimand. The lead singer, Mike Peters, a longtime friend of Dave's, was the perfect person to introduce him. He hollered to the crowd.

"I think with a little encouragement we can get Dave Germain up here. Dave, where are ya, man?"

Dave was still in the corner with Lively, but managed to escape from where she had him sequestered to get on stage for his shining moment. He jumped on stage with his hands raised like David Lee Roth, full of arrogance and bravado. He hugged Mike and then was introduced to the very stately, grey-haired, navy blazer-wearing Corbin Pennington.

"Let me introduce you to this cool dude, Corbin Pennington, who has a special award for The Garage," Dave announced to the crowd gathered in the tightly packed bar.

"By special circumstances, we deem The Garage a place of memorable location in Hoboken." Pennington, who spoke with the New Jersey version of Larchmont lockjaw, announced this grandly as if he were presenting something much more formal.

The crowd cheered. Corbin extended his hand graciously and was greeted by a bear hug from Dave, which he extricated himself from awkwardly. Dave stepped back, realizing that his affection was not quite as rock and roll as he would have liked, backed up and extended a formal handshake and then accepted the plaque. He then held it over his head as if he had just been awarded the Silver Plate at Wimbledon. He looked over at me, over at Lively, and then over at me again. He winked at Bertram, who gave him a thumbs up.

"Speech, speech, speech," the crowd yelled.

"Thanks, thanks, everyone," Dave said, "but things don't just happen. People make things happen. And Jessie, you made this happen," he said, looking down at me. "Thanks again for coming out, it means a lot."

Then he quickly jumped off the stage and into the adoring crowd.

I was overwhelmed. I was appreciated. Maybe it could all work out after all. But somewhere inside I knew my Pontius Pilate moment would be soon. Any hope I had for a good outcome dissipated when the fire chief who I had successfully dodged for an hour finally caught up with me.

"Are you in charge of this circus, young lady?"

"Well, yes, sort of," I demurred.

"Well, you just *sort of* shut down the city of Hoboken to all incoming and outgoing traffic. No one is getting in or out until this party ends. So you might want to end it now."

"Okay, sir, but we're waiting for The Boss. Can't we have a little more time?" I pleaded.

"I don't care if you're waiting for the Pope, no one is getting in and no one is getting out. Consider yourself shut down. Clear it out now, or we will."

I knew it was over, even as I stared at the door and willed Bruce to walk through it. As I looked, the door opened slowly and my heart raced. But it wasn't Bruce, it was Mark Feist, again. He caught my eye and shook his pack of Marlboros at me. As if he needed another bad habit to make him more repulsive, he even smoked. All this waiting, reminded me of a play I had read in high school drama class called *Waiting for Godot*, which is about two characters who wait for the arrival of a character named Godot. Godot could or could not be God and he may or may not show up. Godot never showed up, but in the interim, the characters argue, philosophize and even consider suicide as they wait for him or it. I could relate. Like those characters, I was waiting in vain, along with the entire town of Hoboken, for someone who would never show up.

And just as I was about to get on the stage to announce the bad news, James cued the headliner act. The lights went up and Badlands launched into their cover version of "Cover Me."

The times are tough now, just getting tougher.

This old world is rough, it's just getting rougher.

Cover me, come on baby, cover me.

It took all of three lines for the crowd to realize that they were listening to a cover band, a very good cover band, but it was not Bruce. Bruce, like Godot, was a no-show. The disappointment in everyone's eyes was apparent. They realized that booing a Bruce cover band was not in good form, so they politely listened along. Some people snuck out before they were kicked out. Others looked around, confused and dejected. Some were too drunk to realize anything at all. The media took some photos and then most of them left as well, even most of the stringers.

Not only had I exposed the bar to two possible lawsuits, the first from the bloody- nosed girl who threatened to sue the bar from her stretcher and the second, which I was sure would be forthcoming, from the CBS reporter who'd been manhandled and tossed on the street by Maggie. But I had also alienated the mayor, which left her no alternative but to shut us down. As the crowd dispersed, some of them even demanded their money back. Grumbles of "bummer," "let down," and "buzz kill" were overheard as they were marched out. Daniel and Bertram managed the crowd control along with Maggie and two stringer photographers who had now become her groupies. Dave avoided making any eye contact with me at all as Lively led him to the upstairs office to do God knows what. Derek and Allison were led out by a fireman and waved at me as they left. Somehow I had managed to disappoint everyone. I was at a personal low point as I apologized to whomever would listen at the door, but most of these stragglers just wanted out. The firemen led everyone out on to the street and back to their fruitful lives. My life at the moment had hit rock bottom. And as if I did not feel bad enough, even Corbin Pennington had had enough of me.

He looked at me with a "shame on you" look on his face and, before I could open my mouth, he ripped the plaque from out of my hands and simply said while he shook his head, "You won't be needing this anymore."

The fight or flight impulse is scientifically described as the body's automatic response to impending attack or harm. Some may choose to fight, to dig in, to stick around and weather the storm, or some other display of sporty heroism that you might see in a movie like *Rudy* or *Hoosiers*. But this wasn't a movie, and I was too tired to stick around and fight. When confronted with the last few months of harmful situations, namely single-handedly ruining my friend's wedding, burying a historic landmark bar, trashing any semblance of a love life and sabotaging my new career, I felt like I had no other choice but to take flight or, in my case, to take a flight.

That would have been a great plan if I had enough money to buy an actual plane ticket. But I didn't, I had about $60 for my trip, so flight was not an option, at least via plane. I packed a bag and headed out, impulsively, not really knowing where I would go. I just needed to take action and go somewhere, to distance myself from the misery and failure. I wanted out; I had officially said "uncle" to an uncaring universe.

If you are down and out, there is nothing that makes you feel even worse than bus travel. It's the most time-consuming, least glamorous, cheapest way to travel. Planes have glamorous jet-set efficiency, trains hold a romantic cross-country allure, but buses are common, just a down-and-dirty way to get from point A to point B.

The Port Authority bus terminal on Eighth Avenue in Manhattan is a dismal place despite recent upgrade attempts to humanize the once crime-ridden concourse. But no amount of Au Bon Pains, Tie Racks, and Aunt Annie's were going to lift my spirits. Even the overbearing classical music provided no solace to my troubled escape. In the newly remodeled waiting room, I licked my wounds and reviewed my options. I had about $67 for my trip, which is actually quite a lot for bus travel. If you had a very flexible travel itinerary, you could board a Peter Pan bus and get to Boston for $1. As I tried to come up with a reason to travel to Boston, I looked at my fellow commuters, who all moved with their own purpose. An elderly woman headed for a visit with her grandchildren, two coeds returned to college after a weekend at home, a young couple gathered their twin boys and gear and dashed off to their gate. They all seemed to be living better, more purpose-filled lives than mine. I drank my oversized Dunkin' Donuts coffee in an effort to stay warm in the sub-zero bus terminal.

The newly installed televisions flashed the news of the day. The world's complicated stories were distilled down to a 60-second sound bite. Images of a train derailment in China cut to the English royal family christening a ship and then back to unrest along the Gaza Strip, each given equal gravity, about 20 seconds worth, give or take. The news dulled my senses momentarily, so much so that I might have fallen asleep, because what happened next seemed dreamlike.

Suddenly and without warning, the Governor of New Jersey was in front of me. He even whispered my name. "Pssst. Hey, Jessie, over here." I could see that he was motioning to me from the television screen. I looked around to see if anyone else noticed, but no one apparently did. Since the governor of New Jersey doesn't usually communicate through a television screen in the middle of the Port Authority, I did what anyone would do in that situation. I ignored him. I tried to avoid eye contact, but the governor was persistent and adopted his usual persuasive conversational style—he hollered as if I had just cut him off on the Garden State Parkway.

"Hey, I'm talking to you. Eyes in front. Eyes in front." He meant business. And I knew better than to ignore the man who had gained national recognition as a feisty advocate for his state in the wake of Hurricane Sandy. He wasn't going away, that was for sure. His abrasive style was often spun in the media as strong leadership skills, but despite the public relations designed to humanize him, I felt bullied. I pointed to myself and looked around for a moment as if to say, "Who, me? Are you really talking to me?" Impatiently, he raised his voice. He did not like to be kept waiting.

"Yeah, you. You, the one from New Jersey. What are you doing? We don't bail out, we show up. We don't give up, we get up. If it's a choice between fight and flight, we fight."

Had he read my mind about the fight or flight thing, or what?

"We don't care what people think of us, we know the truth. We band together; when the going gets tough, we DON'T get going. We are from New Jersey, we stay right where we are."

And as if making a personal plea to me alone, the governor asked, "So where are you going? You can't leave. We won't let you. Now get back there." And he shook his chubby fingers at me and pointed toward the door.

I thought to myself, there, where? Get back where? But the governor had disappeared just as mysteriously as he had arrived. I looked down at my nearly empty coffee and inspected its contents; maybe caffeine is more harmful than I thought.

When I looked up again, one of those state tourism commercials was on, a lovely montage of a boardwalk sausage stand, a cranberry bog, and a panoramic shot of the Statue of Liberty (which technically is in New Jersey) against the background music of that Bon Jovi song about not being able to go home. All pretty ironic, really. But before I could get my head around my real or imagined conversation with the governor and the expensively produced tourism commercial which extolled the handful of reasons to visit my home state, there was breaking news on the screen, a live report from Eyewitness News. I looked closer and recognized a familiar scene. The camera zoomed in on The Garage sign and then widened out to a shot of Washington Street, the sawhorses still in place from the fundraiser the night before, the crowd still gathered as if they had stayed there overnight.

"Eyewitness News is coming to you live from Hoboken," a peppy midday reporter shouted so she could be heard over the large crowd that was lined up outside the bar.

"...where Bruce Springsteen has made a surprise appearance. Fans of The Boss will remember that he filmed the "Glory Days" video here in the mid-1980s. When he heard about this New Jersey rock institution being closed, he tweeted a message to his followers promising a free concert to save the landmark and asked for their support. The first hundred people would be treated to a free show."

The reporter cut to the original footage of Bruce's video and then back to the chaotic but jovial crowd on Washington Street. It was kind of like a flashback to the confusing events of the fundraiser.

"So what do you think about Bruce showing up here?" the reporter asked an optimistic fan, clad in an oversized black shirt with a younger Bruce's image on it.

"We knew he would come. We would have waited all night. We thought it would be yesterday, but we knew he'd be here sooner or later."

It took me a moment to process what was happening, and then I leapt to my feet and searched for the door. I dug through my suitcase to find my phone, which I saw had messages and texts from everyone I knew, including Emily, who sounded chipper despite the way we'd left things. In the few short hours away, I had missed five calls from Maggie, ten calls from Bertram, a retweet from James, and three hang-ups from Dave. And now Bruce was at the bar, mid-concert, and I was sitting in the middle of Port Authority destined for parts unknown. Suddenly, possessed with purpose, I ditched my super-sized coffee, gathered my bag, and, with phone in hand, ran full speed to the nearest exit. Outside the Port Authority, on the street, I looked for a cab to take me across the river. Bus travel might have been cheaper, but money was no longer an issue, I had to get back. I just hoped I wasn't too late.

The first two taxis I approached rolled up their window and drove away speechless when I asked them if they would drive me all the way back to Hoboken. The third was more receptive. This negotiation is common among cabbies, who never want to travel to New Jersey. There is some mystery and confusion about cabbies crossing the state line, the general rule of thumb is that they can drive you there, but cannot pick up a fare to come back into Manhattan. This notion only reinforces the idea of New Jersey being somehow a one-way destination that even cabbies hesitate to travel to. But for me, that was all I needed, a one-way trip to Hoboken regardless of the cost. When you do find the right cabbie, be prepared to pay double or triple the amount that a 12-minute fare in the city would cost. Even with that incentive, drivers are reluctant to cross the river, so it often takes the right offer and the kind of person who is apt to ignore the rules to earn a little cash.

"Forty bucks to Hoboken?" I asked.

"Fifty plus the toll," he said in a heavy Jamaican accent.

"Fifty dollars, really? How about $50 with the toll?"

"Plus the toll," he volleyed back.

"Okay, fine, okay. Just go!" I hopped into the backseat of the Ford Hybrid Escape.

He tore down 31st Street and cut west across to Tenth Avenue, which took about five minutes, and suddenly we were in the Lincoln Tunnel. And just a few minutes later, we are out of the tunnel and making the turn at the Hoboken sign that takes you right into town. The ride took about 10 minutes, but I quickly calculated that that could be half of a "Rosalita" or part of "Jungleland," so time was of the essence. In the next 10 minutes, I texted Bertram to tell him about my arrival, so that he could get me in.

"Park on 12th and come up Hudson, I will meet you at the back door. ☺"

It was a good thing that he had given me that instruction, because there was no way to get close to the bar. The roads were again closed to traffic and crowds of people lined the streets for blocks around the bar.

"Just drop me here," I ordered the cabbie and quickly handed him $60, which, for the record, left me with just $7 to my name.

He screeched to a halt and I sprinted the four blocks to the bar with my wheeled suitcase in tow.

"Just in time." Bertram rushed me into the back of the bar, where Bruce was three songs into his short set. The back door slammed as Bruce approached the mic and he looked back at the flash of daylight that opening the back door had let into the dark room.

"Thanks for joining us," Bruce nodded.

"You know I played here once before," he said with typical Bruce understatement as the crowd cheered.

"And I think it's important to recognize that. But it's more than the recognition, isn't it? We get recognized all the time for what we do. I just knew I couldn't pass up a chance to play here again. Places like The Garage are important. They're important to keep around and we need to recognize that too, don't we? But it's more than the recognition you get when you do something right, it's more about doing the right thing. That's what it's about."

And as if time stood still, Bruce Springsteen looked directly at me and smiled. I just stood there, motionless, letting everything sink in, and for a moment it was just Bruce and me, and everything else went quiet. But when you are in the middle of a Bruce Springsteen concert, which is more like a shared religious experience than a musical performance, you are not alone for long. The band broke into a heavy guitar riff and the magic began. The crowd erupted. I looked around and let them envelope me and I knew that I had finally come home.

22

We watched as the last of the cars pulled away from the bar and headed toward the end of Washington Street and out of town. Behind them, a few diehard fans tried for one last photo opportunity. The street cleaners with their heavy wire brushes and power sprayers washed away any evidence of the event that had just taken place. We stood outside the bar and watched for a few moments. The Korean grocer across the street rolled down the metal gate to open his store, oblivious to what had just happened. And then it was just the three of us. I wondered about that time that is spent when you are desperately waiting for something to happen, for something to change; that time seems like eternity when you are waiting. But when the "something" happens, that time feels short, erased as if you never suffered through it.

We slowly moved inside the bar, to the darkly lit empty backroom, where the only evidence that was left were some toppled Rolling Rock bottles and an overflowing garbage can of plastic keg cups. It was as if the echo of the music could still be heard, faintly. Bertram, who had made it his habit to quote only Grateful Dead lyrics, chose that moment to share the words of a new inspirational leader.

"Someday we'll look back on this and it will all seem funny," he said, quoting one of the seminal lines from "Rosalita."

It was actually funny in a way, funny strange, really. Because it was like a karmic switch had been thrown and our lives changed in minutes. Bruce's appearance provided good publicity for the bar, which was like a Teflon coating against anyone in opposition. Going against Bruce was bad for business, any business, and that included Tot Land. Andres Schmidt was going to have to find another place for the town's tiniest residents to hang out. He called Dave and told him, "Maybe you're not so bad after all, you can stick around, for now." I suspected that his persuasive daughter had something to do with his change of heart. Perhaps the combination of Dave's charm and the arrival of a rock superhero had won them over in the end. Whatever the reason, The Garage had been saved, creating a dividing line in The Garage's history as the time pre-Bruce and the time after-Bruce, kind of like BC and AD was for Jesus.

"Congratulations, guys. It worked. It really worked," I said, convincing myself as much as them that the reality matched our shared vision.

"Okay, then...that is that. I'm gonna grab my stuff." And I headed to the office.

Downstairs, the sounds of cleanup were noisily underway, beer glasses clanged together, bar seats shuffled across the floor and tables slid back into the dining room.

Outside, the street cleaning crew gave orders to some pajama-clad residents, who shuffled to move their cars from one side of the street to another to avoid being booted. Being booted was a new convenient way for cars to be fined without having to tow them. The police put a large metal device on your car wheel, which can only be removed by paying the fine and entering a secret code. It's kind of like *The Amazing Race* of car ticketing, where you get clues as you go along. The annoying part of this new system is that the person has to return the boot once it is removed, which seemed a little mean, if you ask me. From the sound of the sirens and car alarms, it seemed like everyone in town was anxious to get things cleaned up and back to normal.

Amid the clatter, the phone rang continuously; I could hear bits of conversation from upstairs as callers were juggled and put on hold. I packed up the few personal belongings I had on my desk into a tote bag and pulled my wheelie suitcase toward the door. I was familiar with quick pack-up scenes and wanted to make this exit as quickly and painlessly as possible. Ironically, just a few months ago, I had landed at this very bar when my world came crashing down, and now here I was again, under much different circumstances, but on my way out again.

Dave lamented loudly, as I reached the foot of the steps, "I really need someone to handle all these details, and I'm just not sure how I'm going to sort this all out. VH1 called to do a documentary on the bar and PBS also wants to film B Roll here for an American Masters series that will feature Springsteen."

"I hear you, I just got three new acts for next month alone. It would be great if we knew someone who could help. Do you know anyone like that?" Bertram added as if playing along.

I cleared my throat as I stood in the doorway. They both turned and looked at me.

"Well, I suppose I could come back here tomorrow to help you out, you know, just until you get things going again..." I hesitantly offered.

"Here's the thing. I don't need you here tomorrow." Dave moved off his barstool to where I stood and addressed me directly for the first time since this roller coaster ride began.

"Oh, boy," I muttered under my breath, feeling awkward, exposed.

And then, in true form, he moved even closer, leaned his hand on the door and stood over me, once again invading my personal space, which I didn't mind, not one bit.

"I need you here, with me, every day." He smiled.

These words were delivered slowly; at least that was how I perceived them. So surprised was I by his revelation that I dropped my tote bag. It landed on the ground with a thud. Dave picked it up, put it over his shoulder and gave me his arm to personally escort me back upstairs.

As the morning light flowed through the stained glass windows of The Garage, Dave looked up and said to me, "Let's get outta here and take a walk to the water."

There is something redemptive about looking at a new day emerging over the New York skyline. The mix of old and new buildings provided a fitting counterbalance. Living on the waterfront never grows old as the Hudson River reflected the early morning light. The morning hubbub signaled the promise of another day.

The ferries made their way across the river packed with Wall Streeters out early to conquer the foreign markets. Runners sprinted down Frank Sinatra Boulevard to get their adrenalin rush in before they, too, crossed the water to their cubicles. Young parents shuffled their children to daycare before boarding New Jersey Transit buses to the city, no doubt to law firms and public relations companies. And as many left our small city to find their fortunes in our big city neighbor, Dave and I sat right where we were on a bench directly across the Hudson from the Empire State Building. Our workday on this side of the river had already begun

"You know what else I love about New Jersey?" he said as he looked at me.

"We have a much better view."

Epilogue

Someone once told me that good attracts good, and in the weeks that followed, that notion became more than just a catchphrase; it became my company's mission statement. (Finally!) I never did come up with an official business plan because I was too busy making Best Friend for Hire into a successful business. I kept the office upstairs from The Garage, but now I paid rent, which only seems fair. And as if karma had intervened once again, new clients arrived daily and the most surprising one of them all was a return client, which made me think I was pretty good at my job and being a good friend, after all.

Dear Best Friend for Hire

I was hoping you could help me with my social life. You see, I just moved to Edgewater, New Jersey, and I don't know anything about the area. I need help getting settled. Would you be able to work for me? Call my cell, anytime!

Dear Best Friend for Hire

Do you have a Soho office? I need help setting up my home office. I live in a studio and right now my headquarters is like a corner of my bed. Are you good with organizing small spaces?

Dear Best Friend for Hire

My good friend and I recently got into a fight over a guy, of all things. I know it's pathetic, but what we really need is a judge, you know, like Judge Judy? Every time we talk, we get into it all over again. Do you have any time this weekend?

P.S. I know you will see it my way, anyway...

Dear Best Friend for Hire

I am the events coordinator for the Bergen County Library System and we need a speaker to do a talk about starting your own business. We offer an honorarium and would be pleased to have you. Please send current headshot and bio.

Dear Best Friend for Hire

I need you! I am pregnant with twins and I need a reliable person to help me set up a nursery. Do you have any appointments available? I heard you are amazing and I am super easy to work with. ☺

Love, Emily

Acknowledgements

This book would not have been possible without my husband Frank, who took the book out of my filing cabinet and pushed it toward publication. To my mother Millie, who provides daily wisdom that goes well beyond the kitchen. To Kenneth Salikof for reading, coaching, and encouraging me page by page.

Thank you to the good people at Post Hill Press, especially the invincible Anthony Ziccardi who gave the book a wonderful home. I would also like to thank Gavin Caruthers for his thoughtful advice, Billie Brownell for her editing guidance, Devon Brown for her boundless enthusiasm, and the amazing Laura Rossi whose kindness pervades everything she does. I am also appreciative of my book publishing friends who supported, read, and advised, especially Jennifer Battista and Babette Ross.

And finally, to the many good people in publishing that I have had the pleasure to work with over the years. Your stories have been the inspiration for this book.

About the Author

Mary Carlomagno is the author of three previous books about organizing, a nationally recognized spokesperson and owner of order (orderperiod.com), a company that helps busy people get organized and live more balanced lives. She has been featured on the *Oprah Winfrey Show*, NBC's *Today*, and National Public Radio. She was born and raised in New Jersey, and currently lives there with her husband and two children.